Beyond The Surface

Felice Stevens

Beyond the Surface (The Breakfast Club, Book 1)
August 2015

Cover Art by:
Reese Dante
www.reesedante.com

Edited by:
Keren Reed

Interior Design and Formatting by:
Christine Borgford, Perfectly Publishable
www.perfectlypublishable.com

Published in the United States of America

On 9/11, firefighter Nick Fletcher's world changed forever. He's unable to rid himself of survivor's guilt, made worse by the secret he hides from his family and co-workers. Nick's life is centered around helping burn victims, until he is reunited with the man he'd once loved but pushed away. Now he has a second chance at a love he thought lost forever.

For fashion designer Julian Cornell, appearances mean everything. His love affairs are strictly casual, and the only thing he cares about is making his clothing line a success. A chance encounter with the man he loved long ago has Julian thinking for the first time in years that there may be more to life than being seen at the best parties or deciding what designer labels to wear.

When Julian's world takes an unexpected turn, it's Nick who helps him regain perspective on what matters most in life. Julian, in turn, helps Nick accept who he is and understand he isn't responsible for tragedies he couldn't prevent. Lost love found can be even sweeter the second time around, and after all the years apart, both men learn to look beyond the surface to find the men they are inside.

Dedication

To the 343 of the FDNY who never came home and all the other first responders who helped bring New York City back from the depths of despair after September 11th. Your sacrifice and service has never been forgotten.

Acknowledgments

Thanks, as always, to my editor Keren Reed.

To Sandy and Lindsey who pushed me for this story from the moment I mentioned the idea, thank you for always being there, night and day. To Hope Cousin, every other Tuesday, baby. To Denise, I can't thank you enough.

To Kade-thank you for everything and for being my friend.

I have to give a shout out to Jessica de Ruiter-I have two words for you—leather pants. Without you, it wouldn't have happened.

To the readers, thank you for the support, the sense of family and the love. I'm the luckiest person I know because of all of you.

Chapter One

IT WAS A cold, gray, windy day in New York City. The kind of day where you smelled the snow coming and couldn't wait for that first cup of coffee to sink through your bones and warm you up. Julian Cornell exited the black car without a backward glance and hurried up the stairs to the diner. Though only eight o'clock in the morning, he'd been up for hours with his design team, directing the final touches on the fashion show that would introduce his summer ready-to-wear line. In his opinion, which was all that counted, it was his best to date.

Julian and his two best friends had set a goal to meet at least once a month for breakfast, either in the city, where he and Marcus lived, or in Brooklyn where Zach was. Today it was Brooklyn; thankfully the diner was right over the Brooklyn Bridge in Brooklyn Heights, so it wouldn't be a hassle to get back into the city.

He pushed open the doors and immediately spotted his friends in their usual corner booth, and a smile curved his lips. At least for an hour he could put aside the bullshit and the back-stabbing of work, and relax with the only people he truly trusted in the world.

"Hey, guys." He slid in next to Zach, who scooted over to give more room to Julian's lean, six-foot-two frame. "Thanks, Zach. How's your mom?"

Zach pushed up the glasses that had been perpetually sliding down his nose since the first day Julian met him, and flashed Julian his usual sweet smile. "She's better. Thanks for asking. And she said thanks for the scarf for her birthday. She showed everyone her original Julian Cornell creation." Zach's blue eyes danced. "All the ladies at the senior center were jealous."

Not for the first time Julian wondered why a nice guy like Zach had never found anyone. Spending all day and night with his computers probably didn't help Zach's chance at an active social life. Plus, guys liked a bit of a bastard. He grinned to himself, recalling the pouting model he'd kicked out of his bed early that morning, and their headboard-banging, hard and furious fucking all night long.

"Ha, Juli, you have some major granny fans." Marcus smirked at him from the other side of the table.

"Shut up, Marcus," said Julian absently as he glanced at the waiter pouring his coffee. "The usual, Peter."

"Yes, Mr. Cornell." The waiter set the carafe down on the table and departed.

"Shut up? Is that any way to talk to your oldest friend?"

It was sometimes the only way Julian could deal with a character like Marcus Feldman. How his friend managed to graduate from college and become the owner of one of New York City's trendiest nightclubs, Sparks, blew Julian's mind. Julian thought all Marcus was interested in was drinking, partying, and fucking the next cute guy he saw.

But Marcus had fooled them all, and now Julian was planning his after-party at Sparks and knew—thanks to Marcus's laser-sharp business acumen—it would be as much of a success as the fashion show would be. His blood quickened as he thought of all the accolades his new, trendsetting designs would receive.

Ignoring Marcus's comeback, Julian instead ran down a list of questions. "Everything is set for tonight, correct? You have the VIP list and the separate waitstaff for their tables?" He held Marcus's gaze. "Nothing can go wrong. I'm counting on you."

"Chill out, man. I'm not worried, you shouldn't be either." Marcus sipped his coffee. "Seriously, Juli, you know I won't let you down. I've handpicked the waiters myself." He took another sip of coffee, his lips smiling around the edge of his cup.

"Oh, Christ." Julian groaned. "Tell me that doesn't mean you've screwed every one of them? Jesus, Marc. Have a little discretion."

The waiter approached with their breakfasts, and Julian kept quiet while their plates were set before them and the man departed, before he continued. "I don't want a group of unhappy, pretty boys fighting with each other over who gets to suck the boss off at the end of the night, when they should be concentrating on my guests."

Zach sat in between the two of them, his gaze ping-ponging from Julian's to Marcus's face. It wasn't often that Julian saw the normally composed, cool Marcus lose his temper, but by the ominous flash in his violet-gray eyes, Julian knew one of those times had come. Zach winced and sat back in the booth, as if anticipating the two men coming to blows.

"By what right do you think you can dictate to me how I run my business, or who I choose to fuck?" Marcus slammed his hand on the table, rattling the coffee cups and causing the diners from nearby tables to throw uneasy glances their way.

"When I'm paying you for it." Julian glared right back at his friend. "This night is very important for me. It needs to be perfect."

"And it will be," said Marcus. "I'm going to leave your show a bit early to make sure everything is in place and the staff is ready for the onslaught of admiring fans and the throngs of press that will be beating down my door to get to you. I won't let you down."

"I'm sorry. I've never been so stressed," said Julian, and turned to Zach. "And thanks to you also, for putting together all the programs I needed, from the lighting to the mix tapes for the music and the slide shows."

"No problem, I'm happy to help." Zach ducked his head and took a bite of his eggs.

"Are you sure you won't come to the show and the after-party?" Julian asked Zach in a gentler tone. He'd been protective of Zach since they all met when he took extra classes in business and marketing at CUNY and then lived together until he moved to Europe. Oddly enough, Julian still felt responsible for his friend, who he knew was socially shy and awkward, preferring to remain at home rather than accept the many invitations both he and Marcus extended to openings, shows, and parties. "I'll have the seat next to me saved for you."

"It's okay, Julian. I-I have stuff to do. Maybe next time, huh?" Zach held his gaze and Julian smiled slightly.

"Sure, Zach. Next time."

But Julian knew the same thing would happen the next time. He'd invited Zach to every one of his shows and parties, and there was always an excuse, or a reason for the man not to come, or to keep himself hidden in the sound and light booth.

His phone buzzed with a text. It was Melanie, his assistant, with a thousand little things that needed to be done before to-night. Much as Julian hated cutting short the breakfast with his best friends, he knew he had to leave to make sure things were proceeding as planned. Part of what made him so successful was how closely he kept on top of every detail. Not that he was a mi-cromanager, but he liked everything done the way he envisioned it.

He shoveled in the rest of his eggs and drained his second cup of coffee, looking wistfully at the thermal carafe on the table. "I'm sorry you guys." He wiped his lips with his napkin. "I've got to go and check that the clothing is all at the space and in the right order, and that the models' dressing area is set up proper-ly." He stood and took a twenty dollar bill out of his wallet and slid it across the table. "Marcus, I'll see you tonight. Zach, I'll keep your seat open if you change your mind."

He strode out of the diner, his mind whirling with all the minute details that required his attention, and hailed a cab on Court Street to go back into the city to his Seventh Avenue showroom. Then it would be back downtown to the magnifi-cent Tribeca loft he'd rented for his show this afternoon, which should already be set up.

Julian never left anything to chance. He anticipated that at any given moment something might and will go wrong. That's why he always insisted on run-throughs in advance with his makeup artists, models, and dressers. They grumbled about it, but it always made for a seamless, flawlessly run show. The cab turned onto the West Side Highway, and the river rushed by on his left, but Julian barely noticed. He was too busy tapping out instructions for Melanie and reading the updates on shows already in progress.

Several of his competitors, designers who would love to see him fail, had already had their shows. Julian didn't care; he knew there were spies, snooping around the dressing rooms, or sitting in the audience, planting little tidbits of doubt about a collection into buyers and fashion bloggers ears. Things like that could ruin an entire season for a designer on the verge of breaking out and into the big times. Like him.

And Julian knew this show was it: the culmination of everything he'd strived for, all the long days and longer nights of blood, heartache, and even, occasionally, tears. The designs he envisioned were outside the box, different from anything he'd attempted before. When he'd fitted them on the models, they'd looked magnificent. Now all he had to do was wait for them to walk the catwalk, and let the naysayers and doubters, the ones who never thought he could make it, eat their words.

He'd taken some risks, he knew, but what was life without them? At least all his risks were on a business level now. He ran his personal life akin to a business, never allowing himself to become too close. Julian had learned the hard way the damage falling in love could cause.

Despite himself, his mind strayed to days gone by, back to those tender years when all that mattered was the look in Nick's eyes when they touched each other where no one else ever had before. Wonder and innocence burned between them like fire as they thought their love would last forever.

It inevitably crashed to earth, incinerating when it touched ground, reality hitting them in the face: life went on beyond the shadows of summer nights and whispers in the dark. Fear and self-loathing, prejudices and narrow-minded values, all prevented him and Nick from walking in the sunlight together, proud and in love.

It had been over eighteen years, yet Julian would never forget the beauty of Nick's deep blue eyes. It was always Nick; beautiful, tortured, closeted Nick, whose tentative kisses made Julian's body burn with a fever he didn't understand. At sixteen years old, as they lay naked on the couch in the basement of Julian's house, touching each other, fumbling and rubbing themselves off to climax together in a marvelous, sticky mess, Julian thought they'd be in love forever.

And Julian, who had never doubted who he was and whom he loved, couldn't understand the shame Nick wrestled with, along with the fear and uncertainty. He'd never dreamed Nick would walk away from him, refusing to admit that what he and Julian had together was real and beautiful.

"I can't." Nick's voice trembled in an agonized whisper as they lay together naked on the scratchy couch. Julian had given Nick a blowjob; his first one, and it was the most exciting and intense experience ever. Their bodies still quivered from the aftereffects of their mutual climaxes.

"You can't what?" Julian licked Nick's nipple, loving the way it budded in his mouth. "You don't have to give me one." He grinned. "Not yet, at least."

"I can't do this. My family . . ." Nick swallowed hard and pushed himself up on his elbows. Away from Julian. "They won't understand this." He motioned between them. "Us. I want a family, kids." He dropped his head between his hands. "I can't see you anymore, Julian. I want to be normal."

Julian scrambled to his feet, the hurt constricting his chest so tightly he could barely breathe. "I thought we loved each other. I love you, Nick."

Nick refused to meet his gaze, saying nothing. He still said nothing, while picking up his scattered clothes from the floor and getting dressed, and nothing before he left, closing the door behind him.

After that, Julian vowed that he would choose his life, live it to the max, and to hell with everyone else. He went to school and met Marcus and Zach. After graduating, he moved to Europe and caught the eye of Lorenzo, an older designer he studied under and screwed silly until he missed New York and his friends, and decided it was time to come home and prove himself to everyone who'd ever laughed at him and called him a fag and a queer.

And if late at night the memory of Nick's sad blue eyes haunted him, keeping him up to stare for hours at the endless night-dark sky, Julian never acted on his feelings. He'd never be someone's backdoor lover, would never hide who he was.

Only once, on that horrible day of September 11, did he pick up his phone a second time after calling his old apartment to make sure Zach and Marcus were both all right. He dialed the only number he had for Nick: his parents' house. It rang without answer for four days straight, and Julian presumed they'd most likely moved.

After that he put Nick out of his mind and closed off his heart, and after another year abroad Julian decided he wanted to come home, back to New York and Seventh Avenue. It was time to show everyone what he'd accomplished; to start his own company, and design for himself and his vision. He was ready to make his dream come to life.

His love life, however, was haphazard at best. He was happy to sample the models who came before him with their tousled hair, bee-stung lips, and oh-so-willing wet mouths, but his heart remained his own. Love was, after all, a farce, like the designs he created. Simply an image, with no substance behind it.

But he took what he learned both business-wise and in love, and lived by that creed: the world was an ocean full of sharks. It was up to each person to learn which were the man-eaters and which were harmless. He'd been ripped to shreds and managed to piece himself back together, but Julian never forgot his scars, or how he came by them. There was nothing left of the wide-eyed innocent boy he'd once been.

The cab pulled up in front of the building that housed his workspace and showroom, ten stories above Fashion Avenue. People who had no clue thought a fashion designer's workroom was a hushed and glamorous world. Julian laughed to himself as he pocketed his credit card receipt from the cab. In reality it was a crazy place, with fabric dummies strewn about, and tables filled with samples, drawings, and computers.

With his trench coat billowing out and head held high, Julian strode into the building, greeting the security guard as he passed the desk. He pushed his hair out of his eyes, debating whether he should have it trimmed before tonight's party, but deciding almost immediately against it. He liked his hair a bit longer so it curled around the nape of his neck. The model he had last night, Lucien or Louis or whatever the hell his name was, liked it as well; he enjoyed pulling and tugging on it while they were screwing.

A smile teased his lips. Hopefully the poor guy didn't think fucking the designer was the way to walking in a major show. Julian kept his work and his cock separate; he didn't fuck where he ate, so to speak. And even though he'd gotten angry at Marcus for having his pretty waiters take care of the VIP table, he'd occasionally indulged with a member of the Sparks staff himself. He knew he'd be flying high after tonight, and he'd need to let off steam, and what better way than to have one or two pretty boys.

The more the merrier.

The rest of the day passed in a haze of clothing changes, makeup artists, and interviews. His excitement grew exponentially with every passing hour. By the time he was behind the scenes, watching the models walk, he was vibrating with an almost orgasmic delight. At the end of the show, walking down the runway with the clapping reverberating in his ears, Julian was at the zenith of his life; a man on top of the world. He caught sight of Marcus in the front row, clapping his hands. His friend gave him the thumbs-up sign along with a huge smile, and left as promised to go to the club.

Six hours later at Sparks, with the music pumping over the sound system and the lights flashing, Julian sat slumped in his chair, staring at the coverage in the various fashion columns in a daze.

"Copycat styling."

"Out of the box? Out of touch more like it."

"Irrelevant, mediocre."

And perhaps the nastiest review came from a blogger whose name Julian recognized as someone he hadn't spared the time to grant an interview to.

"Julian Cornell's show was akin to the geeky guy who never gets the date to the prom. He tries too hard, copying the cool kids, and thinks this time he'll finally make it, only to stumble and fail as usual."

The mood at the table was somber, not the anticipated giddiness of a collection well received. By this time he should've been receiving orders from buyers, but both his phone and Melanie's remained ominously silent.

"I don't understand. Those gilt sweaters looked fabulous on the guys." Melanie waved her phone, which showed pictures of the models walking down the runway. "How can they say they looked too girly? And what does that even mean?"

If she was expecting an answer from him, Julian had no clue. He'd thought those sweaters were fabulous, and when paired with the silk button-fly painters pants and matching short trench coat—Julian had expected those pieces alone to make the night.

Instead he was ridiculed, with one article suggesting he was nothing more than a one-hit wonder from last year's mediocre crop of new talent, and his designs this year were a pallid imitation of another young designer—Devon Chambers.

Almost ten years. That's how long it had taken him to get to this point where he thought he was about to finally do it: break out and take his place among the stars of the industry. Not the front line, but certainly on the same stage. Now he wasn't even sure he'd be allowed to buy a ticket to the show.

A hand slid around his shoulders. "Fuck 'em, Juli. It'll be fine. This will all blow over, and by tomorrow the orders will come pouring in. The clothes were great. Hell,"—Marcus tucked a strand of his sleek black hair behind his ears—"I'll order the entire damn collection." Marcus slipped into the seat next to Julian and placed a glass of champagne on the table in front of him.

And while Julian knew what Marcus was doing—and appreciated it—he couldn't sit there anymore and be the subject of all the pitying glances and fake, reassuring smiles. It ate at his insides and reminded him of all his failures, and how, in the end, he'd wind up once again alone. He loved his friend, but no one knew how close to the edge Julian teetered. He put on a show for the world, keeping them all at the surface, never once letting anyone deep inside; it was an ugly place, full of hurt, betrayal, and loss. He was a master at concealing his true self. Another life lesson from his past.

"I have to go." He downed the glass of champagne and stood abruptly. "Everyone stay as my guests, please." With that he strode off, threading his way past the ropes that had delineated the back area as VIP. What a fucking farce, he thought, viciously tearing himself to pieces in his mind. Very Insignificant Prick. That's what he was.

The coat check girl's smile was sympathetic when he handed over his ticket; shit, even she'd heard how badly it had gone. It made sense; half the people working in these clubs were aspiring models or actresses. They knew the score.

"Juli, please wait." Marcus placed a restraining hand on his arm. Julian jerked it away. The last thing he needed was sympathy, however well meaning it was.

"Come on, man." Marcus insisted. "It's us. We're here for you."

He turned to face Marcus. "I can't. I can't sit there and pretend everything's all right. I've put everything into this collection. *Everything.* I took out loans, thinking I'd get the orders to repay them, no problem. Now?" He huffed out a bitter laugh. "Maybe I should get a job at Wal-Mart, 'cause I'm going to need a way to pay back the bank. It sure as hell isn't going to come from this collection. Not after those reviews."

He took his coat from the girl and without another word, pushed his way past the bouncers and the people waiting outside behind the velvet ropes. A fine rain had begun to fall, the cold misery of the evening matching Julian's mood. Putting his head down, he strode down the block and across the street, heedless of the honking taxicabs and rain splashing on his five–hundred-dollar shoes. Everything—all of it—was a farce.

Shivering and becoming more soaked with each passing block as the rain now began to fall in earnest, Julian spotted a small pub across from a firehouse, tucked in between a sushi restaurant and a dry-cleaning store. He couldn't imagine anyone in a place like that would know who he was. He pushed open the door. Blessed warmth hit him in the face as he stood just inside the doorway and surveyed the room. It had a typical long, highly-polished bar along the wall, with one man standing with the bartender, waiting for his beer. For a moment Julian felt uncertain whether he should stay or leave.

"Come on in, buddy, and have a drink. You look like you could use it." The bartender finished pouring the beer, and the man took it and another one back to a table in the corner where his friends sat sharing a large platter of chicken wings and other appetizers.

Julian hung up his wet coat, sat, and ordered a Grey Goose on the rocks. He drank down half of it in one gulp and wiped his mouth. The bartender raised a brow.

"Rough night?"

Julian smiled faintly. "You could say that." He sipped a little slower now, looking around the bar. The group of men were in uniform; fire department he saw, from their heavy FDNY emblazoned jackets draped over their chairs. Five of them sat around a table, and as Julian sipped his drink, he casually scanned the men.

One had his back to him, but Julian was drawn to his broad shoulders and strong neck. He had short, wavy brown hair that stood up in tufts as if he'd been running his hands through it. Julian craned his neck and glimpsed a powerful thigh.

The models Julian usually took to his bed were slim and narrow hipped, and while they had muscle tone and definition, it wasn't anywhere near such an overwhelmingly masculine appearance. Julian sensed the fireman didn't have to ask for anything he wanted—he commanded.

Electricity raced up his spine. His business may be cold as

death, but Julian's libido ran hot and his cock hardened. The stranger oozed macho and sex, and Julian couldn't help but wonder how it would feel to have all that naked flesh underneath him. Better stop his ogling; this didn't seem like the kind of place to get caught staring at another guy.

He finished his drink and signaled the bartender for another one. At least he'd go home drunk, with a nice fantasy to help him get to sleep. Tomorrow he could begin thinking about the wreckage of his company.

"What do you do?" The bartender took away his empty glass and replaced it with a fresh one.

"I'm a clothing designer; I design men's clothing." *Hopefully that is still true.*

The man's brows rose. "No shit?" When Julian nodded, he added, "I shoulda guessed from how you look. You definitely got more style than anyone else here."

"Yo, Jimmy." One of the men from the table yelled out. "Send another round over and tell the kitchen more wings, huh?"

"Holdja horses, Carlos. I'm talking. I was telling this man here"—he pointed to Julian—"Whaja say your name was?"

"I didn't," said Julian with a small grin, "but it's Julian." He was surprised to find himself enjoying the conversation and the bar in general. It was so far removed from Marcus's trendy club as to be comical, yet much more intimate and real.

Jimmy the bartender continued. "I was telling Julian here, that he's the best dressed guy who's ever come in here. You all look like slobs next to him."

Julian winced, knowing these men wouldn't appreciate that remark.

"We'd hardly need to dress like that when out on a tour." The man named Carlos ran his gaze over Julian, a smirk curling his lips. "We're busy saving lives. We ain't having lunch with the Queen, ya know." The entire table snickered, although Julian noticed how stiff the man he'd been eyeing had become; he'd drawn into himself, hunched over his drink.

The dismissive tone of Carlos's voice set Julian on edge. And the queen remark—was that a subtle dig at Julian being gay? After the worst night of his life, the last thing he needed was to be put down by someone who looked like he bought his clothes at Home Depot and didn't know the difference between *Popular Mechanics* and *GQ* Magazine.

"So sorry my job doesn't fit in with your opinion of what real work is." He straightened his cashmere sweater and flicked his hair back.

"Look buddy, we don't got time to worry about whether our socks match our underwear when we're fighting a fire." A tall, gray-haired man leaned back in his chair and kicked the foot of the man whose back was to Julian. "Tell me, am I right?"

Julian watched the man shrug, but couldn't hear his answer.

He bristled, his blood running hot. "Not everyone can be a life saver. And you're right. I don't save people. But I help them in other ways. Sometimes looking good can make a person feel better about themselves when the rest of their life is shit." Julian dug into his pants and pulled out his wallet. "Thanks for *your* hospitality, Jimmy." He gave him two twenty dollar bills. "Keep the change."

He stood and without a backward glance, lifted his coat off the rack by the door and left the pub. Fucking guys probably didn't even own asuit. Julian buttoned up his coat and hunched his shoulders against the cold as he walked to the subway. No limo for him tonight. His phone buzzed with a text. He checked and saw it was from Zach.

Congratulations on the show, I know you killed it.

Julian laughed so hard, tears came to his eyes.

Chapter Two

THE BEST DAYS of Nick Fletcher's week weren't spent on the job. He enjoyed being a tactical trainer for the FDNY; not as much as when he'd been on active duty as a firefighter, but right now Nick was thankful he could get up in the morning and have a place to go to. It was more than some of his buddies were able to do. Still, Nick thought as he poured himself a cup of coffee, the kids in the burn unit, they were the real heroes as far as he was concerned.

His phone rang, and seeing it was his mother he hit Speaker so he could keep cleaning up in the kitchen and drink his coffee as he talked.

"Hi, Mom."

"Are you coming upstairs for breakfast?" Her loud voice filled the room, and he could hear the sink running in the background. "I have waffles and bacon, and Katie's here and wants to see you."

"Sure, I'll be up in a few." He smiled, as he hadn't seen his sister in a while and missed her.

"Good."

Nick finished his coffee and headed upstairs. He lived in the first-floor apartment of his family's two-family house in Brooklyn. The arrangement worked perfectly for Nick; he was close, but his parents respected his need for privacy.

Upon entering his parents' house he was greeted by the aroma of the aforementioned bacon, and the sound of his sister's laughter. Nick was instantly taken back to his youth, when he and Katie would sit and watch out of the window, waiting for their father to get home from his tour as a firefighter, and argue over who would get to wear his gear.

The sofa with its needlepoint pillows remained the same, although it was a bit more faded now from both sun and age. The photographs along the wall had changed to include his graduation from the academy, his swearing-in ceremony as a firefighter, and the day he joined his firehouse as a probie. The pictures stopped after that.

Nick ran his fingers over the photograph of himself and his parents together, the day he was sworn in. His father couldn't stop smiling—he'd been so proud Nick followed in his footsteps. Nick's throat tightened and his vision blurred with tears.

"Nicky? Is that you?"

No use in dwelling on the past. There was nothing left of that young and carefree man anymore. After last night, wondering if the man in the bar was Julian, *his Julian,* he'd barely been able to get any sleep.

Blinking furiously to hide any telltale sign of emotion, he answered his mother. "Yeah, coming."

The sight that greeted him brought a smile to his face. His mother at the stove and his father sitting at the round wooden kitchen table reading the newspaper, were both comforting sights that once again, brought back memories of better times. But it was his sister, Katie, who lightened his heart. Though five years his junior, she had seamlessly fit in with his friends growing up, and they'd always stayed close. She'd been his support, his best friend, and the only one he was able to talk to.

Katie glanced up from her plate and a smile lit up her face. "Nicky!" Her hug was gentle, and as always he sensed the love behind it. "You big jerk. Why haven't you called me?"

He brushed the dark curls off her face. "I'm sorry. I got busy with my extra tours and then the burn center."

His father put down his paper. The sun streaming in through the large kitchen window glinted off the silver threading through his black hair. They'd all inherited his Black Irish looks, with their inky dark hair and startling blue eyes.

"How's that going? Is it hard for you to be with all those children?"

Nick sat next to Katie and toyed with a folded napkin. His mother wordlessly slid a plate filled with waffles and bacon in front of him, then sat next to his father and looked at him expectantly.

Nick hesitated, wondering how to put into words the emotions that gripped his heart each time he sat with a child who was suffering. The only thing that eased his way was the knowledge that he was helping them and to an extent, healing himself in the process and doing what he knew his buddies, the ones who didn't make it, would have wanted. He twisted the ring on his finger, the ring given to him by Maryann O'Reilly, wife of Brian, one of his brothers, who didn't make it back. Nick hadn't wanted to accept it but she insisted, and he finally relented, vowing never to take it off, and always to make Brian proud of him.

"It helps me, sometimes more than them, if that makes sense." The ache of long-ago pain would remain with him, despite the passage of years. "It helps them see there's life beyond the hospital, skin grafts, and the pain killers."

"As long as it isn't too much for you. I don't want you to think I'm insensitive." Anxious worry etched even more lines in his mother's fair skin. "I love how you've found a passion and dedication."

"It isn't, and I don't." He cut into his food. "To be able to work and give something to these kids who think there's nothing left for them, gives me a reason to get up."

Instead of his words alleviating his mother's worry, Nick caught the glint of tears in her eyes.

"Mom. I'm fine."

And he was, for him. Life had the certainty he now required: get up, go to work, and volunteer. It made sense to him, and that's what he needed. Sense out of the senselessness of life. But then there was last night, and if he was right and it was Julian, he was all jumbled up again.

"Oh, this is terrible." Katie scrolled through her phone, frowning.

"What?" He poured more syrup on his waffles.

"My friend Melanie works for this designer and last night his show was panned by the critics. So bad in fact that she isn't sure if she'll even have a job by the end of the week."

"That sucks." He chewed and took a sip of his coffee. "How do you know her?"

"She was robbed a few years ago when I first came to the office and working nights." Still reading her text, Katie bit her lip. "I worked her case and we became friends."

"I'm so glad you don't work burglary anymore, dear."

Finally putting down her phone, Katie grinned. "Well, honestly, I'm not sure working sex crimes is much better in that respect, Mom."

Nick knew his parents were inordinately proud of his sister's work as an assistant district attorney. She'd prosecuted some cases that had received minor publicity, but more importantly, she enjoyed doing her job and was damn good at it. "I like putting the bastards behind bars" was always her cheerful response when people questioned her long hours and choice of profession.

Nick thought of the man he'd seen last night in the bar. "I heard a guy last night saying he was a men's clothing designer; he seemed kind of obnoxious to me. Very full of himself."

"Most of them are." A surprised expression crossed her face. "Where were you that you'd meet a clothing designer?" She snatched a piece of bacon off his plate and grabbed her empty dish to take it to the sink. "I don't see you hanging out at trendy clubs."

"He came into Backdrafts. He was talking to Jimmy, then Carlos and him had a difference of opinion as to what his contribution to society is. He got very defensive." To be fair, maybe his buddy had been a little harsh on the guy.

"Oh, Nicky. What did Carlos say?"

He shrugged. "Nothing that wasn't the truth. He told him designing fancy clothes couldn't be measured against someone who saved lives, that's all. And we all agreed."

Katie gaped at him. "He didn't."

Unconcerned, he chewed his waffles and swallowed. "Yep."

"That wasn't very nice, Nicholas. People have different skills and talents." His mother shot him a disapproving look over her coffee cup.

Ridiculous. It wasn't as if he disagreed with Carlos and Jensen. Who had time to think about their clothes? Maybe they'd been a bit harsh, but what the hell. It ate at his gut that he'd been too chickenshit to turn around and see if it was Julian after all these years. He knew why he didn't, of course.

If he had and it was Julian, would he have turned away from him? Nick was ashamed to admit he probably would have. He'd caught a glimpse of the man walking out of the bar, and he was tall and lean, with a head full of golden wavy hair. Still, it didn't mean it was his Julian, there were probably plenty of designers with that name. And who knew if he really accomplished his dream?

But Nick knew Julian did. He remembered them lying together, Julian's head on his chest, listening to the passion in Julian's voice; how he'd become this famous designer, and Nick would model his clothes for him. Nick would laugh and then they'd start kissing again and forget what they were talking about.

Those stolen afternoons and weekend nights with Julian were the only times Nick had ever been able to be himself; when he'd let go of his fear and lived only on the bubble of hope and hormones and desire, it all came crashing down. That last day, watching his cock sliding in and out of Julian's mouth, hearing Julian's moans of delight, reality slapped Nick in the face and woke him up from the dream world he was living in. He knew he couldn't ever tell his family he liked men and not women. It wasn't how he was raised.

Worst of all, he knew how badly he hurt Julian. Though he didn't say a word, Nick saw the wetness in Julian's eyes and watched him bite that quivering full lower lip, that mouth that only minutes before had been wrapped round Nick's cock, moaning Nick's name.

Why the hell was he thinking about this and in his parents' kitchen of all places? It seemed indecent to think about sex, gay or straight, in the place where he and his sister had sat doing their homework and eating their after-school snacks. Maybe because it had been months since Nick had sex. People might think it was easier for a gay man these days, but not when you wore a uniform, and certainly not when you've kept your entire life a secret. To be fair, he had no idea how his parents would take the news. But with all he'd put them through over the years, he didn't see the need to tell them, *"Oh and guess what, I'm gay too."*

Nick had gotten so used to hiding things about himself, he often wondered if he even knew who he was anymore.

"To me it seems shallow, that's all. Concentrating on a button, or whether someone's tie is the right color." But he squirmed under his mother's rebuke.

From the sink, Katie added her own opinion. "Melanie says her boss works crazy hours and barely sleeps. He's stretched to the max. But he's nice to her and donates to a lot of charities."

"All right, all right," he grumbled. "Her boss is perfect and I'm wrong." He stood and brought his own plate to the sink, joining Katie. "The man I saw last night didn't act like he cared about anything other than his and everyone else's appearance. And that to me is shallow." Nick quickly washed his plate and cup. "I gotta run now. I promised I'd be at the burn center by noon."

Katie placed her cup in the dish drain and dried her hands. "What are you doing tonight?" Her blue eyes bore into his. "Want to come out with me? I'm meeting Melanie and we're going to a party."

God no. As he opened his mouth to decline, Katie, sensing his answer, hurried her words and cut him off.

"Please, Nicky? It's a charity event to benefit runaway gay youth." She squeezed his arm. "It's at a club, but I promise you won't have to dance or anything. I really want to hang out with you."

Though he cringed at the thought of all those hot bodies

pressed up against his and the dark enclosed space, he owed Katie more than he could ever repay her, so an evening of sitting in a corner nursing a drink and making stilted talk was a small price to pay.

"Sure, what the hell." The delight that flared in her eyes was reason enough to put aside his misgivings and go. "Tell me where and when."

He took down the contact information on his phone. "Sparks. Isn't that one of those trendy clubs in Tribeca?"

"Yes, but the owner is a big supporter of the LGBT community and is throwing this fundraiser tonight. I'll have the tickets, so we'll meet beforehand, say ten o'clock?"

"Works for me." He kissed his mother goodbye and clapped his father on the back. "Thanks for the breakfast, Mom. I'll see you tomorrow, Dad, and we can work on winterizing the house like we talked about."

Once back downstairs in his apartment, Nick collected keys, wallet, and the parking pass for the garage he'd been given by the hospital administrators when he began volunteering. He pulled out of the driveway and started the drive into the city. At the corner, his neighbor from across the street waved to him.

"Have a nice day, Nicky. Say hi to the kids for me."

"I will, Mrs. O'Keefe." All the neighbors knew he volunteered from his mother. That and the fact that in this working-class enclave of Marine Park, Brooklyn, every neighbor knew each other's business.

The drive took close to forty-five minutes from the time Nick left his house until he pulled into a free space in the hospital garage and slapped the parking permit on his windshield. He greeted the security guard and headed toward the elevators, refusing to make a mad dash in through the open doors. He'd rather wait for the next one.

The children's burn unit should've been a depressing place, but the nurses and doctors who worked there always made certain to have balloons about along with fresh flowers and colorful pictures hanging on the walls. These were special people who dedicated themselves to working long hours and providing unequaled care.

"Hello, Nick. Glad you're here." Hannah, the head nurse, approached him with her usual long, purposeful stride. Nick had never seen her not busy with something. He wondered if she ever rested.

"Hi, Hannah. Yes, I promised Jamal I'd be here today when he received his compression bandages. And I want to visit the others as well."

They walked together down the hall toward the rooms, and the nurse's face softened in sympathy. "It's so hard on the younger ones. They can't imagine anything ever getting better for them."

Who says it will? Knowing he should offer up words of encouragement, since that was what he was there for, Nick forced a smile. "It's a tough road ahead of them." As if on cue, the fabric of his thin shirt rubbed against Nick's chest, and he itched to press his hands against his skin. "Nothing can really prepare a person for what lies ahead of them after this happens."

"We appreciate everything you do, Nick, you know that, right? The kids need someone like you." For five years Nick had been volunteering at the burn unit, and Hannah knew better than to ask him any personal questions.

They stopped outside a room. "Jamal's in here." The sympathy in her eyes turned to sadness. "He's having a hard time adjusting to the limitations of his injuries. Plus the compression bandages on his arm and leg . . ." She shook her head. "It's too much for anyone to bear, especially a child. And he is a child despite being seventeen."

Pain, fear, and the cold lonely feeling as you lay in bed at night, tasting the salt of your tears, that you'll never make it back. You'll never be a whole person again.

"Let me see what I can do," said Nick grimly.

Hannah gave him a measured look and walked away without another word. Nick entered Jamal's room to find the young man lying in bed, staring at the ceiling. His eyes barely flickered when Nick sat down next to his bed.

"Hi."

Seconds passed with no response. "Jamal. You don't have to say a word. Listen though. It sucks. It hurts. You feel like life will never be good again. And I'm going to agree with everything."

That got a reaction. If Jamal expected him to sugarcoat it, Nick wasn't there for that.

"It hurts, Nick. And this crap I gotta wear? It's so fuckin' ugly, and it's all itchy and shit." As best he could, Jamal's stiff fingers plucked uselessly at the bandages that wrapped around his fingers and hand. Nick didn't need to be told the bandages wrapped all the way up Jamal's arm.

"Yeah, I know. But you know why you have to wear it right? It helps prevent the scar tissue from forming. Keep saying in your mind it won't be forever."

"But it feels like it. I hate it, I can't do it." Tears trickled out of the corners of Jamal's eyes, and the anger and hurt spilled out unchecked. "I used to be the stylin' one. Everyone in school looked to me; what to wear and how to wear it. The girls . . ." He bit his lip. "Who's gonna want me now, man? I'm ugly." He blinked furiously. Nick knew Jamal didn't think it was cool to cry; not in front of anyone at least. Seventeen-year-olds didn't cry.

The best Nick could do for Jamal was take a tissue, wipe his tears, and be honest.

"It's going to be hard; the hardest thing you'll ever do. And you'll find out who your real friends are; they'll be the ones by your side when you come home, sticking by you and cheering you on." He held Jamal's tearful gaze. "I'll be there, whenever and wherever you need me. That you can take to the bank."

True friends didn't look away in disgust, or pretend like nothing had changed. People had a way of disappearing when shit got real. Jamal didn't ask for this to happen. He didn't ask for his mother's boyfriend to fall asleep with a cigarette burning and have the apartment catch on fire. Not only did he have to contend with his injuries, but he and his mother and little sister were now homeless, forced to live with his aunt.

The small nod he received from Jamal was a victory for Nick. They spent the remainder of the visit with Nick helping Jamal with his exercises to keep his fingers from stiffening. Then Jamal's mother came, and Nick visited with other patients, listening to them, helping them, and offering whatever comfort he could. His mother's delicious breakfast seemed ages ago as he grabbed a container of yogurt from the hospital cafeteria.

The hours he spent here several times a week were as important to him as being a firefighter. Nick needed this; somehow it validated everything that had happened to him. His phone buzzed, and Nick couldn't help but smile when Katie's name popped up.

Don't forget tonight. We'll meet you outside the club. Wear blue to match your eyes.

He'd forgotten her friend Melanie was going to be there. *Shit.* The last thing Nick wanted was for his sister to be setting him up. With a woman. It didn't matter that Katie most likely wouldn't care if he was gay or not; Nick was in no way putting it out there for the world to see. He'd heard enough homophobic remarks on his tours when he was on active duty and now that he was doing training to know how well that bit of news would be received. Not that he would ever say anything; he wasn't going to rock that proverbial boat. Not when the department was doing all it could to help ease him back into active duty.

It may be the age of enlightenment, but that didn't extend everywhere or to everyone, and especially not to people who wore a uniform. And Nick knew his old buddies at the firehouse would freak the hell out if he ever came out as gay.

Too many secrets.

After leaving the hospital, Nick knew he didn't have anything suitable to wear to this club, so he stopped at a store in SoHo. Because of his 9/11 settlement, Nick didn't have to worry too much about money; most of what he'd spent had been for his parents' house and their needs. He owed them everything, and it was the least he could do. He'd hardly spent anything on himself, since he lived in jeans and tee shirts or sweats, so he had no clue what to wear; he'd entered the first trendy-looking shop he passed. This wasn't where he'd typically buy his clothes, but he didn't want to embarrass his sister.

One hour and three hundred dollars later, Nick was on his way home, with a blue silk shirt and a pair of black, snug-fitting pants the hot salesman insisted would be perfect. He knew the salesman was gay and interested by the way he'd let his hand linger while handing Nick the clothes, and his repeated offers of assistance. There'd been one wild moment when his pants were off and Nick had a vision of the guy on his knees, sucking his cock in the dressing room, while customers browsed the store on the other side of the flimsy curtain. Impossibly hard from that thought, Nick had squashed it down and waited until he cooled down and could zip himself up again.

Any hooking up Nick might do was with anonymous guys he met online, or at bars away from where he lived. Besides, sex wasn't high on his list of priorities, never had been. It had always been something done furtively; rushed and against a wall in a club or a bar, somewhere, anywhere but at home. He wasn't looking for anything except release. Nick had given up on forevers and happily-ever-afters once he'd sent Julian away.

He pulled into his driveway and cut the engine. Sitting still in the silence for a moment, Nick took a few deep breaths to calm down, then left his car and went inside his house. New clothes, a club tonight, everything was happening fast. Too fast. He'd take a nap and wake up with a clearer head. He lay down and instantly fell asleep, thinking of Julian's mouth and wide green eyes.

Five hours later, he was outside the club called Sparks, waiting for Katie and her friend. Well-dressed people walked in past the velvet ropes after having their tickets checked by the bouncers. Nick remembered he owed Katie a thank-you for making him look halfway presentable.

"Nicky!" Katie called to him as she exited a cab, and Nick frowned as he watched a passerby ogle her long legs.

"Isn't that dress too short?" He kissed her cheek and put his arm around her in a protective gesture, shooting warning looks at others to keep away.

"One hour of shopping and now you're a fashion expert?"

She was teasing him, Nick knew, but he was still her big brother. "Someone has to look out for you."

"You're sweet." She kissed his cheek and he caught a whiff of her subtle, expensive perfume. "This is Melanie." She beckoned to her friend. "Mel, this is my big brother, Nicky."

A thin, blonde young woman, dressed all in black, with a wide smile and a firm handshake, greeted him. "Nice to meet you."

Nick relaxed, instantly liking her direct and friendly demeanor. "Same. Shall we go inside?"

Melanie took the tickets out of her bag and handed them to the bouncer. "My boss got these for me; his best friend owns this club."

"That was generous of him."

Katie squeezed his arm gently. "You look great."

He smiled at her. "Same to you, even if your dress is too short."

"He's very generous to me." Melanie stopped at the coat check so they could hand over their jackets. "And even with all the horrible reviews last night for his show, he said he was coming here and not hiding away in shame. I know he's in trouble, but he won't talk about it."

Nick stiffened, but allowed Katie to pull him inside. *It can't be.* They walked into the club.

"There they are. Let me bring them over and introduce you." She hurried off.

"She's so nice, don't you think?" Katie took two glasses of champagne from a waiter's offered tray.

"What? Yeah, sure." Nick took a gulp of his drink. The club was well lit, with plenty of flashing lights in a rainbow of colors. And speaking of rainbows, there were pride flags everywhere: hanging from the stage where the male dancers moved to the pounding music, draped as banners against the wall, and miniature ones as centerpieces on the table. Katie was correct, there wasn't a huge crowd; there was plenty of room between the tables and, as Nick always did, he made note of where the nearest emergency exits were.

Just in case.

Melanie returned with two men. "This is Marcus Feldman, the owner of Sparks. This is my friend Katie and her brother Nick."

A tall, well-built man with black hair and odd, gray-violet eyes ignored Katie and gave Nick a slow assessing look. "Nice to meet you." Marcus shook his hand, and Nick instantly knew the guy was gay and a major player. The way he slid his hand out of Nick's grasp, with a stroke of his thumb on Nick's palm, was a nice touch. He ignored it, his eyes widening in shock as Melanie introduced her boss to him. Marcus turned to speak to Katie.

"Nick, this is my boss, Julian Cornell."

"Oh, I believe we've met already." Julian's lips curved in a smirk. "How are you Nick?"

"Out of my fucking mind," said Nick in a voice so low he didn't think anyone heard him.

Julian stuck out his hand and Nick took it automatically. Electricity shot down Nick's spine and straight to his crotch. He jerked away from Julian and gulped down the rest of his drink.

Shit. Last time he listened to his sister.

Chapter Three

WELL, WELL." MARCUS'S eyes gleamed. "This may prove to be a much more interesting night than originally planned."

Julian, who hadn't taken his eyes off Nick, frowned. "What're you talking about?" *Was Melanie his date?* He took a sip of his drink, continuing to study the man as he walked toward the bar with the two women.

Cute as a high school boy, Nick was devastating as a grown man. He was tall and broad in the chest without being overly muscled, and wore a beautiful blue shirt that brought out the glow in his eyes and showed off the breadth of those wide shoulders. Julian imagined the strength of his arms now, and couldn't help noticing Nick's powerful legs.

"I mean, your little assistant's friend is a stunner, and I plan on finding out his story."

That caught Julian's attention, drawing him away from his study of Nick's ass. They'd been together only two years and apart almost two decades. Those high school days were so far away in the past, Julian had no idea who Nick was anymore. He'd never spoken of his broken heart to Marcus or Zach; there'd been no need, since he never thought he'd lay eyes on Nick again. And Marcus would do nothing but laugh at him anyway.

"Forget it, Marcus. That guy would never be interested in you. He's got a stick up his ass a mile long."

The corner of Marcus's mouth tipped up in a smile. "That would make it easier for what I have planned, don't you think?"

Julian shrugged, dismissing his friend's crude joke. Let Marcus find out on his own how Nick would shut him down. He had bigger problems that his friend's overactive sex life. Like how he was supposed to pay off the loan he'd taken when he'd only received a few orders from last night's show, plus pay his office rent, and Melanie's salary, in addition to his own living expenses. He had no family to ask for a loan, no one to fall back on. For perhaps the hundredth time, Julian ran through the stinging criticisms he'd read about his collection, trying to figure out something, *anything* he might have missed. How did that bastard Devon Chambers steal his ideas? He tipped his glass to take a drink, only to find it empty.

"Here." Melanie pressed another glass in his hand. "Even though you won't talk to me, I've worked with you too long and know you too well. Stop second-guessing yourself."

His laugh rang bitter. "I'm all the way up to fifth and sixth. Second-guessing was right before the show started." Half the vodka disappeared in one gulp. "How did it happen? How did he steal everything we worked so hard for?" Julian counted on her for honesty, as well as her innate talent and sense of style. Plus, after working together for three years, she was his friend. "Maybe he is better than I'll ever be and I'm wrong. There was enough of a difference after all."

"Don't be ridiculous; you're miles ahead of him, and I'm not saying that because you're my boss. You're a wonderful designer." She patted his arm. "I'll find out the scoop, I promise."

Humiliating as it was, there were things Julian needed to make clear. This was the hardest thing he'd ever had to say, but he owed it to her. "I won't hold you to your commitment to me. You're starting out, and you need to work where you'll be noticed for your talent. It's hard enough for a woman to be taken seriously designing men's clothing; you don't need to be stuck with me."

"Don't be ridiculous. I love working for you." They stood together, surveying the crowd. "I think for tonight you should forget all the negativity. There'll be plenty of time for us to sort through reality next week. Tonight, let yourself go."

The model he'd had in his bed the other night walked into the club, his eyes scanning the crowd. Julian couldn't forget how talented his mouth was, and the varied ways he'd put his tongue and lips to use. For a second his thoughts flickered to Nick, but he ruthlessly shut that down.

He rejected you. He doesn't want you; he never really did.

"Perhaps you're right," he murmured to Melanie. "What was it that Scarlett O'Hara said, 'I'll think about it tomorrow,' or something to that effect?" Julian set his drink down on one of the many mirror-top tables set about the club. "I see someone who'll be able to take my mind off my problems." He kissed her cheek. "Go flirt with some of the straight guys here. I know they're around somewhere."

Threading his way through the crowd, Julian managed to make eye contact with Lucien. At least that's what he thought the guy's name was. Funny how he could have his cock buried in someone's ass or in their mouth for half the night, and couldn't remember their name, yet exchanging only one or two sentences was enough to conjure up Nick's blue eyes.

"Hey." He grasped Lucien around the neck and dragged the man's slim body up against his. It was only when Julian bent his head down for a kiss that he realized Lucien was pulling away from him.

"Get your hands off me."

The coldness in Lucien's voice startled Julian. "Surely you didn't forget me already?" He held the gaze of the handsome young man's pale gray eyes. "You screamed my name enough times."

Lucien shrugged. "You were a good fuck, but I'm here to meet someone. See you around." He turned, his lip curled in disdain, then glanced over his shoulder. "I gotta thank you for turning me down to walk in your show." His gaze flickered over Julian as though he were no better than a homeless person begging in the subway. "After your reviews, you'd be lucky to get a high school kid off the streets to walk for you." With a toss of his blond curls, he flounced away.

Gape-mouthed, Julian watched Lucien curl himself around the man labeled this year's "it designer," Devon Chambers. Hopeful no one witnessed his small humiliation, Julian couldn't hurry away fast enough. Fate was a cruel bitch as usual, and before he could make his escape, a firm hand clamped down on his shoulder, and Julian heard Chambers' drawling tone in his ear.

"Julian, I'm *so* happy to see you, although I must say I'm a bit surprised." Devon Chambers' dark, close-cropped beard couldn't hide his strong jaw and full lips. White teeth flashed against his tanned skin in a smug, self-assured grin that only someone who'd had his ass kissed all day by the press could possess. Chambers was aware of his good looks, and now with last night's accolades still streaming in from industry professionals, Julian braced himself.

"Surprised?" Swallowing the bitterness that still swamped him, Julian affected his best nonchalant attitude. "Why?" He checked his watch as if to show he hadn't the time to waste on the conversation.

Chambers' black eyes narrowed. "I'm sure you thought no one would notice how your collection, hmm, shall we say—for want of a better word—resembled mine?" The grin on his face grew calculating. "But you got no calls or orders, did you? You thought you'd be the star of the season, instead of fizzling out to nothing." He flicked a spot off his black shirt and leaned in close enough for Julian to smell his subtle aftershave. "A word of advice? Try and come up with fresh ideas."

Lucien—little rat that he was—whispered into Chambers' ear, and he threw his head back and laughed. Julian's hands itched, imagining a nice, hard throat punch. How he managed to hold his temper he had no idea.

"Have fun with your little plaything, Devon. Enjoy my sloppy seconds. Oh," Julian sneered, hoping against hope no one saw his shaking hands. "Make sure you keep an eye on your wallet." This time he strode off, uncaring as to whose shoulder he knocked into, or whose drink he spilled. He could barely see for the blind fury descending over his eyes in a red haze.

How had that fucker snatched his designs? Julian remembered exactly when he came up with the sketches; hell, he still had the napkins from the diner in his apartment. Somehow, that bastard had copied Julian's best work, slightly switching the choice of fabrics and colors. With Chambers' show running earlier in the day, he'd been the first to show the designs, gathering all the accolades and praise.

Which left Julian, who'd been so wrapped up in his own collection, completely unaware it was almost a repetition of Chambers', until the reports started trickling in. Oh, there were some subtle differences, but the influences, the heart and emotion of the collection, were practically identical.

"Julian?" Melanie stopped him by the bar. She stared over his shoulder and her eyes widened. "Is that Devon Chambers? Did he—"

"He told me I should think up some new ideas. That fucker."

Slouched up against the bar, Nick stood, his brow furrowed in confusion.

"What's wrong?"

Melanie began to explain what had happened, but listening to her talk about Devon Chambers and how he'd managed to steal Julian's designs was like a knife to Julian's heart. And with the sting of Chambers' snide comments fresh in his head, Julian was in no mood to act nice. It wasn't his way to conceal and pretend.

"Why would you care?" Julian held Nick's gaze and was inordinately pleased to see the man wince, shame evidenced on his face.

"Julian," Nick began. "I'm sorry."

"Why?" Julian folded his arms. "You don't know what I'm talking about and probably don't care either." He got a perverse pleasure over watching Nick squirm at his words. Julian didn't want to think of the other, more erotic pleasures he got from looking at Nick.

"Julian, that's not nice." Melanie protested.

"I'm being truthful. I know his type."

Nick had the grace to flush. "Doesn't give someone the right to steal. Or be a tool."

"Why do I get the feeling I'm missing something here?"

Melanie asked, her eyes creased with confusion.

Julian shot Nick a sharp glance, and he could see the muscle tense under that hard, stubbled jaw.

"Julian and I knew each other. Back in high school."

"Barely." Julian couldn't resist the dig, and even in the flashing lights, he could see Nick flush.

Melanie's gaze traveled between the two of them, unconcealed delight spreading across her face. "But that's amazing. I can't believe it." She smacked Julian lightly on his shoulder. "How come you didn't say anything?"

"It was so long ago." Nick tightened his grip around his glass and huffed out a small laugh. "I mean, who remembers high school after so many years?"

Julian froze for a moment, then took a sip of his drink, amazed it slid down past the tightness in his throat. So while he had mourned the death of their relationship, Nick had barely given it a second thought. He hadn't suffered the way Julian had; he'd probably started dating as soon as they stopped seeing each other.

Seeing each other. No use in thinking about that. Julian surreptitiously stared at the strong cords of muscle in Nick's neck, as he tilted his head back to drink his whisky. There was so much restrained power in the man's body, and Julian, who was used to dealing with highly strung models who needed constant reassurance, sensed there was something else, something hidden.

Melanie's eyes flashed at him. "I hate this. You've proved yourself over and over to these bastards for years, how brilliant you are, and now that miserable excuse for a designer up and steals your designs with no repercussions, and you can't enjoy what's rightfully yours."

He wavered between anger and humiliation, as Nick stared at him. Though he worked in a public industry, Julian was a very private person and didn't get close to many people. 'Trust no one' was his motto, and except for Marcus, Zach, and Melanie, he didn't.

"I don't get it," Nick said, putting his empty glass back

down on the bar. The muscles in his biceps rippled through the thin, silky fabric of his shirt, and Julian had to force himself to look away. "I mean it's only clothes. Like, who cares how many ways are there to make a shirt or a pair of pants?"

"It isn't only clothes." Julian enjoyed watching the discomfort on Nick's face. "It's the whole persona. We're selling an outlook on life." Julian loved talking about the emotional aspect of clothes. "Don't you feel better when you put something on your body that fits well? Or when you put a color on and it brightens up your mood? Like your shirt." Without thinking, Julian reached over and grabbed the material between his fingers. "This color makes the blue of your eyes pop, and the whites even whiter, and I'm sure the silk feels good against your body."

When he received no response, Julian realized not only was he standing way too close to Nick, but his hand was touching his chest. His fingertips brushed the whorls of dark hair against Nick's skin and the warm, soapy scent of him surrounded Julian. Nick stood frozen, his eyes a dark mask. The heat of Nick's whisky-tinged breath blew against Julian's face.

Nick jerked away, his shirt sliding through Julian's hands. "I don't give a shit what I wear," he said brusquely. "I only dressed like this for Katie, so I wouldn't embarrass her."

"Oh, Nicky," Katie said, materializing at his side.

Julian stood silent and watched as Katie spoke quietly to Nick and gave him a hug. He raised a brow at Melanie who shrugged. There was a story here he was missing. The strobe lights couldn't hide the deep grooves cutting furrows alongside Nick's firm mouth, or the coiled intensity of his body. Nick was a man on the edge, Julian sensed, a powder keg only a spark away from igniting.

A fire burned inside of Nick, and Julian sensed if it was ever to be released, there would be an explosion.

"I only meant people's perspective on life can change if they feel strong and powerful, and that can come from looking at yourself in the mirror and being positive about your appearance."

Nick snorted. "You still believe that crap? I mean you dress nice, but you think if you walked around in a pair of old jeans and a tee shirt you wouldn't sound as pompous as you do right now?"

A familiar cackle rang out behind him. "Damn, Nick. You haven't spent more than five minutes with Juli and you've got him pegged."

Marcus had no idea of his and Nick's past together. When Marcus slung an arm around Julian's shoulder, for some crazy reason it pleased him to see Nick's eyes narrow.

"He's not so bad, but if you really want to torture Julian, make him go shopping to one of the outer-boroughs, or Jersey."

"How long have you two been together?" Katie smiled at Julian.

Now it was Julian's turn to choke back the laughter. "Me with Marc? Not in a million years." The two of them looked at each other and broke out in hysterics. Julian put his hand out, as if to indicate Katie should never say that again. "Never. He's too much of a man-whore."

"Bullshit, man. I'm too much for you to handle." They bumped shoulders, the gesture familiar to them from years of friendship.

"We met when we took classes together, then the two of us and our other friend Zach became roommates, but we're not together. Never even considered it." Julian wiped tears of laughter from his eyes. "The first time I saw him he was hitting on an assistant professor."

"Aim high I always believe." Marcus drained his drink, wiped his mouth with the back of his hand, and to Julian's shock, grabbed Nick by the hand and pulled him onto the dance floor. Julian stood, watching Nick stand uncomfortably for a few moments before turning away from Marcus and walking away.

Knowing Marcus—flirt that he was—possessed an ego that would never allow a man to walk away from him, Julian wasn't surprised to see his friend grab onto the back of Nick's shirt, pulling it free from the waistband of his pants. Nick froze and turned around, spitting out angry words Julian wasn't close enough to hear. And Marcus, oblivious to anything except himself and his cock, chose to ignore Nick's obvious fury, and tugged the front of Nick's shirt up, as if to yank it over his head.

Which was when Nick hauled off, hit Marcus square on the jaw, and stormed away, leaving him flat on his ass. And instead of helping his friend, Julian took off after Nick who had fled to the back of the club.

Chapter Four

F*UCK.* BY SOME miracle, Nick found himself at the door to the men's restroom and pushed his way inside. The lights were bright and Nick blinked hard, unsure if what he was witnessing was real. Two men were up against the wall, hands down each other's pants, tongues down each other's throats. Fascinated, Nick stood, watching the intensely erotic scene unfold in front of him.

His cheeks warmed as he listened to their escalating groans echoing against the tiled walls. Nick's cock throbbed and he adjusted his tight pants, giving himself a firm squeeze to soothe the ache. The mutual rub-off came to a frenetic, explosive climax, and the two men sagged against the wall, bracing themselves from sinking to the floor.

Fearful of being caught, Nick hastened into one of the stalls and sat breathing hard, more turned on than he would have liked. The sink ran and he could hear voices whisper and then the sound of low laughter and kisses. Finally, the door opened, the two men left, and he was alone.

His hand was on the latch of the stall when he heard the door to the bathroom open. *Damn.* Hopeful the man had just come in to take a piss, Nick waited, but heard nothing except for breathing.

This was ridiculous. He couldn't sit here all night, hiding out like a child who knew he'd done something wrong. Nick had to swallow his fear and his pride and go back outside and apologize to Marcus, then go home.

"I'm wondering how long you're planning on sitting there."

Nick froze at Julian's soft, mocking tone.

"Knowing Marcus, whatever you hit him for, you probably

had a good reason."

Nick couldn't help the flicker of a smile before he flipped up the latch on the door and walked out. Dressed all in black, which Nick was beginning to think was the only color the man wore, Julian looked like a somber angel, his face set in an expression of cautious sympathy. Nick had had enough compassion in his life and had grown to despise it and all the false enthusiasm that came with it.

It made him angry and defensive. "Why are you here?" he blurted. "Shouldn't you be with your friend?" But he was inordinately pleased Julian had chosen to be with him over Marcus.

Julian shrugged. "Marcus is a big boy. If you decked him, I'm sure he had it coming." He smiled then, the corners of his eyes crinkling in genuine amusement, and in a flash Nick recognized Julian's charm and the person he might actually be away from this world of surface gloss.

The boy he'd once loved.

"God knows I've wanted to do it often enough."

Nick couldn't hide his grin. "He can be a dick, huh?"

"Especially when he's thinking with it, which is ninety percent of the time." The amusement fled from Julian's face, replaced by an anxious, concerned expression. "Are you all right, though? I know Marc can be hard to take, but he's a good guy. He didn't mean—"

"I'm fine." Nick growled. "I don't like it when someone gets too physical, that's all." Even he could hear how lame that sounded.

"Must be hell on your girlfriends," muttered Julian as he faced the mirror to adjust his sweater.

What possessed Nick to answer he had no clue, but the words tumbled out before he could stop himself, and he shot back. "If I ever had any, maybe it would be." Stunned by his admission, Nick met Julian's gaze in the mirror.

Holy hell. All traces of sympathy had been wiped clean from Julian's face, replaced by a slow, assessing gaze, and desire blazing from those striking, dark-green eyes. How had Nick forgotten the sexy little mole right under Julian's cheekbone? It had driven him crazy, and he recalled tracing it with his tongue the first time they kissed.

He tensed, feeling his cock twitching and thickening at the thought of Julian's mouth wrapped around its hard length, swallowing him whole. Nick's entire body burned with need, and he craved the taste of Julian, and the power of those muscles flexing and bunching beneath his fingers.

Fuck, fuck, fuck. Rein it in, buddy. This is so not going to happen. Nick had no intention of outing himself; after all these years, he was fine with his life and the equilibrium he sought to achieve to make it through each and every day.

Even as Nick continued to convince himself, Julian took a step toward him. "Nick—"

"I gotta go." Without another look at Julian, Nick escaped, hurrying out of the bathroom and back into the bowels of the club. Spotting Marcus talking to one of the bartenders, he approached, unsure if the club owner was truly as forgiving as Julian had made him out to be. When he caught Marcus's eye, the man said a few more words to the bartender, then held up his hands in mock surrender to Nick.

"Don't hit me. I promise not to touch you again." His smoky eyes darkened. "Not that I don't want to, but I've no interest in forcing myself on someone who isn't interested." He flashed that winning grin which Nick knew got him whoever and whatever he wanted in bed.

Nick stuck out his hand. "I'm sorry. I, I'm not into the scene and it got a little much for me, but I shouldn't have hit you."

"Well never let it be said I don't enjoy a little spanking every once in a while," Marcus's eyes sparkled with amusement. "But I get it. And I am sorry I overstepped your boundaries."

They shook hands. "Friends, then?" Marcus asked as he signaled the bartender to give them both drinks.

Nick supposed so, although he doubted he'd be seeing any of these men after tonight. "Sure."

Marcus handed Nick his drink. "Juli, come over. All's well,

I promise. I even apologized." Julian came up from behind Nick and said nothing, but Nick could feel his presence and it disturbed him. For all these years he'd been fine, managing to get through each day, one at a time. Now? He was edgy and uncomfortable, his mind filled with thoughts of touching Julian, kissing him, seeing him naked. Wondering what he looked like as a man, and not the boy he once knew.

"I've always told you to think before you act. Finally someone decided to explain it with a bit more emphasis." Julian tipped his glass to Nick and smirked. "Point to Nick."

Nick met Julian's eyes over the rim of his glass for a moment, then hurriedly gulped his drink. Once again that damned uncomfortable sensation of being off-kilter hit him, making him crave Julian's mouth on his dick.

"So, tell us Nick." Marcus scanned the crowd, then returned his gaze to the two of them. "What do you do again?"

"I'm with the fire department."

"A fireman?" Marcus sipped his drink and waved to someone on the dance floor. "You ride on the truck and wear the cool jacket and everything?"

His hand shook a bit. Being interrogated about his life and job was not how he'd intended on spending his evening. Where was Katie? He scanned the crowded dance floor and found her dancing with a man. She seemed happy, and he didn't have the heart to ruin her evening by behaving badly again. Punching the owner of the club who'd given them the tickets to this fundraiser was bad enough; Nick knew they were at least $100 per person.

"I always wanted to date a fireman or a cop so I could wear his gear." Marcus licked his lips. "Umm. I love me a man in a uniform."

"What do you care? You never keep them in their clothes long enough that it matters what they wear." Julian patted Marcus on the shoulder and winked at Nick. "I'm sure he has the full getup and looks hot in it."

Heat rose in Nick's face. "It's only a uniform," he mumbled. He was well aware of the groupies who loved men in their full dress gear. When he was a probie at the firehouse, women would stop by all the time, ostensibly to say hello, but time and time again he'd find phone numbers and addresses slipped into his hand or pocket. A few of his fellow firemen had gotten in trouble for becoming a little too friendly with the neighborhood ladies.

"Nothing is sexier than a strong, confident man in a uniform." Julian's eyes held his, and Nick's heart began to thud in heavy, almost painful beats. They stood close, Julian's warm scent teasing him. "Put a man like you, with your build and face, in well-tailored clothes or a uniform, and you can have your pick of the ladies." Nick's gaze followed the tip of Julian's tongue as it licked those firm lips. "If that's what you're into, of course."

Their eyes met and damn Julian to hell for playing this game with him. It had been years—not since that last time with Julian on that basement couch had he been so uncertain about who he was and who he wanted.

When he and Julian split, he made a point of going out with as many girls as he could before he graduated to prove he could do it; he'd even managed to sleep with one or two. The experience had been less than satisfying for both him and the girls. There were some gay guys and organizations he could've joined in the fire department, but he chose to keep to himself, sneaking off into town to hook up with random guys.

At that moment Katie and Melanie bounded over, with several other people they'd met while dancing, and dragged him away to sit with them. For the rest of the evening he smiled and made noncommittal small talk with people, but by one in the morning he was ready to call it quits.

"I'm heading out." He put his hand on Katie's shoulder. "How are you getting home?"

"I'm taking a cab; Melanie and I are sharing it uptown." Katie lived in the East 20s near Second Avenue, so it wouldn't be a far ride.

"Text me when you get home, so I know you're all right." He kissed her cheek and said goodbye to the other people at the table. He searched the bar area and found Marcus chatting up some guy in a suit and glasses who looked almost as uncomfortable at being there as Nick did. He went over to him to make his goodbyes.

"It was nice talking to you, but I'm heading out."

"Hey, it's early. You really have to leave?" Marcus's arm rested casually on the other guy's shoulder. Nick didn't think he'd ever met such a touchy-feely man before.

"Yeah. I'm beat; I've been doing training classes nonstop for a week, so I'm still catching up on my sleep." Nick took out his claim check for his coat.

"Um, hi, I'm Zach." The guy with Marcus's arm over his shoulder shook his hand.

"Sorry." Marcus ruffled Zach's hair, and Nick saw the guy shoot Marcus an annoyed look. "Nick, this is the other one of our friends, Zach. Julian, myself, and Zach were in school together and roommates for a while. I'm just so happy you came tonight, Zach."

The smile on Marcus's face was so genuine, Nick wondered why Zach wouldn't want to come. It didn't matter all that much to him, and he vowed to put these people out of his mind for good once he left.

"Nice to meet you. Have you seen Julian? I'd like to say goodbye."

Marcus pointed his finger to the dance floor. "He's over there, laying the rest of the groundwork for his evening. Laying being the operative word."

Confused, Nick looked over and almost stopped breathing. In the center of the dance floor Julian had his arms around a tall, willowy young man and was being kissed within an inch of his life. He watched as Julian's hands caressed the man's back, traveling downward until they cupped his ass. At that moment he opened his eyes and met Nick's gaze. A small grin teased the corner of his mouth and he licked his lips.

Behind him, Marcus leaned in close to whisper in his ear. "I'm an ass man myself. How about you?"

In shock, Nick's body clenched, watching Julian caress his

dance partner, their gazes locked across the club's dance floor. Heat flooded Nick's body as he imagined Julian touching his ass, dipping inside, spreading him wide. Where no one had ever been before.

Without another word, Nick took off, fleeing the club so fast, he left his coat behind.

Chapter Five

"I DON'T UNDERSTAND." Julian sat across from his bank representative, in an uncomfortable chair. He glanced quickly around him, but there was no one within listening distance.

"It's very simple, Mr. Cornell." The smug banker laced his hands together and placed them on the desk. "You made us certain assurances when we lent you the money that you'd be able to pay us back. Your first payment is now a week late, so we need to know when the bank will receive its first payment." His thin lips curled in a smile.

Bastard. It seemed like he almost enjoyed making Julian squirm in his seat. Summoning whatever haughty pride he could dredge up, Julian straightened in his seat and smoothed his suit jacket.

"I'm sure you're aware of the overall downtrend in the fashion market, Mr. Milne. It isn't only my company that's having problems. Retailers have closed their doors, making for stiffer competition." He gave the man a tight smile. "I'm sure if you give me another six months—"

"Oh, no, Mr. Cornell, that's out of the question." Milne leaned forward and tapped on his computer keyboard, frowning as he squinted at the screen. "We need to receive a payment immediately." He smiled at Julian. "With interest, of course."

Though his heart beat frantically, Julian somehow managed to keep his demeanor calm. Calculating swiftly in his head, he determined that if he maxed out on all his credit cards, he could at least make a two-month payment and still pay his showroom rent and Melanie's salary. Thank God New York was such a pro-tenant state, or he'd be out on his ass, since he had no way to pay the rent for his apartment.

Standing abruptly, he leaned over the somewhat startled banker, the man's muddy-brown eyes widening a bit with anxiety. The thought that Milne could be afraid of him was laughable; Julian couldn't even step on a spider, but it didn't hurt to play a part.

"You'll have your money by the end of the week."

He held his head high and walked out of the bank. Humiliation burned through him, but Julian had learned to never let his emotions show. It made you weak and easy prey. Another life lesson he'd learned from his past. Shame was to be kept discreet and private.

The day hovered in that in-between season he loved about living on the East Coast. You knew it should be cold because it was October, but the temperature was reluctant to give up on the almost long-forgotten summer's warmth. The sun still shone with that fierceness you longed to see in a fall sky. It let you hope it might stay warm, if only for a little longer, and the days of snow, howling winds, and heavy clothing were still far, far away.

Julian twined his scarf around his neck and set off down Seventh Avenue, past all the shlock stores and cafes, and headed east. He had no destination in mind but he couldn't return to the showroom and think about a new collection right now, nor face Melanie's expectant expression wondering if he'd been able to miraculously pull another extension from the bank out of his ass.

All his hopes and dreams to make it in the business had been tied up in the show last week. He'd received a few orders, but nothing that would pave his way to breaking even, or get him past the debacle of the show. Julian knew he had it in him; his designs were good enough weren't they? Obviously, if someone wanted to steal them.

He grimaced, recalling Devon Chambers on television. The man had the nerve to smile and say how hard he worked for his success, and how he knew this last collection would put him over the top.

Of course it would, Julian fumed as he increased his stride. It must've taken a lot of hard work to figure out how to steal Julian's designs and alter them just enough so that Julian couldn't accuse him outright. The rumor that morning that Chambers might be named Coty's Top Young Designer of the year, a title Julian had longed for, only made him angrier.

When he looked up, Julian found himself on the East Side on a side street in the forties. This was the old garment district and though there were still some old-time factories left, most were now gone, leaving in place an era gone by of fashion when it was all done behind closed doors, no glitzy shows and after-parties on the internet. Fashion was revered and somewhat mysterious; no one knew how their clothing was created.

Now, with the advent of reality TV, the entire world watched how things were done, and in Julian's opinion, it did a disservice to the industry to see designs created in half an hour, or out of outrageous materials. But the public loved it, so who was he to criticize. He'd met several of the winners of these shows and some of them were nice enough, but Julian believed there was enough drama in real life without the need for a television show about it all.

He kept walking and passed a firehouse. A vision of Nick, all dark and brooding in his uniform, popped into Julian's head and he wondered where the man worked. Did he work in a firehouse? He'd been so close-mouthed about his job. And sad. Nick seemed unhappy, something he'd never been when they were together. There'd been light and laughter in those beautiful blue eyes, a softness and heat that made Julian's breath catch until he found himself faint with desire.

Now there was nothing. No light, no spark. Nothing more than a reflection of whomever Nick was speaking to. A blank canvas. Whatever it was, seeing Nick again had ignited something inside Julian that had been dead for years. He'd had many lovers, some he'd been fond of and, maybe if he'd allowed himself, he might have loved one of them. But no one had led him to that place where he might miss them when they were gone.

Though he'd never been one to deny himself the pleasures of a man in his bed, lately Julian found himself going through the motions. He'd seen many of his acquaintances settle down with husbands; buying homes and setting up cute little domesticated lives. He shuddered; so not his thing. He brushed aside the little dart of envy that wedged its way into his mind. Bored and edgy, Julian wondered if this was all there was in life; get up, work, eat, find someone to fuck, and sleep.

Seemed kind of pointless.

He stopped in front of the opened doors, hesitating, uncertain.

"Can I help you, sir?" A stocky, dark-haired fireman in uniform approached him, a curious expression on his face.

The firehouse was a haven of activity. Shouts and laughter could be heard from the back, and there was the crackling static of a radio off in the distance. Julian supposed that was where they received their calls from. A big firetruck was parked in the middle and Julian saw several firemen on it, presumably checking to make sure it was at the ready.

Julian had nothing but the utmost respect for the FDNY. He knew he wasn't the type of person to go running into danger, and he gave them all the credit in the world for choosing this as their profession. Like the millions of others on 9/11, he'd cried buckets of tears in the aftermath of the carnage. Not for the first time he wondered where Nick had been on that horrible day.

Julian could only imagine nowadays firehouses had to be wary of any strangers randomly walking in, and he made sure to smile and be respectful. "Yes, please. I'm trying to find a fireman. How would I go about it?"

"What's the guy's name?"

"Nick Fletcher." Julian realized how long it had been since that name had been on his lips.

A closed look replaced the friendliness in the fireman's face. "How do you know Nicky Fletcher?"

Why would they know Nick? He wasn't anyone special as far as Julian knew. "We grew up together."

The fireman gave him the eye and Julian bristled. He knew that look and what it meant, and he glared back at him with defiance. *Yeah, I'm fucking gay. Tough shit. Deal with it.*

You can live in the most liberal city in the world and still have to deal with assholes. There's no getting away from it.

"He works Training and Tactical; with the probies on Randalls Island."

"Did he use to work here?" Julian couldn't rid himself of his curiosity. Some might call it nosiness.

Ignoring Julian's question, the fireman widened his stance and folded his arms. "Anything else I can help you with, sir?" The man couldn't be faulted for his courtesy, but there was something odd about his behavior; a subtle wariness in the way he carried himself now, that hadn't been present before he'd mentioned Nick.

Julian wasn't one to be sloughed off and asked his question again.

"Did you know Nick? Did he work at this house?"

The lieutenant's eyes narrowed. He looked around as if to check no one was near before he stepped closer to Julian. "Look, mister. I don't know you from atom; maybe you're okay and maybe you're not. But Nicky's a good guy and he went through hell. So leave him alone. I'm trying to be nice and polite, ya understand?" Without waiting for a response he turned on his heel and strode away, yelling out to the men in the firehouse.

Stunned for a moment, Julian could only stare after the man, then he shook his head and left, wondering what the fuck had just happened.

What hell had Nick been through, and why did the fireman give him such an odd look when Julian asked about Nick? All these questions ran through his head as Julian realized he was hungry. He went into a diner a few blocks from the firehouse and ordered a turkey sandwich. As he waited for his food, he wondered how much longer it would be before he couldn't afford to eat even in a place like this. Certainly the places he frequented nightly in the past were no longer an option for him. He couldn't afford the twenty dollar cocktails or the tiny meals at outrageous prices. But if he didn't show his face, he'd be forgotten even quicker.

The waiter brought his sandwich. "Something to drink, sir?"

"Just the water, thanks." He'd better start saving in every way possible. Two years ago, if someone would have told him that he'd be worrying over ordering coffee at a neighborhood diner, he would have laughed in their face and walked away from them without a second thought.

Now he had to look at himself and things around him in a different light. Until he could build himself and his business back up, he'd have to think of other sources of income and ways to make money to survive. Never, of course, forgetting his ultimate goal of becoming the best designer he possibly could.

Nick's words played again in Julian's mind. He wasn't a shallow person because he cared about fashion. At least he didn't think so. It was all he knew, all he'd ever wanted to do. And he was a good person; he donated to charity. And no matter what Nick or anyone else thought, he did make people feel better about themselves.

He chewed his sandwich and thought about Nick instead of his money problems. There was no use trying to resurrect what might have been. Their lives had gone in such different directions there was nothing left of the boys they'd once been, and the men they'd become traveled in different circles now. Happy as he was to have seen him again, a part of Julian was grief-stricken that a man like Nick still believed he had to live a life of lies.

He paid his bill and left the diner. At this point he could go back uptown and begin the daunting task of making calls to all the buyers, bloggers, and fashion editors, and kissing their asses. That is, if they even took his calls now those fickle, two-faced fucks. They loved you when you were on the way up, but couldn't scurry away fast enough, like cockroaches, when you were free-falling. Shit, he was exhausted thinking about it all. Maybe he should go back to bed. Or get drunk.

"Julian?" A woman's voice stopped him before he stepped off the sidewalk at the corner to cross Second Avenue. The cars whizzed by, and he took a few steps back.

His eyes widened with surprise as he saw Nick's sister. "Katie, how are you?" Sometimes lady (or lord as the case may be) Fate played right into a person's hands. If he thought too much, Julian knew he'd stop himself and simply smile, say hello and walk away.

"I'm fine, but what are you doing in this neighborhood?" She tucked a dark curl behind her ear, and Julian couldn't help but notice the striking similarities between the siblings. "I didn't think you ventured away from Seventh Avenue unless it was to go to SoHo or Tribeca."

She had a point. Julian hardly ever took advantage of all the city had to offer, preferring to remain within the confines of Seventh Avenue, Marcus's club, or the trendy places written about in the press.

"I needed the exercise and figured the fresh air would clear my head." There was truth to that statement. Unfortunately, the walk had done little to clear his head, only adding more to the clutter within. And he still had no idea how he was going to save his company, once the money he had in the bank was used up. Unless he made some sales, he might be sunk.

Katie's dark brows knitted together and her clear blue eyes held his. "Is everything okay? Mel told me all about the show and how that designer stole your ideas." She grimaced. "That's horrible. We used to have people in law school who'd hide books in the library and never share notes, but what he did was pretty heinous."

That's the business. It could make you a star or spit you out like bad fish. If ever there was an industry where one day you were flying high and the next you were six feet underground, that was the fashion industry. "There's little recourse. The designs aren't copyrighted and the slight change he incorporated in them was enough for him to show everyone his originality."

"Which he no doubt stole from other people as well," Katie said. Her staunch defense of him warmed Julian's heart. There was something comforting about another person believing in you unequivocally.

"Thanks for your concern. My main problem now is finding enough backers and/or orders to hold me through until I can make the next big sale."

"When is that?" She leaned against a mailbox, but her eyes never wavered from his face. She was like her brother in that respect: when they spoke to you, their concentration was only on you; it was as if no one else around mattered. Only Julian didn't react to Katie the way he did to Nick.

"I have no idea," he sighed. "I have a small showing coming up in a few weeks, but that was supposed to be gravy. Extra cash, not the main source of income."

Her expression softened, and she reached out and squeezed his arm. "Well right now everything helps I'm sure, so I would concentrate on making that the best you can." She glanced down at her watch. "Shoot, I'm late. I promised to meet Nick for coffee. He finished early with training and I'm off today."

"Well, thanks, it was nice seeing you again." Julian turned to leave.

"Hey, Julian?"

He stopped and looked back at Katie. "Yeah?"

"Want to join us? I mean . . ." she bit her lip. "Maybe it'll take your mind off your problems."

"I'd love to."

Chapter Six

YO, NICK, HEADS-UP." Carlos Hernandez called out to him from the opposite end of the locker room.

Nick looked up from tying his sneaker to see a football sailing over his head. He reached up and snagged it, hefting the ball in his hand.

"Man, the way you throw this it's more like a deadly weapon than a football." He tossed it back to his partner, Jensen, and slammed his locker shut. They'd spent a rigorous day training the new recruits, and he was looking forward to his time off. He had no plans other than to sleep and see how Jamal and the others were doing at the hospital.

"Whatja think of the new crew we got?" Jensen braced his foot on the bench behind Nick. "Some of them run like faggots, but for the most part they seem okay."

Nick stilled, his breaths slow and careful. "What did you say?"

Jensen flipped the ball back to Carlos. "Some of the guys, they look like they're tiptoeing around. All they need is a tutu." He held out and flopped his hand. "Real limp-wrists, especially that Barton kid." He winked and whistled. "I think he's got a thing for you, Nicky."

"Shut the fuck up, man. You can't talk like that. You'll get all of us in trouble." Carlos darted an anxious look around the room.

Jensen's face turned red. "Can't say fuckin' anything these days anymore." He stormed out of the room, banging the door behind him.

Stunned, Nick shot a quick glance at Carlos, but said nothing. He finished tying his sneakers and muttered "bye," not waiting for a reply, before walking out through the swinging doors.

He checked his watch and saw he had about forty-five minutes before he was supposed to meet Katie for coffee in downtown Brooklyn. Nick texted her.

On my way. Just finished training for the day.

He received an answer almost immediately.

K. We'll see you soon.

We? What does she mean, we? Knowing his sister's less than stellar typing skills, she probably meant "will" not "we'll."

With his brow furrowed, Nick hunched his shoulders against the brisk wind coming off the river. Though the guys had invited him out for a beer, Nick knew it would lead to another evening of hanging around and making useless, fake small talk while they picked up women. There was nothing he wanted to do less in this world than that; it wasn't fair to the woman or to him.

By some miracle there wasn't much traffic on the FDR Drive, and he made it to Brooklyn in a little over thirty minutes. Darkness was slipping slowly over the city, and the necklace of lights across the Brooklyn Bridge had begun to turn on. Downtown by the Brooklyn Courts was now a thriving tourist area, with the addition of restaurants and new stores that had sprung up in the last few years.

Nick also noticed the increased security presence around the courts and the bridges, something that hadn't been there before 9/11. No matter how he tried not to see, his eyes always became automatically drawn to the sight of the bomb sniffing dogs or the undercover cars he knew how to spot. And reflexively, he couldn't help but look toward the river and the empty place where the Towers had stood, still irreplaceable for him, no matter the glorious sight of the Freedom Tower lit up against the night sky.

He pulled into a parking spot and, after checking the traffic and the people around him, Nick crossed the street and entered the little coffee shop he and Katie always chose for its quiet atmosphere and off the beaten track location. Nick didn't like to be surrounded by too many perky, smiling people. It set him on edge.

The sight of his sister sitting at the table with her coffee in front of her, checking her phone, brought a smile to his face; it faded quickly when he saw Julian Cornell cross the coffee shop to join her, cup in hand.

Fuck. The last time he'd seen Julian, Nick had been watching him devour the mouth of a young, beautiful man on the dance floor at Sparks. Had they spent the night together?

Why the fuck did he care?

Julian, returning to the table with his coffee, hesitated, his smile turning wary. He remained standing, which caught Katie's attention, and she turned around.

Her face lit up and Nick couldn't help but smile back at her. "Hi."

"Hi. I hope you don't mind. I ran into Julian when I was coming over and invited him to join us." She faltered and Julian stepped in.

"Your sister is too polite to say the truth. She found me walking the streets and took pity on me."

Nick laughed. "You sound like a lost little puppy."

"Nicky," Katie admonished him with a frown. "That wasn't nice."

"It's all right." Julian twirled the thin wooden stirrer between his fingers, and Nick was drawn to his hands. He'd expected them to be soft looking and prissy, like the hands of a man who'd never lifted a finger in his life. Instead, there were callouses along his right index finger and several scars on his thumb. They were workingman's hands, and Nick was caught off guard. He'd never before thought of hands as sexual and attractive, but Julian's were rough and masculine. A definite turn on, imagining them stroking his body, jerking him off.

Hot with embarrassment, he mumbled, "I'm gonna go get my coffee." Nick fled to the back of the line and ordered his coffee. He paid extra attention to stirring in his milk and sugar, gathering his racing thoughts. For Christ's sake, he had to get his act together. He couldn't walk around with a hard-on for Julian.

When he felt sufficiently calm Nick walked back to the table and sat down. "Sorry about that crack."

"It's all right." Nick followed the movement of Julian's hand as it raked through his blond waves. "It's been a crappy day, and I may have looked like a lost puppy, who knows?" He sipped his coffee, staring off into the distance.

"What's wrong? You're not still moping about those stupid reviews are you?"

Whoops. Wrong thing to say, he realized, as Julian's mouth thinned to an angry white line.

"Those stupid reviews are my life blood. I told you already, these reviewers determine how or if I make a living. I don't owe you an apology for that."

"By why involve yourself with something that's so petty and mean spirited? Surely you think you're worth more than that? I know you are."

"Nick." Once again, Katie shot him a warning look, but this time he didn't stop.

"I never knew you could be so shallow. Your entire focus is caught up in appearances and what others think of you. There are people out there who are hurting, with real issues. They're the ones who should be getting attention from the newspapers, not someone deciding whether a tie is skinny enough." Why the fuck did he keep talking? Nick should never have started this conversation. Inevitably Julian would want to know what happened to him; find out things. The truth was, there was nothing left of the man he used to be.

"You're very passionate about this. Is it something personal?" Julian held his gaze, and it might have been only the two of them in the room. Nick swore he could feel Julian's breath brush his cheek although the man hadn't moved from across the table. "You were with the FDNY during 9/11 weren't you?"

A humming sounded in his ears, yet he managed to remain calm. Katie slid her hand over his and his tension eased. An idea crossed his mind. A crazy, fucked-up one to be sure, but Nick blurted it out before he could stop himself.

"I'd like to take you somewhere."

Katie gripped his hand, and for a second Nick wanted to yank back the words, or pretend he hadn't said them, but Julian brightened.

"Yeah? Where?" There was animation in his face, a spark that hadn't been there before.

Katie squeezed his hand. "Jamal?"

Nicky nodded and stood up, coffee in hand. "Come on. After this, I guarantee your outlook on life will be different."

Julian glanced between him and Katie, then stood. "I don't know where we're going, but sure. I'm game."

Nick bent to kiss Katie. "Love you, Kiki."

Her breath caught. "You haven't called me that in forever." She clutched him tight.

Since before he was hurt. Since before he lost himself. He extricated himself from her grasp and gestured to Julian. "Come on, we'll take my car."

They walked outside, and Nick liked how Julian followed him no questions asked. There was an inevitability—from the moment Nick laid eyes on Julian at the club the other night—that the two of them would have time alone together and talk about their past. "Does it feel strange, being together again?" His gaze flickered to Julian at his side.

"It's not like we're together because we're walking next to one another on the street." Julian didn't meet his gaze, and Nick's light mood turned dark again. They continued to walk down the street, past homes and stores, many of them closed now that it was dark. Dried leaves, picked up by the wind, swirled around their feet, coming to rest and lie strewn upon the sidewalk, like the little broken pieces of his heart, scattered along the ground.

Nick licked his lips. "I-I didn't mean it that way."

"So how did you mean it?"

Julian wasn't pulling any punches, and Nick realized there was little left of the loving, lighthearted young man he once knew.

"Do you have any idea how it felt when you pulled away from me that day? Even though it was in secret, we'd spent all our after-school time together and then suddenly I had nothing, nobody. You at least had football and friends. You could hide who you were."

Nick's heart hurt from the pain in Julian's voice, but he kept silent.

"You weren't the strange kid, the one people were only nice to so they could copy from in class. The one they called queer and homo when they thought I wasn't listening."

"I never called you that, Julian. I couldn't—I didn't . . ." Nick stopped walking and stood helpless on the street.

"You never told them to stop; never defended me. That's why I asked my mother to transfer me to another school after that year." Julian rocked on his heels with his hands fisted at his side. "I couldn't take it anymore, and to see you every day, knowing you didn't want me . . ." Julian inhaled and scrubbed his face with his hands. "I vowed no one would ever use me again or make fun of me."

"I'm sorry," Nick whispered. "I never meant to hurt you." Voices screamed inside his head, *Tell him you loved him, tell him you still care for him.*

Nick stayed quiet.

"It doesn't matter does it?" Julian gave him a tight little smile. "We're different people now, with different lives."

Nick said nothing, but began walking again and stopped by his car. After they'd seated themselves and he started the engine, Nick couldn't leave that conversation as it had ended.

"There never was anyone after you."

Julian said nothing for several minutes as Nick navigated the car through the streets and onto the Brooklyn Bridge.

"I doubt you're a virgin, Nick. I don't believe it."

"No, of course not. But it's all been random hookups; never anyone serious. I meant I've never had feelings for anyone like I had for you."

"Don't worry about it," Julian waved his hand in the air as

he stared out of the window at the East River. "We were kids. It was never going to go anywhere."

They sat the rest of the way in silence as Nick entered the ramp for the FDR Drive and drove toward the hospital.

Chapter Seven

WHY THE FUCK had he agreed to go anywhere with Nick? The blackness of the river at night matched Julian's mood. Maybe when they stopped he'd thank Nick for the ride and be on his way home. The yawning emptiness of what he had waiting for him there proved one thing to him. He needed help fast. If he didn't figure out something, he'd be broke within the month.

Nick pulled into a parking lot and Julian snapped out of his reverie.

"Where are we?" Julian peered out of the window, as Nick parked the car and shut off the engine.

"Bellevue Hospital. I come here at least three times a week." Nick got out of the car, and Julian unbuckled his seatbelt.

"Are you sick?" With lightning speed, Julian scrambled out of the car and hurried around to Nick's side. "Is something wrong? Oh God, Nick, I'm sorry."

The thought of Nick being ill, subjected to horrible tests and drugs, spiked a terrible fear through Julian. He grabbed Nick's shoulders, his fingers crushing the fabric of his shirt. "You can tell me."

Julian held his breath. Something akin to fear flashed through Nick's eyes, and he jerked away from Julian and turned his back on him. Nick's shoulders heaved slightly and he braced his arms against the roof of his car.

"Nick?" Julian reached out as if to touch Nick's back, but pulled his hand away. "Is everything okay?"

A quick shake of Nick's head. "No. I'm not sick. Not the way you think at least."

Relief poured through Julian. *Thank God.*

"What's wrong then?" Julian leaned up against the car. If it took all night, he wasn't leaving here without some explanation for Nick's freak-out when Julian touched him.

"I, I don't like people touching me. I'm sorry, Julian, it's nothing personal to you."

What had happened to Nick to make him this way? The Nick Julian remembered loved to be kissed and touched. All over.

"Did something happen?" Julian's fingers curled into his palm; he itched to place his hand on Nick's shoulder, to give him comfort. It was in his nature to touch—Julian was a sensory person; he and his friends touched each other all the time with friendly gestures. Not being able to offer a gentle hand to someone in such obvious pain was a foreign concept to Julian.

Something was going on, something he didn't understand, and Julian had to find a way to get Nick to break down the barriers he'd set up to keep people away.

"How about we table this for later discussion, and you can tell me now why you brought me here?"

Nick sagged a bit, as if relieved Julian had stopped harassing him. "I come here to visit kids in the burn unit." He finally turned around and leaned against the car as well, side by side with Julian. "I talk to them, help them with their exercises. Be there for them when it all gets too much."

Oh God. OhGodohGod. That's what happened to him. And then Julian remembered how Nick had gone deathly still when he'd mentioned 9/11, and Julian's world veered off its axis and he almost passed out. Drawing in a deep breath, Julian concentrated on Nick's shuttered face.

"I'm honored to come with you."

Nick shot him a questioning glance, but said nothing and nodded. "Let's head inside." He straightened up, ran his fingers through his hair, and walked away.

Julian hurried after him, keeping pace with his long strides. They entered the hospital and from the friendly way Nick greeted everyone—from nurses to security guards—Julian guessed he'd been coming here a long time.

"You're a little late today, Nick." An older nurse approached them.

"Sorry, Hannah. I wanted my friend to meet Jamal." Nick gestured to Julian, who stayed several feet behind him, studying a poster on fire prevention. "Julian, come and meet the head nurse here."

"Hello," said Julian extending his hand. "Nice to meet you."

"Hello, same here." Her cool assessing gaze unnerved Julian; he felt like he was under review, but for what he didn't know.

"Jamal had a bad day. His mother lost her job because of all the time she spends here with him." Hannah walked with them down the hallway.

"Damn."

"Plus, his skin grafts are itching under the compression bandages, so the poor kid is a mess today. I think seeing you will cheer him up."

Doubtful, thought Julian as he followed in their footsteps.

"What does his mother do?" asked Julian as they stopped in front of a room with the door closed.

"She was a housekeeper to some woman on the Upper East Side. When Sonia had to keep taking time off, the woman just up and fired her."

"What a bitch." Julian heard Hannah chuckle, only then realizing he'd spoken out loud.

"She sure is."

"We'll see what we can do. Thanks, Hannah." Nick pushed open the door.

"Nice to meet you." Julian smiled at her.

"Be good to him." Hannah left before Julian could respond. Why wouldn't he be good to a child? Pondering that question, Julian entered Jamal's room.

The young man sat in one of those ubiquitous beige vinyl chairs with the wooden arms. Everything in that room was a variation on the color beige: walls, curtains, bedding, and furniture; Julian couldn't imagine spending time there and not going insane with boredom.

Jamal was at the point in his adolescence where he hadn't yet acquired bulk to his frame. His legs were long and gangly, like a yearling horse, and his torso lightly muscled. His hair had been done in tight cornrows against his scalp, except for a large part on the right side, which had been shaved. Julian could see the skin was pink and healing from a burn.

Nick sat on the bed and the two were talking quietly. Julian hesitated by the door, suddenly uncertain as to whether he really belonged here or not. Why did Nick bring him here?

Jamal glanced at him, and Julian was taken aback by the young man's good looks. His light brown skin set off large hazel eyes that shone with intelligence, as well as pain and fear. This young man could walk the runway at any show and be a star.

"Hi." Julian walked forward. "I'm Julian. I'm a friend of Nick's." About to offer his hand, Julian saw the bulky bandages encasing Jamal's right arm, running from his fingertips to disappear into the elbow-length sleeve of the beige hospital gown.

Shit. How horrible.

"Jamal." The boy licked his lips and leaned back in the chair, shifting his right leg which, Julian saw, was also wrapped. "You're a friend of Nick's?"

Julian took out a small moleskin notebook and a pen. "Yeah. We've known each other since we were kids." He started sketching as he spoke, not unmindful of Jamal's and Nick's curiosity as to what he was doing. After a few minutes he was done.

"What do you think?" He held the notebook up to Jamal, who stared at it wide-eyed.

"Holy shit man. Is that me?"

"Yeah. What do you think of the outfit?"

"This shit is trippin'." Jamal's eyes kept shifting from the pad to Julian. "You're pretty good." His face fell. "I used to love clothes. Before." His gaze skittered down to his bandaged arm and leg.

"No reason you still can't be when you go back to school." Julian made some small adjustments to the sketch, his pen moving rapidly over the page.

"Damn. You're really good." Jamal craned his neck to try and see what Julian was doing.

"I should hope so," chuckled Julian. "It's what I do for a living."

"Julian's a men's clothing designer." Nick ran his hand through his short hair. "You might have even heard of him. Julian Cornell."

Jamal's jaw dropped and the way his eyes bugged out of his head was almost comical. "You're Julian Cornell? Shit! I saw you in *GQ* the other month. The lady my mom worked for used to give her the old issues when she was finished with them so I could have them." His face fell. "Mom lost that job because of me."

And Julian, who hadn't thought of this side of life for years, suddenly felt shame course through him hot and strong. He understood now why Nick had brought him here. This was real life. Not the bullshit he dealt with everyday like the inseam of a pant leg. What Nick said was true. Not only was his business going up in flames, his whole fucking life was shallow and a waste.

"She'll be able to find something soon, I bet."

Jamal's jaw tightened and his eyes darkened. "Whatever. She needs to stop thinkin' about me and worry about my little sister." He lifted his bandaged arm. "I'm never gonna be normal, or be able to be like everyone else. I'm gonna be all scarred and ugly. I gotta wear these bandages for two years the doctors say." His voice caught on a sob. "Two years of this ugly shit on my arm and leg. Everyone says it'll be okay, but I can't do it."

Damn. Julian stood helpless as Nick knelt by Jamal's chair and put his arm around the young man's shoulders, talking to him in a quiet, soothing tone. Wanting to give them some privacy, Julian turned around and walked to the opposite side of the room, his sketchpad in hand. He idly flipped through it until he reached a blank page and drew an arm and a leg. He'd seen the bandage Jamal wore and it was tight to the body, probably made of some neoprene type of fabric. And while it was bulky along his fingers, it lay close to the skin, not unlike the material models wore to smooth out any bulges in their skin. *What if . . .*

An idea formed in his mind and before he knew it, his pen flashed across the pad and he'd drawn half a dozen different types of compression legwear and arm sleeves, visualizing in his mind the varied colors, some with designs. He returned to the two men, and Nick gave him a curious look.

"What were you doing over there? You looked intense."

Julian chose to ignore him for the moment and walked over to Jamal. "What do you think of this?" he handed the sketchpad over to Jamal.

The young man's brow furrowed. "What is this . . . wait a minute." He stared hard at the pad in his hand, then back up to Julian who smiled broadly at him.

"Are these like the bandages I gotta wear only like with designs?"

Julian nodded. "I think if you wore ones like this, it almost looks like a tattoo sleeve on your arm or even your leg. And I could customize it for what you would like. We could even make it in the colors of your favorite sports teams."

Jamal couldn't stop looking at it. "This is amazing. I can't believe you did this right in front of me."

Nick pulled him aside as Jamal continued to study the sketches Julian had drawn. "This is the most engaged I've seen him since I met him. How did you do that? It's a brilliant idea." Nick's eyes sparkled and his whole face was alive with happiness. It took all of Julian's willpower not to pull him close and kiss him.

"It's what I do."

Nick shook his head. "No, it's not what you do. Not that I've seen. This isn't the Julian Cornell who hangs out in trendy clubs and only cares what some fucked-up excuse for a human being thinks is important in life." His blue eyes blazed with unexpected passion and Julian slipped back in time, becoming captivated all over again by this man. "This is what you can do to make a difference. Stop worrying about being famous, Julian. You should worry if your life is relevant."

The intensity between them flared. "I want that too. But I'm scared." Julian swallowed hard. "I'm almost broke, Nick." The shame of this admission, out loud in the open, and to Nick of all people, was greater than anything Julian had ever experienced.

"Let's talk later tonight, okay?" Nick held his gaze, and Julian fell into the blue depths of his eyes.

"Yes."

It might cost him his heart, but Julian could never say no to Nick.

Chapter Eight

NICK SPENT ANOTHER hour with Julian and Jamal. To Nick's surprise, Julian also helped Jamal with his hand and leg exercises. Begrudgingly, Nick admitted to himself that Julian was a complete surprise. Here he thought the man had become a self-absorbed, shallow human being, and instead, Julian's compassion for Jamal had blown apart whatever negative stereotypes Nick had conjured up in his mind.

After promising to come back soon with Julian so he could show Jamal more designs, Nick ushered Julian out of the room, said goodbye to Hannah, and they left the hospital. Julian was unusually upbeat, and for the first time Nick had a feeling he was seeing the real man behind the sharp suits. There was a glimmer of the Julian he used to know.

It was late by the time they pulled into the garage across the street from Julian's building. He gave the keys to the valet, and they walked across the street to Julian's loft on the Lower East Side.

He'd pictured Julian living in a luxury high rise in one of the more trendy or elegant areas of the city. It was a surprise therefore to find that Julian chose to live here and not in a chicer area like SoHo or Tribeca. Though hot little restaurants and clubs had popped up over the past few years, the Lower East Side was a much grittier area of the city, with a diverse population.

"I have to thank you for bringing me tonight. Jamal is a wonderful kid and I'm going to do my best to help him." Julian took his keys out of his pocket to unlock the front door of his building. "If I'm still in business that is, by next month."

Nick's breath came in shallow pants. He'd hoped that Julian lived on the first floor or even the second, so he could suggest taking the stairs, but he was heading for the elevator. *Fuck.*

Face your demons, his therapist said. Except for the hospital, Nick had yet to be able to use elevators—he couldn't take being in an enclosed space like that. Yet as much as the gorge rose in his throat at the thought of rocketing up in a steel cage, the shame of his fear prevented him from telling Julian. So he squeezed his eyes shut and, controlling the wild panic zinging through him, followed Julian into the large service-type elevator.

The door clanged shut and Nick imagined it was how the gates of hell sounded behind a sinner when he entered, never to escape.

Open your eyes. If you freak out, he'll know something's wrong.

Gulping down his anxiety, Nick forced himself to look at Julian who had stopped speaking and was staring at him with concern.

"What's wrong? You're pale and shaking."

Nick opened his mouth to speak, but found he couldn't talk. His body was wracked with shivers, and sweat poured off him.

When would this fucking ride end? It must be half an hour already that they were in this rattling, groaning death box.

It shuddered to a halt, and Julian slid the door to the side, opening the elevator up directly into his apartment.

"Come with me."

Without protest, Nick allowed himself to be led to the sofa. Julian settled down next to him, placed a throw over him and took his hand, rubbed it in between his palms. Nick was so cold and Julian was so very warm.

Pain rose within him, clenching his chest and throat, making it hard to breathe. He wanted to curl up underneath the blanket and stay here, on this sofa, with Julian holding his hand forever.

"Nick," said Julian, his voice hesitant. "Talk to me?"

But Nick didn't want to talk. He'd been talking for forever to his therapist. The coldness never left him and he almost broke apart sitting there, next to Julian. He wanted to be normal again; to walk around and see the beauty in life and be free of the suffocating fear, guilt, and loneliness.

His eyes met Julian's, watched the heat and desire kindle and flame in those green eyes that haunted his dreams, and without thinking, Nick cupped the nape of Julian's neck and pulled him close, their lips barely touching. "No talking." Without waiting for a response, he crushed his mouth over Julian's.

Julian moaned his acceptance and pressed his mouth harder against Nick's, opening his lips, giving Nick's tongue free access. Nick plunged inside Julian's mouth, tangling with Julian's velvety smooth tongue, drinking in his wet heat. Long-dormant emotions thundered through Nick and his blood heated. He gently touched Julian's face, skimming his fingertips across Julian's cheekbones, brushing up against his brow, while his mouth moved harsher and more firmly against Julian's.

"Fuck, you taste amazing." Nick broke away, gasping, and pushed Julian underneath him on the couch, straddling him, then leaning down to attack his mouth again. With a long, wet lick of his tongue, Nick kissed and nuzzled a hot trail down Julian's neck, nipping at his throat and sucking the tender skin by Julian's ear. Julian writhed beneath him, his groans escalating in the quiet apartment.

"Hold still," muttered Nick. He sucked the lobe of Julian's ear in his mouth and bit down on in lightly. The sound of Julian's cry of pleasure beneath him caused Nick's cock to throb. His hands roamed over Julian's torso, touching him lightly, feeling the hardness of muscle, the softness of his skin. It was a wonder to him to have this man in his arms after all these years. His fingers circled the flat pad of Julian's nipple and tweaked the tip.

Julian squeaked underneath him, then croaked out in a disbelieving voice, "Hold still? Are you fucking kidding me?"

Nick grinned, his heart suddenly lighter than it had been for years. He braced himself on his arms and rotated his hips, rubbing his dampening, jean clad erection over Julian's. The pain and longing in Julian's bright green gaze almost took Nick's breath away.

"You fucking broke my heart the last time you walked away from me, Nick. Don't you dare disappear on me again."

The heavy sound of his own thumping heart pounded in Nick's ears. Each day he barely existed, moving through the hours without making an imprint, trying only to survive. There was no future with Julian, no happy ending, and Julian deserved to know that. It was the least Nick could do.

With more regret and pain than he'd ever imagined possible, Nick kissed Julian desperately, knowing it would likely be the last time. He memorized the shape of Julian's warm lips, the sweetness of his mouth, his heated breath. Nick drank in Julian's scent, soaking in his warmth, wishing he could capture and keep this moment for a lifetime.

With the last of his dwindling resistance Nick pulled away to stand and gaze down at the beautiful panting man lying on the couch. All the garbage running through his mind that he'd managed to hold at bay for so long reared its ugly head, whispering how he didn't deserve this second chance at happiness. It should've been him running up those steps in the Towers, searching for people. He was the probie, he didn't have a family, never would. He had nothing to lose.

"No." He shook his head, hoping the nightmare wouldn't rise up to choke him now, but he could feel its insidious creep inside his body. What made him think he should enjoy his life, when his buddies, those men, had died? The guilt slammed into him and he gasped, sinking to the floor.

From a distance, he heard his name called, but he couldn't answer. All he saw before him was the rubble; he smelled the burning. He'd lain still, trapped beneath a twisted pile of burning debris for hours, thinking he was going to die. Wishing near the end that he did, to stop the pain.

Strong hands had pulled at him finally, calling his name, giving him comfort. Unashamed, he'd cried tears of thanks and relief. He was saved. Then he'd learned of the catastrophe and the carnage. None of the men in his firehouse who'd gone into the Towers that day had made it. So many gone; 343 lives, 343 brothers lost forever.

Why him? He had no wife to miss and love him, no children

left behind. Why did he—a gay man, afraid to live his life—make it home, while others who had so much to live for, so many people who loved them, never came home?

"It should've been me." He reached out and grasped hold of the outstretched hands.

"Nick, shh. No, come here."

For the first time in years, he allowed himself to be held. Warm arms, strong arms closed around him, holding him like a child. His shivering ceased and he blinked, life coming back into focus; minute sounds of the traffic below and the humming of the refrigerator, shockingly normal considering how he felt. Nick tensed, suddenly aware he was in Julian's arms. He tried to sit up, but Julian held him tight.

"Lie still and relax. I'm not letting you go. Not yet."

Mortified, he nodded and said nothing, merely sitting in the circle of Julian's arms, drenched in perspiration and wondering how he'd allowed his life to descend into such a black abyss.

Several minutes passed before he sighed and pushed at Julian's chest. "Let me up, please. I'm all right, I promise."

After only a slight hesitation, Julian released him. Embarrassed, Nick stood on shaky legs, his gaze flitting around the loft—at the wide open space, high ceilings and modern, sleek décor.

Anywhere but at Julian.

There was no room he could escape to, no place to hide.

"The bathroom is behind the kitchen. I'll get you a different shirt to wear." Julian stood and walked to the back of the apartment, leaving Nick to stare after him.

He hurried off to where Julian indicated and shut the door behind him. Grateful for the moment alone, Nick braced his hands along the marble topped vanity and took deep, cleansing breaths, like his therapist told him to do after an attack. His racing heart steadied after several minutes. When he looked up and gazed into the mirror, Nick saw the ravages of his fear: his skin was pale, deep lines etching grooves like harsh parentheses on either side of his mouth. His eyes peered out, sunken and dark, the right one twitching a bit.

"You're a fucking mess. What made you think you could do this?"

He jumped slightly at the knock on the door.

"Nick? Can I come in for a sec?"

He opened the door for Julian who had a sweatshirt in his hands. "Here. If you want to take a shower, feel free."

"Thank you," he said softly, seeing and ignoring the unasked questions in Julian's eyes, knowing how once again, he was going to hurt the only man who'd ever meant anything to him. "I'm good. I'll put this on and be out in a minute."

Julian closed the door and Nick blew out a breath, grateful he didn't insist on staying. With only a little hesitation Nick pulled the damp shirt over his head and faced the mirror. A litany of scars crossed his chest, some thicker than others, mostly pale pink, fading to white.

The skin grafts had done their job for the most part, but even fourteen years later his chest was numb and felt strange to the touch. The hair hadn't grown back where the burns and grafting had occurred, but he didn't care. He was alive, and he supposed he should be grateful. He could barely look at himself anymore and tugged the sweatshirt over his head, having seen enough.

Julian was in the kitchen, sitting on one of the stools by the counter. He had a glass in front of him filled with what Nick presumed was vodka, having spied the Grey Goose bottle.

"Would you like a drink? I have beer, wine . . . anything you'd like."

Nick shook his head, regret piercing his heart as he watched the hope drain from Julian's eyes.

"I don't think so. I'm going to head home. I want you to know how much I appreciate what you did for Jamal tonight."

Julian stood abruptly, kicking the stool away from his feet.

"Don't treat me like I'm some fucking stranger, Nicky. You owe me. It's been eighteen years; you think I'm going to let you walk out on me again like you did before? After what just happened between us? After you fell apart? No fucking way. I'm not that same person and neither are you, obviously."

Taken aback by Julian's anger, Nick remained mute.

"What the hell is going on with you? One minute you're tongue fucking me into the next century and the next you're freaking out. I know I'm a damn good kisser, but this isn't about us, is it? It has nothing to do with our past and everything to do with you and the shit that's floating around in your head."

Julian stepped closer to him and Nick, who normally couldn't stand people near him, was rooted to the floor, unable to move.

"Talk to me, Nicky. Tell me what happened to you."

He was so tired of holding himself together, feeling like at any moment he'd shatter into a million tiny pieces, leaving nothing behind but a pile of dust.

Ashes to ashes, dust to dust.

The words poured out of him, flowing unchecked this time. "It should've been me. We all went to the Towers to save them. It was my day off, but I went anyway. I heard and couldn't stay home; I had a duty to help, you know? But I lived and they all died. Why, Julian? Why did I live and they didn't?"

"Oh, Nick." Julian held him close. "I don't have the answers for you. No one does. But I'm going to be completely selfish and say I'm so thankful you did make it and we're here together after all these years."

Unflinching green eyes gazed back at him. Clever, beautiful eyes that Nick could never stop dreaming of. Eyes that at one time had held the promise of forever, until Nick ruined everything with his cowardice and shame. Unable to maintain Julian's scrutiny, Nick broke away and ran to the elevator, his chest heaving, eyes stinging with tears.

"Let me out. I need to leave here. NOW."

Chapter Nine

HIS HEART WAS breaking and Julian could barely catch his breath. It had nothing to do with the soul-stealing kiss from moments ago, and everything to do with the total breakdown of the man in front of him.

"Nick." Julian wanted to put his arms around the man, but he was afraid Nick would fight him. But Julian couldn't let him leave. "Nick, please. Come lie down. You're wiped out and in no condition to drive anywhere."

He approached the trembling man with caution, unsure of his mental or physical state. Julian had dealt with high-strung models, but this wasn't anything even close; he wondered if he should call a doctor or maybe Katie.

Coming face to face with Nick, Julian could see he was in another place inside his head. With caution, he placed a hand on Nick's arm, and when there was no response, Julian slid his arm around Nick's shoulder, drawing him near. Nick let out a heavy expulsion of breath and sagged into Julian's arms.

Unprepared for Nick's dead weight in his arms, Julian staggered, then caught himself, hugging the heavy body close. "Let's go." Together, they made a slow but steady progress back into the apartment. Nick headed toward the couch, but Julian deftly steered him to his sleeping area instead. He stopped at the bedside, intending to convince Nick with quiet words and gentleness to rest for a few hours before going home.

Nick grabbed him hard and pushed him down on the bed, covering Julian's body with his. With almost violent desperation, Nick slammed his mouth over Julian's and Julian, still struggling to catch his breath, found himself responding at first. He wrapped his arms around Nick, sinking into the kiss and embrace, loving the harsh neediness of Nick's mouth on his, until Julian sensed wetness on his cheeks. Julian opened his eyes and spotted tears at the corners of Nick's eyes, his brow furrowed as if he were in pain.

Julian pushed at Nick's shoulders, twisting away from Nick's grasping hunger. It wasn't that he didn't want to kiss Nick. God knows his body throbbed and his cock ached. But Julian knew he was being used; right now he could be any warm body for Nick to hold on to. And Julian didn't want that. Nick needed help; he was drowning in a sea of survivor's guilt. And Julian wanted to be his rock to climb onto, that log Nick could hold on to. Julian would be Nick's shelter from the storm. He wanted Nick to want him for the right reasons, not because Julian was the only one around.

Nick reached for him again, but Julian rolled away, coming up on the opposite side of the bed, and stood. Silence reigned in the apartment, broken only by the sharp inhalations of Nick's breaths. With regret, Julian looked down at the dark figure of Nick sprawled out on his white sheets, his face a study in sadness.

"It isn't right, Nick. I'd be lying if I said I didn't want you, but I'd be a lousy friend to take advantage of you now. And more than anything, I think we need to be friends again, don't you?"

Julian searched Nick's face, almost missing his imperceptible nod. Relief poured through him and muscles he wasn't even aware of loosened the stranglehold they had upon his chest.

"Try to rest. In the morning we can talk. Sound good?"

Once again, Nick tipped his head in accord, then toed off his sneakers and without undressing, bunched the pillows under his head and closed his eyes. By the steady rise and fall of his chest, Julian knew the exact moment Nick fell asleep. Julian undressed to his boxers and pulled a tee shirt from his dresser. He went to the bathroom and brushed his teeth, contemplating the events of the day.

What had started out so perfectly miserable, with the visit to the banker about his loan, had ended, if not happily, on a better note than Julian had expected. He rinsed his mouth and spit, then washed his face and brushed his hair. Meeting Jamal earlier had sparked something within him, not just the obvious sympathy for the young man's plight, but the itch to create something new and innovative. Something meaningful.

After turning down the lights, he slid under the comforter, listening to the sound of Nick's breathing. It was peaceful and nice, having someone share his bed after so many years. Julian turned on his side and stared out of the windows, watching the blinking lights of the city stretch out before him. Fatigue washed over him and before he closed his eyes, Julian thought about where he and Nick could have breakfast nearby, and talk about how they'd begin to find their way back, not to where they once were, but perhaps to a better place.

JULIAN AWOKE AND checked the clock next to the bed. "Ten? Jesus. I was tired." He yawned and stretched. Hopefully he and Nick could talk over breakfast and begin to work on rebuilding from their tenuous infrastructure. He raked his hand through his hair, pushing the tangled strands out of his eyes, and looked forward to seeing Nick in the morning, sleep-rough and stubbled.

He rolled over to poke Nick awake and instead faced an empty bed.

Fuck.

Julian scrambled out of bed and raced to the bathroom, knowing in his heart Nick wasn't there. The empty room validated that.

"Where the fuck did you go, Nick? God damn it." Wild at the thought his friend was out there somewhere, suffering the aftereffects of their rough night together, Julian glanced around the loft, hoping against hope Nick might've left a note. He spied a piece of paper propped up against the bowl of fruit on his counter.

Sorry I fucked up last night. Thanks for everything—Nick.

What the hell? *Thanks for everything*?

Julian ran to his phone to call Nick and see what was going on in his brain, when he realized he'd never taken Nick's number. He had no way of getting in touch with him to find out if he was well, or if he'd gotten home okay.

"Damn." He threw the phone onto the couch.

He texted Marcus and Zach.

Are you busy? Can we have breakfast? I need advice.

And like always, they were there for him.

Marcus texted back first.

The usual place in the Village?

He agreed and Zach pinged back a few seconds later with his agreement. The panic in his chest lessened, his heartbeat returning to its normal steady rhythm, and he was able to shower, dress, and make it to the restaurant within the hour. It was somewhat crowded, but he spotted Marcus in the back, waving to him, and he hurried over to his friends.

"Juli, I ordered you coffee and a mimosa."

Three flutes graced the table, filled with the pale orange sparkling liquid, but Julian gulped down the coffee before anything else. He waited for it to warm him up, before settling into the cushion of the booth. The murmur of the other diners was loud enough around them for Julian to feel comfortable to speak frankly.

"Thanks, you guys." He now took a sip of the mimosa, savoring the bubbles sizzling on his tongue. "I have to tell you some stuff, but I need to speak without interruption." A quick glance at Marcus garnered an almost immediate protest from his friend.

"Hey. I can keep quiet."

Zach snorted into his coffee cup, laugh lines crinkling the skin around his big blue eyes. Several years younger than both him and Marcus, Zach possessed an air of gentleness, and neither Julian nor Marcus could ever get angry with him.

"Yeah, I'm with Zach." But Julian knew when it came to personal matters, Marcus could be extremely discreet.

"Last night, I met up with Nick, and—"

"Nick?" Marcus's voice rose in delight. "Gorgeous Nick? Hunky fireman Nick? Juli, you bastard. Holding out on us, huh?"

"Marcus . . ." Julian attempted to cut his friend off, but Marcus, assuming they'd end up discussing something sexual, rolled on.

"I knew you had a thing for him. Mmm, those blue eyes and those big shoulders. That is one delicious piece of man-flesh."

"Marc, shut up a second. I met up with Nick, and he took me to the hospital where he volunteers helping kids in the burn unit." The image of Jamal's agonized face as he exercised his tortured fingers and hand flashed through Julian's mind. "We talked, and he came back to the loft with me."

"Did you score? Are you feeling guilty now?" Marcus drained his champagne and held it up to the waiter standing a few tables away, wiggling it as a signal for another. "You shouldn't, you know. Even if he isn't gay, I could tell from the night of the party he had a thing for you. He watched you all night long."

"It isn't like that." Julian waited for the waiter to finish taking his order and refill Marcus's drink before he spoke. He'd never told his two friends about Nick and what happened when they were young. Now that they were grown, it seemed so silly to go back and talk of high school days, yet somehow he knew that experience had shaped him into the man he'd grown to be.

"Nick and I . . ." he bit his lip, weighing his words carefully, and began again. "Nick and I know each other. From high school. We were kind of together, but he could never admit to anyone he was gay so we broke it off. I transferred schools and we lost touch. Before that night at Sparks, we hadn't seen each other in eighteen years."

Much to Julian's surprise, it was Zach who spoke first. "But you never forgot him, did you? The connection between you two is still there, right?"

Zach might spend most of his time talking to people online, but it didn't prevent him from having an innate insight into people's behavior. Julian knew how shy Zach was, but his observations were as succinct as if he'd been studying relationships for years.

"I was so hurt when he broke it off between us," Julian began. "It was like he was denying the time we spent together meant anything. The rejection was immediate; one day we were together, laughing and hanging out, and the next he told me he couldn't do it anymore and he wanted to be 'normal,' as he put it." He took a sip of his coffee. "I wanted to hate him, and for years managed to an extent to put him out of my mind. I never thought I'd see him again, but when we met at Sparks, I don't know . . ." He fiddled with his knife, spinning it around on the tablecloth.

"It was as if the years fell away," Zach said, softly. "And you were right back there with him all over again."

"Yeah," said Julian with a sad smile. "Exactly."

Marcus remained silent, his eyes focused on his champagne glass. He didn't fool Julian, though. He could see the wheels of that keen mind working. Marcus would speak when he was ready, so Julian sipped his coffee and waited.

"And what makes you think he's ready to welcome you with open arms?" Marcus pinned him with a dark look. "He's uniform and you know how they are about gay men. I don't care what they say about diversity and all their bullshit."

Julian thought back to the kiss he and Nick shared last night. The taste of Nick's tongue and the feel of his lips spiked a shocking rush of hunger within Julian. "I—I know."

"Son of a bitch. You screwed him, didn't you?" Marcus stared at him.

"No, absolutely not." Not for lack of desire. "Nick was injured in 9/11. Somehow he made it out, but members of his firehouse didn't, and he's living with enormous guilt; survivor's guilt, the guilt of being gay and living while those men had families and died." He shook his head and accepted his plate from the waiter. "It's a fucking mess."

"So why are you involved? I don't understand. Unless you

want to start screwing him again. And recognize that if you do, you'll be his little secret, because I doubt after all these years he's coming out of the closet for a gay, clothing designer boyfriend." Marcus attacked his eggs with angry stabs of his fork.

"Our relationship in high school never got that far; it was physical to an extent, but it was on a more emotional level. And I feel for him, Marc. Can't you understand? It's impossible for me or any of us to imagine what he went through. I want to help him in any way I can. I think I found something, but I'd like your opinion."

"So tell us." Zach cut into his steak.

He told them all about Jamal and his injuries. How defeated the young man was, and how he'd given up on life, until Julian showed him the sketches.

"I think they could work." He pulled out his pad and showed the designs to Zach and Marcus. "I'll have to do some research into the fabrics and requirements for the compression."

Marcus looked through the pages, glanced up at him, then handed them to Zach. "This is quite a departure from silk pants and glittery sweaters. It will take up most of your time as I see it."

Julian's hands tightened on his fork. "So?" He tried to keep his voice light. "It's not as if the orders are pouring in. If not for some pre-orders on the collection before the show, I'd have had to close up already."

"It's great that you want to do this, I'm proud of you," said Zach. "So many designers branch out into the usual perfume, or home goods, but this is coming from your heart, I can tell." He gave Julian a big smile. "I think it's amazing."

Warmth settled into his chest at Zach's praise.

"How are you going to manage it? Do you have the money? Does Nick?" Marcus eyed him speculatively and Julian flushed.

"I haven't spoken to him about it. Last night when he freaked out, I had him sleep over, 'cause I was afraid for him to drive home by himself." The eggs tasted like sawdust, and the toast like Styrofoam. He was so worried about Nick, but didn't know what to do about it.

"So where is he? Or did he have someplace better to be?" asked Marcus.

"That's just it." Frustrated, Julian threw his napkin on the table. The little appetite he'd had, had vanished. "When I woke up he was gone. He left a note, but I have no idea how he's feeling, or where he is."

"If he wanted you to, he would've let you know, don't you think?"

Julian gave Marcus a sharp glance. "I don't know if he was in the right frame of mind for anything. I have no way of getting in touch with him to even know if he's okay, since I never took his number."

"Isn't your little assistant friends with his sister?" Marcus asked, draining his second glass of champagne. As if he'd been waiting for Marcus to finish, the waiter appeared immediately and refilled it. Once again, it seemed Marcus had made a conquest. Julian watched Marcus cover the waiter's hand with his, a slow smile breaking across his lips. "Perfect timing, thank you. I love a man who's so attentive to my needs." The waiter blushed and walked away, casting looks over his shoulder at their table. Marcus turned his attention back to Julian. "She can find out from her."

Shooting his friend an evil scowl, Julian pulled out his phone. "You're right, and why do you keep calling Melanie that? She's not my little assistant; she's a damn good designer and has been with me through all the problems with this show."

"She doesn't like me." Marcus scratched his fingernail along the table cloth, a frown tugging his lips down. "I never did anything to her, but I get the sense she's protecting you from me and that's bullshit."

Julian knew Melanie didn't like Marcus because she thought he was a player (which he was) and wanted to get Julian into bed (which he didn't). "Try being a little less of a dick sometimes and maybe you can get along with her. You're both important to me."

He texted Melanie for Nick's number, and she texted him back immediately.

Why do you need his number?

He gave her a brief rundown of last night's events.

I'm having brunch with Katie. Want me to ask?

It hit Julian right then, how stupid he was.

Never mind, thanks.

"Here." Zach handed Julian his phone. "I guess you forgot about looking him up on the internet."

"You know, it just occurred to me to look him up online. I'm hopeless with crap like that." Julian grabbed the phone and took down the information. Shit, Nick still lived in the same house from when he was a kid. Not that he'd ever been there. Julian hadn't been invited over, had never met Nick's parents as Nick had been too afraid of them catching him and Julian together. Julian's father had disappeared even before Julian's birth, and his mother worked long hours as a legal secretary, so she was almost always absent. They'd had the house to themselves and taken full advantage of it.

"I don't need his phone number." He drained his coffee and stood up. "I'm going over to his house."

"Are you sure that's a good idea?" Zach peered at him anxiously. "What if he gets angry again?"

"Don't worry." Julian patted Zach on the shoulder. "I'm a big boy. I can handle myself."

Marcus was busy getting his fourth glass of champagne, along with the waiter's telephone number. "Remember you have a business to think of first. That comes before everything else." He winked at the waiter. "Well, not everything."

Julian knew aside from his business, Marcus thought with his dick first, and that's where the two of them always differed. Marcus professed to love all the men he took to his bed, and couldn't understand why anyone would ever think of settling down with only one person for the rest of his life.

Julian never pretended with his lovers. They knew it was a purely physical relationship right from the start. Julian's heart remained firmly planted in his own chest; he had no intention of losing it to anyone. He took some bills out of his wallet and slid them across the table. Marcus slid them right back.

"My treat, Juli."

Julian's jaw tightened. He knew it was his friend's way of helping him out with his financial difficulties. Normally he would argue, but right now he didn't have the time.

"Thanks, Marc."

But Marcus was already nuzzling the waiter, whispering God knows what in his ear. Zach sat blushing and rolling his eyes. In other words, a normal get-together for the three of them.

"I'll talk to you guys later." Julian took off. It would take him close to an hour to get to Nick's house in Brooklyn, and he didn't want to waste any more time.

Chapter Ten

NICK DIDN'T PLAN to leave his house for the rest of the day. Somehow he'd managed to make it back from Julian's apartment to his house, stripped to his boxers, shut himself in the bedroom, and lay staring up at the ceiling. By sheer luck, his parents were out for the day on some home improvement expedition to Long Island, so he wouldn't be expected to make an appearance upstairs.

What the fuck had he been thinking to kiss Julian? Even now, his cock sprang to attention, remembering the hot wet kisses they'd shared in Julian's bed. Thoughts he hadn't permitted to enter his mind began attacking him from every direction.

What if he told his parents he was gay—would they still love him? It hadn't ever been a subject they'd discussed as a family; gay rights, *being gay*, had never come up as a topic of conversation at the family dinner table, along with the score of the latest Mets baseball game, and whether or not his father was ever going to paint the house.

Nick had heard enough however, around the station he worked at, and now with his training team, to know the department had a long way to go in gay rights education. Like the way Jensen had behaved the other day, calling some of the trainees limp-wrists and fags. That's what he'd heard through the years.

Not that there weren't plenty of men and women who'd stand up for the brave individuals who decided to come out. Nick recalled one of his academy brothers, a big, beefy guy he'd trained with, named Paul, who confided in him over a beer one night that he was gay. Paul had been literally shaking when he told Nick the truth.

And Nick merely sat and said, *"It's no big deal,"* when in fact, if he'd had the courage to man up and instead say, *"Hey, me too. Let's show those bastards,"* maybe he wouldn't feel so lost and alone right now. He might know what to say to his parents and Katie.

In the darkest corner of his mind, Nick had never forgotten those times with Julian. Nick couldn't admit that since those sweet years of exploration, he'd been living a hollow life, stunted by shame and doubt. What he did with those men in back rooms and in his car when the loneliness threatened to choke him was for pure physical release. It was all taking and no giving on his part. And there was always someone willing to open themselves up for him.

Julian was different, and it scared the shit out of Nick, because by looking deep within himself like his therapist had always told him to do, everything Nick wanted had somehow become wrapped up in Julian. Nick wanted to be held by Julian, taken by him. For Julian, Nick would give of himself. He'd give and give until there was no telling where one of them ended and the other began.

What the hell had happened to him?

Nick's stomach growled; he saw it was after two already and he hadn't eaten. He rolled out of bed, put on sweatpants and a sweatshirt, and shuffled to the kitchen where he made himself a sandwich from some questionable meat and a bagel. He guzzled a bottle of water and the cold liquid woke him up a bit.

Julian, the grown man, shocked him. As teenagers, they'd talked about their dreams, and Nick had winced when Julian discussed becoming a fashion designer. He'd always pictured those men to be what people stereotyped as gay: feminine, dressed perfectly, hair always styled. Because to Nick, that's what gay men were. And Nick hadn't thought of himself as gay then. He'd told himself he was curious, experimenting. It didn't mean he'd end up like that.

But it had hurt so damn much when Julian left; no one understood him and laughed with him like that ever again. Their closeness defined Nick, the fumbling and kisses they shared more real to him than any sex he'd had since. It took years before Nick could admit to himself he was gay, and before he understood he'd loved Julian and lost him to stupidity and self-hatred.

He'd tried to force himself into a picture of normalcy by pretending he was straight. Going out with the women he'd been set up with, either by Katie or well-meaning friends, had resulted in nothing more than endless evenings of awkward conversation. Yet he still couldn't bring himself to say the words.

As if not saying them meant he wasn't gay.

Meeting Julian, discovering the man he'd become, the person he was, Nick was overcome by shame. Julian lived with his head held high, while he, Nick, still hid in the closet.

He heard a car door slam outside. His parents must've returned home. Nick threw his half-eaten sandwich in the trash and went into the bathroom to brush his teeth. He didn't even bother to glance in the mirror, knowing he needed a shave, but couldn't muster up the energy. Before dinner he'd make sure to take a shower.

At the expected knock he sighed and mentally shored himself up to face his parents. With a smile firmly planted on his lips, Nick swung open the door.

"Hi Mom—"

He stood gaping at the sight he never thought would come to pass. Julian Cornell on his doorstep, his blond hair windblown, messy waves lying haphazardly across his forehead. There had always been a hint of laughter in his green eyes, but now he looked tired, hesitant, and never more fucking gorgeous in his life.

"I've been called many things, but 'Mom' has never been one of them," said Julian with a wry smile.

Heedless to the cold air, Nick continued to stare, until Julian cleared his throat. "Umm, can I come in?"

Jerking himself out of his trance, Nick stepped aside. "Yeah, sure, sorry." He closed the door behind Julian, drinking in the man's scent. When Julian took off his leather coat and turned to toss it over the chair, Nick's mouth dried.

Leather fucking pants. Julian's ass, that perfect round ass Nick had smoothed his palms over last night, was encased in tight black leather that cupped its delicious curves and hugged his strong thighs. Every ounce of blood in Nick's body rushed south to pool in his groin. It was impossible to hide what the sight of this beautiful man did to him.

"Nick?"

He blinked, tearing his thoughts away from throwing Julian down on the bed and ripping off those pants to expose his beautiful body.

"Yeah?" His voice croaked, and he scrubbed his face with his hands. "Come on inside." He spun on his heel, walking with long strides into his bedroom, hoping Julian didn't see his erection. He stood for a moment, gulping down deep breaths, until he calmed down and was able to walk without pain.

Julian had taken a seat on the couch, and Nick had a crazy thought of the two of them together, having dinner, watching movies, like any other couple. Yeah, crazy, that's what he was. All these fucked-up ideas that he could have a normal life? He should be punched in the face for even thinking about it. He hadn't earned the right to his life; not when others had given theirs so selflessly.

"Why are you here?" Wary, Nick stood, rather than sit down next to Julian.

"I was worried about you. Are you surprised?" Julian held his eyes, and Nick could see the truth that had always been there. The truth he'd hidden from and pushed away.

"I'm fine."

"Fine?" Julian's voice rose as got up from the couch. "You think you're fine? You had a near breakdown in my apartment and then sneaked out in the morning without waking me up to say goodbye. And you think you're fine?"

"I don't owe you anything." He did though. He owed Julian the only bit of love he'd ever had in his life. Their brief time together was as if he'd touched the stars. But it wasn't right for him to have it. Normal didn't belong to someone like him.

"I never said you did." Julian looked at him with sorrow. "I'm not here to keep score. I'm worried about you, though."

The apartment suddenly seemed too small; Nick's breathing quickened. "There's no need to be." He sidestepped away from Julian and those leather pants and walked into the kitchen. "I was going to make some coffee. Do you want any?"

"Sure." Of course Julian followed him, not waiting in the other room like he'd hoped. "Can I ask you a question?"

He poured the water into the coffeemaker and measured the grounds. *No,* Nick wanted to scream. *No. Go away and leave me alone. I was okay with my life before you came back into it. Seeing you again, kissing you last night—you've made me want things. Want you.*

"What?" Nick bit out the question. Yeah, he sounded testy, but right now it was the best he could do.

"Don't get angry at me, but are you seeing anyone? Professionally, I mean."

The coffee sputtered as it hit the pot. Nick didn't like those little cup things. The coffee never tasted right to him.

"You mean a shrink?" His laugh echoed against the walls, but there was little humor there. "I've seen psychologists, psychiatrists, grief counselors; you name 'em, I've seen 'em." So not to face Julian, Nick busied himself at the refrigerator, getting the milk out, but when he turned around Julian was standing right there.

"And?" Julian leaned his hip against the counter, effectively blocking Nick from moving past him.

"And what?" He skirted past Julian, careful not to touch him. "I'm a mess, can't you tell?"

"What happened to you? I know you freaked out in the elevator in my building. Did you get trapped in one during a fire or something?"

"Or something." He huffed out a laugh, running his fingers through his hair.

"Please," begged Julian, refusing to let Nick ignore him and standing in front of him again. "Why won't you tell me? It's just the two of us. I'll never breathe a word to anyone. You know I can keep a secret."

Nick raised his gaze from the floor to meet Julian's eyes. He did know, and Julian didn't deserve to be sloughed off like a one-shot stranger Nick might have picked up in a bar. The shitty way he'd treated Julian the last time they'd talked in high school, telling him he wanted to be normal . . . when Julian, now standing here in Nick's kitchen, so fucking gorgeous Nick could come just from looking at him in those God damn leather pants . . . Nick owed Julian.

"I know." He reached down and before he could think too hard about what he was doing, he pulled his sweatshirt over his head and bared his chest.

"This." He pointed to his chest. "This is what happened. I was caught for hours under a metal support beam when it crashed on me. I wasn't working on 9/11; naturally when I heard what happened I rushed to the site to help the other firefighters. I caught up with my guys, and they laughed at me since I was a probie. They told me to stay back." He touched his chest with the tips of his fingers, letting them rest over his heart.

"They were looking out for you, Nick."

"They saved my life. I should've been with them. They went up and I stayed down at the base, helping the people when they came off the staircases, directing them to ambulances and the doctors. But then the Towers rumbled and began to implode."

"Oh, Nicky."

He was caught up in the memory of that day. He'd never told anyone, not even his doctors. Somehow, though, telling Julian seemed the right thing to do.

"I tried to run back in, but everyone was running away, so I circled back around. I realized then it was too dangerous, and that I didn't want to die, so I ran away and left them there to die." He broke down and Julian took him in his arms. "I didn't want to die, Julian. I should've been there with them, but I got scared."

"Of course you did, anyone would have."

"No, I was trained to help, but I ran. And afterward, after the

Towers collapsed, I went back and started searching. But it was unstable and I got trapped under some burning metal beams."

"Is that what the scarring is on your chest?"

It was a relief to talk about it after all these years. Julian didn't try and make him feel good about himself; nor did he analyze why Nick got so scared that day. He accepted it as a fact. Something anyone might feel. Maybe he wasn't wrong to have run. It was something Dr. Landau, the FDNY psychiatrist, had been trying to get him to see for years, but Nick fought him on it and refused to accept it as truth.

"Yeah. They're third degree burns. I had skin grafts and wore compression bandages like you saw Jamal had on the other day." Months of pain and physical therapy. The utter loneliness of the hospital late at night when Nick was left with nothing but his guilt. Days of pretend cheerful visits with his family.

"Is that when you started volunteering at the burn center?" Without Nick realizing it, Julian had steered him back to the couch where they sat next to each other. "You wanted to give back to those people."

"The kids. I felt so badly for them." Nick stared unseeing at the floor.

Julian kept his hands on Nick, the roughness of his caressing fingers strangely comforting.

"You've made a difference in Jamal's life. I can see it. He looks up to you."

Nick shrugged. "I don't know. I'm no one for anyone to look up to." He watched Julian's long fingers stroke his hand, each touch a lick of fire against his skin. "Remember how I said I wanted to be normal?"

Julian nodded.

Wasted, lonely years of pretending, when all along, no one had ever come close to making Nick feel like he did right at this moment, simply from the touch of a hand.

"I don't even know what that is anymore. Is it normal to live a lie because you're too scared to tell the truth?"

"What are you afraid of, though? Your family? Your job? I

don't get it, Nick."

"You wouldn't. You've always been very clear about who you are."

Julian cupped Nick's jaw with his hand and Nick luxuriated in his touch. "Look at yourself, Nick. Feel it. You're clear about it as well. Say it out loud for once. Admit it when it's only the two of us here."

Nick breathed in Julian's scent and turned his face into Julian's palm, his lips sliding over the warm skin.

"I want you."

"Not that, Nick. I know you do. I didn't forget that kiss last night. Say it out loud, if not outside of this room, then to me at least. Be honest with me. I'll go first."

Julian took Nick's face between his hands. "I'm gay. I'm a gay man."

The blaze of emotion, pride, anger, and fear was all there in Julian's eyes, waiting for Nick to step up and take control of his life. It had taken him almost eighteen years to get to this point—more than half his life. He'd lived through unimaginable loss and pain, all the time hiding the most important thing about himself from everyone. Despite the heat in the apartment, Nick shivered.

He'd been chasing the wrong dream all along, looking for that pot of gold at the end of a rainbow that didn't exist. Often the riches that will bring you the most happiness are right in front of you, and you only have to have the courage to reach out and take what's offered, until, like the rainbow, it disappears from your life forever.

"I'm gay."

Julian expelled a long breath and leaned his forehead against Nick's. "Thank God." He kissed Nick then, a soft sweet brush of his lips like the wing of a bird. "It's the first step. I'm so proud of you."

Nick kissed Julian back, and he knew he'd finally come home.

Chapter Eleven

THERE WAS ONLY so much he could be expected to take, Julian thought, his head spinning as Nick plunged his tongue in Julian's mouth. He allowed Nick to push him down on the couch until Julian was captured between Nick's powerful thighs; Julian hadn't been able to erase them from his mind since last night. Once Nick cupped him through the leather pants, stroking Julian's cock until he was ready to shoot in his pants like a kid, all thoughts except getting Nick inside him escaped Julian.

Nick's gaze left a burning trail as it raked down Julian's body; his skin pebbled with goosebumps. "Take off the sweater, but leave those fucking leather pants on."

"Bossy SOB, aren't you?" Julian muttered, yet he took off the sweater and tossed it on the floor. With a grin, Julian joined Nick in stroking his cock, their fingers brushing together, until Nick knocked Julian's hand away, and with a very deliberate finger, traced the outline of Julian's swollen erection through the softness of the clinging leather.

Julian writhed, his ass pumping up to thrust harder into Nick's touch, but the bastard kept just the right pressure on his cock until Julian was nearly out of his mind with desire.

"Fuck, Nick. Please." Never one to beg, Julian was practically whimpering with the need to get more friction on his dick. Nick, though, took his own sweet time and continued that maddeningly soft to firm touch on Julian's cock, but thank fuck, finally unzipped Julian's pants.

"Lift up," Nick whispered, his hands skimming over Julian's stomach, his blue eyes dark and hungry. Julian's cock peeked above his underwear, and Nick thumbed the swollen head, spreading the precome that had already dampened Julian's briefs.

Hunger twisted in Julian's stomach as he complied, and soon he was bare-assed, Nick having pulled off his briefs as well as the leather pants. Nick stood and held out his hand.

"Let's move this to the bed?"

Julian heard the question in Nick's voice and understood the uncertainty. He didn't need Nick to tell him no other man had ever been in this apartment or in Nick's bed. There were so many firsts Nick was going through today; showing Julian his scars, admitting he was gay. Having Julian here might be overwhelming for Nick, but in a way it was the same for Julian. He'd waited over eighteen years to have sex with Nick. It was a dream Julian had let go of long ago, and still had a hard time believing it was now there within his reach.

Julian stood and hugged Nick close, unashamed of his nakedness, and whispered, "We don't have to rush this."

Nick pulled him close and buried his lips in Julian's hair. "I've waited my whole fucking life for this; since I sent you away. You bet we aren't going to rush it. Come to my bed."

Nick stepped out of his sweatpants and then he was naked. Damaged as Nick's body was, Julian saw only beauty in its strength; the wide shoulders full of power from years of carrying heavy equipment, strong arms corded with muscle from lifting and pulling weights. Nick's thick legs and flat stomach made up a mouthwatering package Julian couldn't help but run his hands over, though he was careful to skirt the damaged part of Nick's chest. He was still unsure how Nick would react to being touched.

Nick took his hand, and together they walked to the bedroom and sat on the bed. "You're afraid to touch me."

Julian nodded. "I don't want to do anything to hurt you. I don't know your boundaries."

Nick yanked him close and took Julian's mouth in a punishing kiss. It seemed every time this man touched him, Julian lost all that self-control he prided himself on. When they were young he'd never been able to resist Nick, and the passage of time had proved no different. He buried his fingers in Nick's thick, short hair and pressed up against him, desperate and needy, while their lips and tongues clashed.

Nick broke away and held him at arms' distance, his face grave and harsh. "I have no boundaries with you, that's what's scaring the hell out of me. I want it all."

Those words set Julian's blood on fire. "Fuck it, Nick. I want you so bad, I'm not gonna last. My whole damn life . . ." His voice caught for a moment.

Without another word, Nick took the lube and condoms from the table and tossed them on the bed. Nick loomed over Julian, his firm hands running over Julian's chest, fingers skimming lightly to trace the quivering muscles. Julian shuddered and arched up into Nick's touch, groaning when Nick tweaked then rolled his nipples, the pleasure pain shooting through his body, straight to his aching cock. Nick tickled his thumbs over the slant of Julian's hipbones, and Julian's cock jerked and swelled against his stomach.

"Touch me, for Christ's sake," Julian begged, any ounce of shame he might have had long gone. "Come on."

With a wicked smile lighting up his normally solemn face, Nick bent down and took Julian's cock in his mouth, electrifying every nerve in Julian's body. Unable to formulate a coherent thought with Nick lapping at his erection, Julian moaned, thrusting deep into Nick's throat. Nick took it all and grasped Julian with one hand while he sucked him down, his tongue swirling around the head of Julian's cock while his fingers danced and stroked along Julian's length.

The wet suction, the heat, and the realization that it was Nick, finally Nick touching him, sucking him, loving him, sent Julian spiraling out of control. His body tightened as his orgasm ripped through him, his cock erupting inside Nick's mouth.

"Oh God." Julian cried out as he came, the rush of sensation overpowering any wish he might have had to hold out longer. He lost control, giving in to the fire that raced through him. It incinerated any doubt he might have had about how much he cared for Nick. He'd never stopped.

Nick swallowed, never hesitating, licking Julian down to the last drop. He released Julian's softening dick from between his full lips with a wet plop. Nick sat back on his haunches, his eyes gleaming in the dim light of the bedroom. Julian's gaze was drawn to Nick's erection, so beautiful, flushed and swollen. With avid eyes, Julian watched Nick take himself in hand and stroke his length, his thumb smearing the liquid seeping out from the slit over the blunt head of his cock. Dizzy with desire, Julian's body clenched at the thought of Nick inside of him.

Holding Nick's gaze, Julian lay back and offered himself up, his heart beating a rapid tattoo. After eighteen years, their story would be complete. All the other men he'd taken to his bed over the years had been a stand-in for Nick; he was the only man Julian had never been able to forget.

Slick and cool with lube, Nick entered him, sinking one finger then two, deep inside. He hesitated.

"Is that okay? Does it feel good?"

And Julian understood there most likely hadn't been loving times for Nick when he'd been with other men. Not if it was all done in secretive places, rushed and hurried in the bathrooms of clubs and parking lots. His heart went out to Nick who, though over thirty, had probably never known a real lover's touch, or heard loving words.

Julian pushed up against Nick's hand, unashamed to show his greediness to be filled up by this amazing man, wanting to make this experience good for Nick, so he'd never forget.

"Do it, come on." Julian urged Nick on, sliding down on the bed. "God, yes. Want you now."

Nick said nothing but fluttered his fingers, and Julian felt those wicked, twisting fingers curl inside him, reaching deep. Julian rarely bottomed, preferring to take control and set the pace, but here he was unapologetic in his hunger to be driven over the edge of reality by Nick.

Nick pulled out and Julian felt the round, sheathed head

of Nick's cock push up against his hole. He reached out and grabbed hold of Nick's thigh, giving an insistent pull, impaling himself on Nick's rigid shaft. The sting and burn of the initial entry fell away, replaced by the incredible fullness; that marvelous, all-encompassing feeling of his passage gripping Nick's thick cock as it entered and withdrew, rocking him back and forth.

Julian lifted his legs, folding them against his chest, to enable Nick to slot himself further and deeper inside Julian's body. He watched Nick, loving the serious intensity on his dark face as Nick plunged inside him. Julian knew the exact time Nick entered that point of no return, when he began to drive himself hard, the bed squeaking as it jumped on the downward thrusts. He'd never had a man so supremely masculine before and Julian reveled in it. Nick threw his head back, wide neck straining, eyes squeezed shut, and he gripped hold of Julian's shoulders, digging his fingers into the muscle. "Julian, Julian. God." Nick's strangled cry echoed in the room.

A few more deep pumps and warmth filled the condom as Nick came hard and strong. He collapsed on top of Julian with a noisy expulsion of breath, and Julian hugged him close, heedless of the sweat pouring off Nick's back. It was enough to hold him after all these years.

They lay together for a minute, Julian listening to Nick breathing in his ear. Nick shifted and eased out of Julian; he removed the condom and tossed it in the trash. Instead of coming back to lie by Julian, he sat on the edge of the bed and stared at the floor.

Julian sat up behind him and placed his arms around Nick's neck, careful, once again, not to touch Nick's chest. "What's wrong?" He kissed the side of Nick's jaw, the late afternoon stubble scratchy against his lips.

For a moment Nick remained motionless, then covered one of Julian's hands with his. "I don't know."

"Don't know what?" Julian pressed into Nick, molding his chest to Nick's body. "Talk to me."

Nick threw him a sideways glance. "Neither of us are

virgins. But whenever I needed to get laid, I'd go to a club and find someone to fuck and be done with it."

Julian could imagine that easily enough. Nick was a gorgeous specimen. All he'd need to do at a gay bar is show up; he'd have his pick of whomever he wanted and they'd be on their knees.

"And so?"

"So it's easy for you; you've always known who you were."

While Julian's heart went out to Nick, he had some misconceptions that needed clearing up. And he wasn't about to hold back for Nick's sake.

"You think it was easy for me because I knew I was gay and admitted it? What rock did you crawl out from under?" He scooted back to the top of the bed and leaned against the headboard. "You ruined me for years; I had no one after you didn't want to see me again. I couldn't trust anyone not to hurt me. Until I met Marcus and Zach, I was alone."

"Why do you trust them?" Nick lay down and propped his chin in his hand.

Julian shrugged. "Sometimes you meet strangers and you know they're going to be the most important people in your life. There's no explaining it; it's how it is. Zach is the sweetest guy in the world and I'd do anything for him. And Marcus." He laughed. "You've seen him in action. He's a character, but loyal to a fault and fiercely protective of his friends. We all mesh."

The harsh lines around Nick's mouth softened. "I think we mesh, don't you?"

Don't fall for it. He's not coming out of the closet simply because he fucked you and told you in the privacy of his home he was gay.

"I think we proved that." Julian kept his voice deliberately casual. "Can I take a shower? You gave me quite a workout and I'm all sweaty."

"Yeah, sure. Use whatever towels and stuff you want."

Nick lay splayed out naked on the bed, and Julian had to control himself from pouncing on all that warm, muscled flesh. His scars were devastating, but to Julian, who rarely looked beyond a face or body, it didn't seem to matter. He saw only the courage it took to overcome the pain Nick must've endured, the sacrifice he'd made.

"Thanks." Julian stood, picked up his clothes, and headed to the bathroom. "I won't be long."

"Take all the time you need. I'm gonna have some coffee."

Julian turned on the shower and stepped in as the water turned warm, letting the water sluice over him, wondering what else this remarkable day could possibly bring.

Chapter Twelve

LYING IN HIS bed, listening to the water run in his shower, an unusual peace settled over Nick. The few times he'd tried to be with a woman had ended so badly—with him mumbling excuses for his poor performance or lack of interest—he stopped trying at all.

It had taken him years to admit to himself it wasn't breasts and soft, perfumed skin he craved, but hard muscles to grasp and stubbled skin to lick and kiss. He couldn't imagine anything better than sinking inside the tight velvety heat of a man. The problem was, Nick also couldn't imagine telling anyone.

He rolled off the bed, slipped on a tee shirt and sweatpants, and closed the door behind him when he left the bedroom, figuring Julian might want some privacy when he came out of the shower.

Nick did some stretches, enjoying the unaccustomed ache of muscles he hadn't used in a while. Sex with Julian had proved to be what he'd imagined: crazy, off the charts hot, better than what he'd ever thought it could be.

But could he do it? Could he admit to his family, the guys on the job, everyone, that he was gay? The thought of having that conversation with his parents and sister cramped his stomach with nerves and fear. It wasn't that he didn't think they'd still love him; Katie, especially, he felt would be cool with it. Probably.

His parents were so old-fashioned in their views about marriage and family, and it had been such a disappointment to his father when he'd been unable to remain on active duty as a firefighter . . . Nick's anxiety level rose exponentially just thinking about it. Right now, he'd have to let things lie quiet.

Besides, there was no indication this was anything but a

one-time thing with him and Julian. Nick sipped his coffee. Maybe they'd needed to have sex; now that they got it out of their systems, they could put it behind them and be friends. A fresh start.

Nick jumped at the sound of knocking. He scrambled to the front door and yanked it open to find Katie.

"Hi." She breezed past him like she always did, heading for the kitchen table. "I took the chance you were in and brought some doughnuts from that place you like by my house." The sugary, yeasty smell reached him then, and he couldn't help but smile at his sister. No matter how busy she was, Katie always made time for him.

"I wanted to know what happened when you and Julian went to visit with Jamal after you left me so abruptly yesterday. What did Julian think?"

Nick chose a doughnut from the box. The glaze melted in his mouth with a burst of cinnamon and vanilla.

"Damn these are so good." After washing it down with some coffee, he wiped his mouth. "It went fine. Surprisingly enough, Julian and Jamal took to each other, and Julian even thinks he may be able to design compression bandage sleeves to make them look more stylish."

Katie's eyes sparkled. "Oh that would be amazing. I'm sure people would snap them up. But is he really serious about doing it, with all the troubles he had lately?" She held the coffee cup Nick had set out for Julian. "Pour me a cup please."

"I believe so." Nick got the milk from the refrigerator. "I didn't know his financial situation was as bad as all that, though." That's because Julian didn't speak about himself, concentrating mainly on Nick's troubles.

But Katie wasn't paying attention to him; her head was cocked as if she was listening to something. "Is someone here? I thought I heard a noise in the bedroom." Her blue eyes grew wide and a delighted smile broke out on her face. "Nicky. Do you have a woman here? Who is she? Why have you kept her a secret?"

Katie put her untouched cup down. "Tell me. How long have you been seeing her?"

Maybe Julian would take his time getting dressed and stay in the bedroom until he could persuade Katie to leave.

No such luck; Nick heard the bedroom door fling open. "Hey, that coffee smells great." Julian came barreling into the kitchen, towel slung around his neck, dressed only in his boxers. His skin glowed pink from the heat of the shower, and his hair lay in damp waves, curling around the nape of his neck. At the sight of Katie at the table, Julian's face shut down and turned guarded and wary.

"Katie."

Nick, frozen in his seat, snuck a glance at Katie's face. Not surprisingly, her stunned expression set his heart lurching in his chest. She gnawed on her full lower lip, shifting her gaze back and forth between Julian and Nick. Smarter than anyone he knew, Nick had no doubt it wouldn't take her long to figure out what was going on.

"Julian."

Nick said nothing and Julian, perhaps sensing the tension, muttered something about putting on some clothes and disappeared back in the bedroom.

A few heartbeats passed before Nick could meet Katie's confused expression. "Julian came to visit me this afternoon. I kind of had a little breakdown last night and Julian was worried, so I guess he wanted to check on me and make sure I was okay."

All true.

"And then he decided to take a shower?" Katie's knowing gaze held his, but it wasn't time. Nick wasn't prepared to have that conversation with his sister or anyone else yet, so he remained silent.

"Are you all right now?" Katie asked. "Why didn't you call me?"

That annoyed him to no end. He wasn't some basket case destined to forever need coddling and protection. Nick had proved to himself he had regained some control over his life, and it was time for his family to know and recognize it for the accomplishment it was and cease fussing over him. After his accident and recovery, he'd never set any limitations or boundaries between him, his parents, and his sister; they were always there for him. Maybe the time had come to rethink that part of his life as well.

"I was fine. I worked through it with Julian's help."

Julian chose that moment to reenter the room—at this point fully dressed—and sat down next to him in silence.

"Really?" Katie focused her attention on Julian now, and Nick braced himself for her interrogation. "It's hard for me to believe someone you barely know could help you when your own family has tried for years and couldn't."

Nick needn't have worried about Julian. He was no longer that shy boy who'd gotten pushed around in high school. Julian was a businessman who owned his own company and swam with the sharks on a daily basis.

"You don't know?" Julian's expression was inscrutable. "Nick and I knew each other in high school. We were friends for a while."

"You were?" Katie couldn't keep the shock from her voice as she shot Nick a confused look before fixating on Julian again. "Why didn't I know this? I know I'm younger, but I don't ever remember seeing you at the house. Were you on the baseball team together?"

That brought a chuckle from Julian. "You must be kidding. I was the scrawny kid; a little too different, too out of the normal social scene. Back then, kids weren't so accepting of gay kids as they supposedly are now. They didn't have to come right out and bully me, but being ignored and whispered about in the hallways was almost as bad. I didn't have the best high school experience."

Sympathy softened Katie's face. "I can only imagine. This wasn't the most liberal neighborhood; it still isn't."

"I know."

"So you and Nick were friends . . . ?" Katie left the question hanging, and Nick knew her curiosity wouldn't wane until she got some kind of satisfying answer. And Katie wasn't easily satisfied.

"We'd study together after school until I transferred in junior year."

It was supposed to make him feel better to have his secret kept, yet hearing Julian's abbreviated version of their friendship tore at Nick's heart. People might think Nick was a hero, but he was such a fucking coward. Julian had been nothing more than a child when Nick had tossed him aside like trash, forced to live life the hard way, and he did so with his head held high, proud and unashamed of who he was. While Nick play-pretended, hiding from the truth, and died a little more every day inside.

It wouldn't take much for her to put the pieces together and figure out that Julian and Nick might have been more than study buddies together. Nick was so fucking tired of it all; Katie was his sister. She loved him and would want him to be happy. *Shit.* He hadn't been this scared since he thought he was going to die. Was he really ready to say it out loud? He couldn't take it back once the words were out there. But Nick knew it was time. It had nothing to do with Julian, and everything to do with him and coming to terms and admitting who he was to his family, his friends, and in some way himself.

"Every day of my life has been like a war for me," Nick began. Julian had been reaching for a coffee mug but halted, his fingers curling until he made a fist, and rested it on the table. There wasn't a sound in the room, and no screams from the usually noisy children filtered through his window.

"I spent my entire childhood in camouflage, hiding from who I was and what I wanted, letting fear dictate every major decision in my life. Along the way I hurt not only myself, but my friends"—Nick turned to Julian, his heart beating madly—"this person who did nothing wrong but love me when I was too fucking much of a coward to admit it back to him."

When he shifted his attention back to Katie, her eyes were filled with tears. "Nicky. Tell me. Let it out already."

"I'm gay, I've always been gay. I'm sorry if I'm disappointing you."

The chair scraped against the floor as she flung it backward, then raced around the table to sit at his side. Katie took both his hands, squeezing hard. "Don't be an idiot. You think I won't love you? What have I ever done to make you think you couldn't tell me this?" Tears streamed down her face.

"I'm so fucked up in the head. It wasn't that you wouldn't love me; I didn't want it to be this way. I wanted the normal life; wife, kids, family. That's what we were programed for by Mom and Dad, by everybody. But even in high school I knew something wasn't right with that equation for me."

"So you and Julian?" Her gaze darted back and forth between the two of them.

"We were close, but I pushed him away when I saw how serious it was getting. I knew I couldn't be brave like him and admit it. Plus, I thought if I tried hard enough, maybe I could like girls and be normal." He blinked against the stinging in his eyes. "It doesn't work that way, though. Some guys can fake it, but I didn't see that as being fair. To me or the woman. So I chose nothing."

"And all these years you told no one, not even your therapist? Maybe it would've helped, although I have to admit I'm still hurt you didn't think you could trust me." Her unwavering gaze met his. "There isn't anything you could do that would ever change how I feel about you, short of murder. And even then." She smiled through her tears. "I don't care who you love, Nicky. I only care that you're loved by someone worthy of the wonderful person you are."

She fell into his arms and he held her slim body and kissed her fragrant hair. The warmth of her acceptance seeped through him, unknotting a few of the stranglehold cords he'd wound around himself.

"It had nothing to do with you and everything to do with me and my perception of the world. I love and trust you and know you feel the same way about me. But until I could start to learn to trust myself and accept who I really was, I couldn't tell you or anyone else."

Katie wiped her eyes and blew her nose on a napkin. "I understand that." She sat in her chair again, her smile tender and loving. "And I've been waiting for the day when you could finally say you trust in yourself. You've made so much progress, and if Julian has helped you, then I'm ready to love him as well."

Nick shot a quick glance over to Julian who returned his look with a reassuring smile of his own. "Ahh, Katie . . ." He didn't know what to say to that. He and Julian weren't in love, they were merely having sex, but that was a bit more information than Nick was willing to share.

Julian saved his ass, once again. "Thanks, that means a lot to me. I can't speak for Nick, but I know I'm looking forward to us becoming friends again. For me that's the most important thing right now."

The sound of a car door slamming broke the silence. Nick heard his mother's voice and immediately tensed. "Don't say anything to them, Katie, please," he begged. "I can't do all this at once."

Julian gave his shoulder a quick squeeze, and Nick relaxed into his touch. It didn't go unnoticed by Katie who remarked, "I promise, but they're going to want to know who Julian is, and if you're going to be yourselves in front of them, they'll notice the connection between you two." She stood and went to the door. "I'm going to go help them. I'll see you later. Bye Julian." And with a wave, she was gone.

That startled him. Connection? They had the tentative beginnings of a friendship, nothing more. Julian removed his hand, but not before giving him another squeeze.

"Don't worry. I'll keep my hands to myself." His lips skimmed Nick's ear and despite the heat in the apartment he shivered, recalling the taste and touch of Julian. The man's rich scent was still all over him like a second skin, and he had no desire to wash it off.

Nick turned his head and placed a kiss on the edge of Julian's mouth, feeling his lips soften. "I'm not trying to keep you as a dirty secret. You understand that right?"

Julian said nothing. He grabbed Nick's shoulders and proceeded to take his mouth in a hard, deep kiss that left them both breathless and Nick shaken when they pulled apart.

"I hope that'll hold you while you're with your parents."

Without thinking, Nick blurted out, "Come upstairs with me and meet them?" He snapped his mouth shut as Julian leaned back in his chair and raised his brow.

Shit. Did he really say that?

Chapter Thirteen

WELL WASN'T THIS a day for surprises. First, the off the chart, heart-seizing sex had Julian wanting more time with Nick rather than closing the chapter on their story and moving on. Julian pushed that to the back burner, as he had no room in his life at the moment for any involvements that weren't relevant to getting his business back on track.

Coming out to Katie took all kinds of courage on Nick's part, but doing so didn't fully solve his emotional problems. Katie was the easy one. There would be far more ramifications Nick would have to face in the future when he decided to open up about his sexuality to his parents and at his job. Nick had already mentioned someone he worked with who'd made homophobic remarks. Those shark-infested waters needed careful treading.

"I mean, you don't have to. I know how busy you are with the problems your company is having." Nick flushed and Julian's back stiffened. "Shit. I-I'm sorry. That didn't come out the way I meant it."

Julian gave him a tight-lipped smile. Nothing like being brought back to reality. "Don't worry about it," he said waving his hand breezily. He pushed back his chair and stood, walking to the front door. "If you want me to say hello, I will. I can't stay; I have things to take care of at home as you're aware."

"Julian. I said I was sorry." Nick got up and circled around the table to grab his arm, forcing him to look Nick in the eyes. "I didn't mean to insult you. I was only thinking you wouldn't want to waste your time, when I know you have a lot of things on your mind."

It wasn't Nick's fault Julian's business was collapsing around him. He'd been so wrapped up in Nick today he'd almost forgotten how his own life and business had gone to shit.

"It's okay." Julian allowed Nick to hug him, and for once it felt good to be taken in someone's arms and held for no other reason than to receive comfort. The scent of sex and sweat and Nick were a heady perfume to Julian's starved senses, and he gave himself permission to bury his lips in the thick silken tufts of Nick's hair. "It's not your problem, it's mine."

"I'd like to think you'd let me help you."

No one could. But meeting Jamal yesterday had awakened a fire within Julian; one he hadn't felt since his first show. His fingers itched to create something for that sad young man and all the other people suffering through the same circumstances.

It was time to go before he let Nick draw him into the rhythm of an everyday, normal life. This wasn't a place for Julian; he'd left it all behind years ago and had no wish to return. "I'll go upstairs and meet the parents and then go back to the city."

Nick gave him an odd look. "Let's go then."

Julian followed him out the door and up the narrow flight of stairs to the apartment above. Pictures lined the wall as he climbed the steep steps. He didn't stop to look carefully at each photo, but he caught a glimpse of a smiling, happy nuclear unit, arms around each other at milestone events; Nick's and Katie's various graduations, baseball championship games, backyard parties.

The stairway opened up to a living room with a large bay window overlooking the street. Sunlight beamed onto the carpet, dust motes dancing, and highlighted the glistening dining room tabletop. Warm smells of roasting meat and other delicious food hit him; the house spoke of family times, talks around the kitchen table, and after-school snacks. Things Julian never had, since his mother worked late to support them. He was an original "latch-key" kid; on his own for as long as he could remember.

This would be what Nick had wanted when he spoke all those years ago of being a family, being normal. Julian was in no position to make Nick give it up.

A middle-aged woman, her brown hair curling in soft waves

about her head, was engaged in a lively conversation with Katie on the sofa, while a stern man who looked a bit like an older version of Nick, sat with his feet up in a well-worn leather recliner, reading a newspaper and drinking a beer.

Nick's mother stopped talking to Katie and looked from Nick to Julian with an expectant expression. Nick's father lowered the paper and peered over the rims of his bifocals.

"Hey, son. I picked up a new door for the back entrance."

"Great." Nick glanced over his shoulder with a slight smile, then faced his family again. "Mom, Dad. I want you to meet a friend of mine."

Julian raised his head high and stood next to Nick. His heart beat a bit quicker, almost as if he was backstage, waiting for a show to begin and the models to walk.

"Mr. and Mrs. Fletcher, nice to meet you." He smiled at Nick's mother with all the charm he normally saved for store buyers and special customers. "I'm Julian Cornell."

"Julian's an old friend from high school I ran into recently. He's a fashion designer, Mom. He designs men's clothing."

Nick's mother's eyes lit up. "Really? That's so exciting, to be surrounded by all those handsome models and beautiful clothes."

Julian laughed. "It's not as glamorous as you might think. Between the designing and getting ready for the shows, not to mention dealing with the models and their crazy temperaments, it could drive most people crazy."

"Julian just had a show and his clothes were wonderful, Mom. He's exceptionally talented." Katie gushed.

Warmth stole through Julian at this unexpected praise. Nick rested his hand on his shoulder. "Come sit down next to my mom. She'd love to hear some stories, if you have the time."

Katie had moved, and before he knew what he was doing, Julian found himself sitting in between Nick and his mother on the plump-cushioned, flowered sofa. There were so many stories he could tell about the behind the scenes activity of a clothing shoot or a show, but Julian didn't think Nick's parents would appreciate the raunchier exploits. Especially if Julian was involved. A few PG-rated, yet still funny jokes that would be appropriate to share came to mind, when Nick's father folded the newspaper and stared, his surprised gaze roaming over Julian's leather pants. Anticipating a taunt or some cruel jab, Julian gritted his teeth.

In a voice tinged with curiosity, Nick's father asked, "Since when have you been into that stuff, Nick? I can't remember the last time I saw you in anything other than jeans and a tee shirt."

Nick's thigh, which happened to be pressed against Julian's, tensed. "I never said I was into that stuff, Dad. I said Julian is an old friend and he's a designer."

"Well, you wouldn't catch me in a pair of pants like that, and I don't know many men who'd wear them either," he grumbled.

"Thank God for that," whispered Katie, and Julian bit his lip to prevent himself from laughing out loud.

"Brian, that's not nice." Nick's mother glared at his father, then turned to Julian with a smile and patted his knee. "Go right ahead, I'm dying to hear your stories."

He soon had Nick, Katie, and their mother laughing about his first attempt at fitting a model, which was done right on the man's body. The strategically placed pins fell out and the model's clothes fell off as he walked for a client.

"It all turned out for the best, though. The buyer asked the model out on a date, and they've been together ever since." Julian chuckled as he told the story. "Seems the buyer had a crush on the model, but was too scared to ask him out, while the model later confessed to me he loosened the pins deliberately hoping to get the buyer's attention."

"That's so sweet," said Katie. "It's like true love conquers all."

Nick's father snorted and peered at them over his glasses. "Oh, please, those guys change partners like I change socks."

Julian had no wish to argue with the man, especially as he was Nick's father, but he needn't have worried.

"What are you talking about, Dad? What do you mean by

'those guys'?"

Julian heard the increased cadence of Nick's breath; the tension rolling off his body was almost palpable. "It's all right. It's nothing I haven't heard before," he murmured to Nick. Now he understood a little better the latent hostility Nick was confronted with. The subtle digs were almost as hurtful as the outright rude and nasty comments.

"You know, the gays." Brian Fletcher shifted in his chair. "They say they want marriage, but they're always running around without their shirts on, kissing and hugging in public." He shrugged. "That's not what normal men do."

"What do you mean normal? I see plenty of men and women kissing and hugging on the street. Why is it any less normal when people of the same sex do it?" Julian wanted to mentally slap himself. He didn't want to get into a discussion of gay rights with Nick's father or anyone else. "People should be able to live their lives the way they want as long as no one gets hurt."

"Well, the sanctity of marriage gets hurt. And I got a problem with that." Fletcher's jaw thrust out in a pugnacious tilt.

"Brian, please." Nick's mother placed a hand on Julian's arm. "I'm sorry. You're a guest in our house and I don't want you offended. It's a new world we live in and some of us,"—she scowled at her husband—"have a harder time accepting it than others. I think it's wonderful." She squeezed his arm. "Do you have a special person in your life?"

"No. I'm too busy with my business right now."

"Oh, that's terrible. You must make room for your personal life. If you don't take care of the inner you, you will have a hard time creating beautiful things. All your energy gets blocked."

"Mom reads a lot of self-help books." Nick grinned.

"I know you're making fun of me, but it's true. You have to open yourself up to finding happiness, and when you least expect it, it will happen. Take you and my son."

Julian froze and Nick choked out, "What are you talking about?"

"After all these years you ran into each other and now you

can be friends again."

"Yeah, right," said Nick weakly. "Friends again."

"Christ, Marilyn, I thought you were telling Nick to be the guy's boyfriend." Fletcher shot her a disgusted look.

And Julian knew at that point it was time to leave.

LATER ON THAT evening, after he'd returned home from Nick's house, Julian sat by himself, drinking a glass of wine, thinking about his life, and what the future held after the debacle of his show. Everything he'd ever wanted was wrapped up in being the top designer, a way to prove he could be the best, that he was someone worth remembering.

Meeting Nick had wrenched him away from the world he'd immersed himself into, a world that from the outside looked glittering and beautiful, yet was so ugly and decayed underneath. Julian found himself back in that hospital room, watching Jamal's agonized face as he concentrated on simply trying to bend his fingers and his elbow.

How could he go back to worrying about whether silk or linen was best for summer, when what really mattered was if a young girl would get asked to the prom with an arm so badly burned she may never be able to regain its full function?

He should be in the showroom, calling up buyers, boutiques, anything and everything he could, to get his clothing into stores. That all seemed unimportant compared to figuring out how to sew onto the fabric of the compression bandages to make the sleeves he'd sketched out for Jamal.

Julian drank down the rest of his wine, then reached for his sketchbook. He hadn't had this burst of quickening excitement to create something meaningful, rather than something purely for its aesthetic sense, in months. Like it had in Jamal's hospital room, the work flowed effortlessly from his pencil to the paper. The next time he looked up, it was pitch black outside and the clock over his stove read 1:02 A.M.

He stretched and tossed aside his pencil. This was work he

could be proud of and for no other reason than it might help someone. For one fleeting moment Julian wished Nick was there so he could show him. He texted Melanie, asking her to meet him at the showroom in the morning, and be prepared to work all day.

He went to bed, more alive than he had been in years.

Chapter Fourteen

GOOD MOVES TODAY, Barton. You've been paying attention," said Nick, smiling with approval. He clapped the man on his back. "You really improved with your skills and search techniques."

"Thanks." Barton's face shone with happiness. "I've been hitting the gym trying to build up my strength. You're a great instructor; you show us how to do everything so clearly."

"Well, keep up the good work. You and your guys are doing great." He turned to stow away the training gear. Seagulls swooped above, and the brisk, cold air off the river had him shivering slightly. When Barton didn't leave, Nick gave him a questioning look. "Something else?"

The man flushed, the dull red creeping up his throat to tint his pale cheeks. "Umm, well." His eyes darted side to side.

"Spit it out, Barton. Is there a problem?" Nick straightened up and leaned on the tree trunk next to him.

"No, not at all." The man took a deep breath, then let it out in a rush. "A bunch of the guys are getting together afterward and I wondered if you wanted to come."

Adam Barton's hesitant, hopeful smile left no doubt now in Nick's mind that Jensen was probably correct in his assumption that Barton was gay. Nick recognized the look of interest in the man's eyes and wanted to make sure he understood Nick's reason for not going had nothing to do with Barton being gay.

"Barton." Jensen's big booming voice forestalled any answer Nick had planned. "Ass-kissing Fletcher ain't gonna help you, although I hear you guys like that. Now get back with your team." His raucous laughter floated through the air as he walked away. Nick winced and wished he could punch the guy right in his nice square jaw.

Barton, now bright red and breathing heavily, gazed with utter hatred at Jensen's back. Nick knew that feeling. It was one of helplessness, while inside dreaming about ripping the offending person to shreds.

"I'm sorry, Adam, but I can't go tonight."

Barton blinked, then shrugged, as if he'd already guessed the answer. "Yeah, sure, whatever." He picked up his gym bag and hurried off without saying goodbye.

What a fucking coward you are, Nick chastised himself, as he finished putting away all the training gear. Heading back to the squat gray brick building where the lockers were located, Nick struggled with his shame. He should've said something to Jensen; he'd heard enough remarks over the past few years to know the man was a homophobic, racist idiot, and Nick should have had the guts to stand up to Jensen and tell him to shut the fuck up.

Julian would have. It had been over a week since he'd seen or heard from the man, and Nick missed him and his honest clarity in the way he looked at life. Julian had no shame or fear in living his life as an openly gay man, and Nick could see him flaying Jensen to the ground with his sarcastic tongue. He'd hoped to run into him when he went to the hospital to see Jamal, and even dropped by on the days he didn't normally visit, but no luck. No Julian. Not wanting to get Jamal's hopes up anymore, since it looked like Julian had abandoned the project, Nick never mentioned the designer, or the idea of the designer compression bandages.

There were quite a few people still milling about the building, hanging out on the sofas in the lounge, watching TV, and grabbing a quick cup of coffee before heading home. Nick nodded to them on his way to the locker room, but didn't stop. He heard some whispers and laughter and wondered what the joke was, but he had no desire to listen to firehouse gossip. When he pushed open the door to the locker room he saw Adam Barton standing in front of his locker, his face crumpled with hurt.

Condoms of every color hung on the door to his locker, covering it from top to bottom. Some were still in the packages, but most were loose and lay limp, like flaccid, multi-colored balloons. It was a vaguely obscene sight and one Nick knew was meant to shock and titillate. There was also a crudely lettered sign taped to the top that said, "FDNY FAGS GO HOME."

At least ten men, men who were supposed to have his back, men who were on his team, stood around him doing nothing. Some were laughing, but that quickly died out when Nick stormed over. Some at least had the grace to look uncomfortable. Only one stood next to Barton and had his hand on his shoulder in a gesture of comfort.

"What the fuck is going on here?" Vibrating with restrained fury, Nick gestured to the locker. "Who did this?" It was worse than he'd thought. They were supposed to be a brotherhood, comrades. A family. Did these people remember nothing about what the department went through over a decade ago?

"No one has the balls to take responsibility here, I see." He took out his phone and took pictures of the locker. "On 9/11 the guys in my house died for our country's freedom. *Everyone's* freedom. Who or what gives any of you the fucking right to do this to Barton or anyone else?"

Dead silence now, save for the sounds of the men shifting restlessly. "I'm going to report this, and every single one of you are going to retake EEO training. Obviously you were all asleep during the last classes. Now get out of my sight."

The men scurried away, all except for Barton and his friend. The man wasn't on Nick's training team, but he'd seen him around and thought his name was Gentry. First, he had to make sure Barton was all right.

"You okay?" He began to pull the condoms off the locker.

Barton slumped onto the bench behind him. "Yeah. Thanks. I never did anything to any of them. Why do they treat me like there's something wrong with me? I've never said I was gay or anything."

Before he could stop himself, Nick blurted out, "Are you?"

Immediately he wanted to take it back. "I'm sorry, man. It's none of my business. Forget I asked."

Wariness crept over Barton's face. "Yeah, I am." His voice grew defiant and Nick's admiration for the man increased. Adam Barton had more backbone than Nick did. "But I've never said anything to them or talked about my life." He raked his hand through his hair. "What gives them the right to do this and think it's okay?"

"I won't let them get away with it. No one should be treated like this. I promise it won't happen again."

"How do you deal with it?" Barton's blue eyes met his. "They have such respect for you."

"I don't know what you're talking about," said Nick, his gaze skittering away from Barton's. "Listen, I've got all the pictures I need. I'm gonna go report it." He stood and slipped his phone into his jacket pocket.

"No." Barton stood as well. "If I want to get along with these guys I have to learn to roll with it. There will always be people who hate. Do you think some stupid class telling these guys to change a lifetime of prejudices is going to make a difference?" His eyes held Nick's. "It's only when enough people show everyone that being gay isn't being wrong or bad that it will begin to be accepted as the norm."

The kid had more guts than Nick that was for sure. "I have to report it. It's the law."

Barton shrugged. "Whatever." He fished his jacket out of the locker and slipped it on. "I'm leaving to meet my friends." His eyes turned dark. "I'll see you around." With that dismissal, Barton walked away from him and out of the locker room.

"Don't do it, Nick."

He whirled around and found Jensen leaning against the doorway, his arms folded, a smirk across his face.

"What are you talking about? You know I have to report it."

"Kid's a faggot. If he can't keep up, let him put on his tutu and leave the FDNY to the real men."

You never really knew people it seemed. All the years of

working with Jensen, Nick had never paid much attention to his ramblings. He was the type of man who blamed others for his own shortcomings in life. A bitter, insecure man.

Spittle flew from Jensen's lips as he continued to rail against Barton. Nick had never known a man to spew such vicious hatred against another human being. Funny how Nick never thought he'd end up in this position, defending a gay colleague, but he couldn't stand by and let this asshole win. He may not be ready to come out, but he could sure as hell be an ally.

"Fuck off, Jensen. I'm no probie you can bully. You need to keep your mouth shut and learn to act like a human being." With that, he turned on his heel and left a shocked Jensen standing red-faced in the locker room. Nick's heart lifted, but his soul was weighed down by guilt over his inner conflict.

It only took Nick a few minutes to call Human Resources and make an appointment to come in the next day to fill out the paperwork. Maybe he wasn't changing the world, but Nick wanted to think this small step would help start the process of change.

It was dark when Nick got off Randalls Island, and he had no plans for the evening. It was nothing new; he liked his orderly life. He could've gone with Adam, but he wasn't interested in making new friends and hanging around with a bunch of people who'd want to know his history. Plus, he didn't want to encourage Adam when there was no chance in hell they'd ever get together.

Nick knew what he wanted; what he didn't know was how to reach out and grab it. Perhaps the time had already passed for him and Julian. Plus, Julian wasn't the type to remain in the background; he'd want to make sure everyone knew they were together, and Nick wasn't prepared for that just yet. Still, it didn't prevent him from directing his car to the Lower East Side, and Julian's apartment, instead of over the Brooklyn Bridge and home.

What he planned to say to Julian was another story. He had no fucking clue what to do. There had been no relationships in his life; when he needed sex he'd go to a bar. This was beyond the physical though; he'd felt it the afternoon when Julian had come to him. The connection they'd had as young men had never disappeared. It may have lain dormant, but one look from Julian and Nick's blood bubbled with heat, rekindling the fire Nick had never been able to fully snuff out.

By some magic, Nick found a parking spot across the street from Julian's apartment. Light glowed through his windows, five stories up. At least he was home. Perhaps he wasn't alone tonight; that thought had never occurred to Nick. Julian was a very handsome and desirable man, with a life Nick knew nothing about. Certainly he had his pick of beautiful men; it was his business. One doesn't become immune to the sight of gorgeous models strutting around half-naked, and Nick's anticipation faltered. He couldn't compete with perfection.

What was he thinking coming here to see Julian? He couldn't even make it up in the elevator without shaking. It had taken him a year to muster up the courage and ability to get inside the hospital elevator; he'd yet to try another. Somehow that morning he'd left Julian's, he'd managed, so he counted on that infinitesimal bit of nerve he'd dug down deep to find to rear its head once again and allow him to get inside that enclosed space.

He got out of the car and approached the building. This all could be moot as Julian might not have any desire to see him tonight; he might have another man up there. Better to know it now, than play mind games with himself. The outside of the brick building had a listing of the residents' names, and Nick pressed the button next to the one reading "Cornell" and waited.

"Yes?" The static-y voice of Julian came through the little tin speaker.

"Julian. It's Nick."

There was no sound and Nick deflated. *Too late,* he thought and with shoulders sagging, he turned to walk away.

"Nick. Christ. Yes, come up." The buzzer sounded and Nick pushed open the door. With trepidation he approached the large elevator and wondered again what he'd done in his previous life to be subjected to this hell on earth; he pushed the button, wincing as he heard it lurch to life and descend.

He stood waiting, folding and unfolding his arms, rocking back and forth on his heels, as the sweat began to pool underneath his arms and dampen the back of his shirt. With a grinding, guttural sound the elevator shuddered to a halt. Nick made no attempt to open it, eyeing it instead as if it were a ravenous beast come to swallow him up.

Dr. Landau had told him the only way to face your fears was live through them. Rationally, Nick knew that to be true. He'd never had problems with elevators when he was young. And it wasn't the elevator itself, Nick told himself as he reached to open the door. It was the fear of enclosure and darkness; of being caught in a space he couldn't get out of. If Nick thought carefully, he could work through his anxiety and take back a part of himself.

Before he had a chance to turn the handle, the elevator door opened and Julian stepped out, his face a mask of concern.

"What's wrong? Are you all right?" His gaze flickered over Nick's body causing a stirring deep inside.

"Yeah, I'm fine. I wanted to see you. We hadn't talked in a week and . . ." He drifted off, not sure he could put into words why he had this need to see Julian, as if being in the man's presence would make his own life more bearable somehow.

The furrows lining Julian's brow relaxed and his face softened. "Hey, that's nice to hear. No one's ever said they missed me before." He hesitated for a second. "Do you, um, want to come upstairs? I came down to meet you knowing you might not want to come up in the elevator by yourself."

Nick nodded and Julian pulled the door open. "Come on then. I have something to show you."

Nick chuckled, his heart suddenly lighter. "Your etchings? Are you going to use that old line on me?"

Julian's smile lit up his face. "Funny you should mention that." There was the old laughter in his eyes, a lightness Nick remembered from years ago.

The door shut with a thump and though his heart raced, Nick wasn't at all sure it was from fear, or the anticipation of the night that lay ahead.

Chapter Fifteen

JULIAN HAD NEVER been a great believer in God, fate, or mysticism, call it what you will. He was too pragmatic a person, having been knocked down more times in his life than he'd care to remember. If fate did exist, something or someone could've intervened to allow his mother to enjoy a moment of her life, instead of having her die of a heart attack at the age of forty-five. Whip-thin from stress over her ability to pay their bills, her fingers stained nicotine-yellow from the ever-present cigarette, Emma Cornell never got the chance to see him graduate from high school.

Though she hadn't been able to be around much, he understood why, and knew she loved him fiercely and was incredibly proud of him. On the rare occasions she had an evening off and they'd make popcorn and watch a movie together, she'd always tell him the same thing.

"Whatever you do, make sure you don't end up like me. Make your life count, baby. Leave your mark so that when you're no longer here, they'll always remember you."

"You're special to me, Mom."

She'd wipe her eyes and give him a kiss. Julian hadn't thought about those days in years. He'd spent too much time clawing his way to the top of what turned out to be a dung heap of the most shallow, evil people he could ever imagine.

After the chance meeting with Nick, and learning his personal suffering and the heroic and selfless work he did with those children in the burn unit, Julian had taken a week to reevaluate what was important for his own life to have meaning, and in what direction he wanted to move forward.

He could continue on and hopefully garner enough interest

in his next collection, making sure this time no one outside of his trusted circle had access to his ideas, apartment, or his life. He'd need to borrow from the bank, if they'd even allow it, at a ridiculously high interest rate that would take years to pay back. It would mean endless nights spent sucking up to people he personally detested but were professionally necessary to further the career he'd been striving for his entire life.

Or he could put it all aside and capture that excitement at creating something for these people he'd been visiting at the burn unit. He'd made sure to time his visits when he knew Nick wouldn't be there. This had to be about doing it for the right reason, not to get close to Nick again. Jamal had become his personal assistant, the liaison with other people in the hospital. The young man had a tremendous sense of style, and Julian marveled at how he'd show him the rough sketch of an idea, and Jamal would have the perfect suggestion for what to do.

Julian had taken a risk and asked to meet an old friend, Helena Weinstock, a style icon he'd met studying under Lorenzo in Italy, and he'd given her a brief rundown of his plans. When he'd finished speaking she'd studied him for a moment, then kissed him and told him whatever he needed from her she'd give him. Dizzy with shock, he left her magnificent Upper East Side townhouse with the promise of a loan.

After meeting with Jamal and a young woman, Kayla, who'd been burned terribly across her chest and arm, Julian had bought several yards of fabric in different colors, materials, and weight. Tonight he was planning on sewing the fabric onto the bandages themselves. Tomorrow he would bring the samples to the hospital, and let Jamal and Kayla try them on.

Now, unexpectedly, Nick had shown up and Julian, who hadn't yet been ready to reveal all he'd done and the decision he'd made, had the chance to present all his hard work and prove to Nick there was more to him than that shallow first impression.

The elevator ride ended and Nick, whose jaw clenched and unclenched rapidly throughout the ride, wiped the glistening sweat from his brow and cleared his throat.

"Can you open the door? I need some air."

It must be a terrible thing to battle demons for so long. Julian ached for Nick, but knew pride stood in the way of Nick's asking for or accepting help. "Let's get inside and I'll get you a cold drink."

He took Nick by the hand, led him into the kitchen, and gave him a bottle of water. After he'd chugged down half of it, Nick wiped his mouth on his sleeve and seemed much more relaxed. He glanced up and smiled into Julian's eyes. "Thanks."

Julian's heart did a funny flip in his chest; a lazy somersault that set his pulse racing and fired his blood. For all his insistence that love was a farce and he wanted no part of it, Julian had been fooling himself for years. It only took Nick's deep blue eyes glowing like a twilight night, the deep laugh lines crinkling in their corners, to shock Julian like a dousing of ice cold water.

He was in love with Nick, all over again. Julian swallowed his own water, amazed it made it through the tightness in his throat. He'd gone ahead and done the exact thing he swore he'd never do.

Fall in love. And with the only man who had ever taken possession of his heart, and in the process, broke it to pieces.

Lesson barely survived and learned. The mistake Julian made years ago was in telling Nick how he felt about him, allowing his feelings to override his brain. That won't happen here; his dick wouldn't rule his head. Julian had no desire to be locked in a closet, even if it was with the very sexy firefighter Nick. He wouldn't become someone's back door dirty secret. What they had years ago was gone.

Julian steeled himself against Nick's masculine presence, which seemed to shift the air in the loft from casual to sexual tension and heat. First, Julian needed to find out what unexpected circumstances brought Nick to his door.

"Is everything all right? You seem kind of nervous."

Nick scratched his head, his fingers sliding through the short strands. "For years my training partner has made anti-gay remarks I let slide. I never let it bother me and hoped it would stop. I should've known better."

Julian wasn't surprised. Not by the fact that remarks were made, nor by the fact Nick said nothing. He wasn't angry, just not surprised.

Nick prowled around the loft, restlessly pacing back and forth. "I never had the guts, you see, to tell Jensen to shut up, that his remarks were out of line and offensive. But you already know that about me. I'm selfish and would rather let other people suffer than out myself and pay the price."

"Ahh, Nick, stop being so hard on yourself." There wasn't much Julian could do to change Nick's self-image. That would come with hard work, therapy, and a willingness to do it.

"Hard on me? This isn't because Jensen's been hard on me. Today he blasted one of my trainees, Adam Barton. A good guy and a hard worker who's been pushing himself to excel. When we came back to the locker room, Barton's locker was decorated with condoms and a fucked-up offensive sign. Instead of standing with me to try and find out what's wrong, all Jensen focused on was that Barton is gay, and he ripped him a new one, telling him to put on a tutu if he can't handle the job."

"And you did what while Jensen was saying all this?" There was a part of Julian that wished Nick would leave right now because to allow this to happen with no repercussion was something Julian wouldn't stand for.

"I told him off. Said I was reporting it, and he'd better change his attitude. Barton didn't want me to, but how in good conscience could I stand by and let it continue?"

Thank God. If he couldn't admit his own sexuality, at least Nick had the guts to stand up to the bullying homophobes.

"And did you?"

"Yeah, I did. Walked right into the office and made an appointment tomorrow with Human Resources to fill out the paperwork."

"I'm proud of you."

Nick shook his head. "Don't be. I don't have the guts to come out and admit who I am. This guy Barton asked me to hang out with him and his friends and I said no. Then he tells me it's only when people can be proud of who they are that the fuckers like Jensen will have no power anymore." Anguished eyes met his, and Julian could see the emotional struggle play on Nick's face.

"Don't you see, Julian? I'm still living a lie after all these years. I was a fucking coward at 9/11, and I'm still a fucking coward."

"Enough."

Nick glanced at him in surprise.

"Maybe it's because I haven't seen you in years, but the Nick I know would never wallow in self-pity. You may be afraid to come out, whether it's family you think won't be supportive, or fear of the job backlash. Whatever the reason, it's legitimate, real, and not cowardly."

Nick said nothing. Encouraged by his silence, Julian continued. "What you do, by going to the burn center, should be healing you, and giving you perspective. Those people are living proof that true courage isn't always in the grand show but in the everyday scope of life. Jamal learning to bend his fingers again, or Kayla going out in public with a sleeveless top, exposing her bandages. That's courage."

Nick slumped onto the sofa. "You're right, I know."

"And you."

"Me?" Nick's incredulous voice rang out. "I've done nothing."

"You're so hard on yourself. You're not responsible for what happened to the men in your firehouse. They were doing what they were trained to do." Julian sat next to Nick, careful not to get too close.

"I was trained to do it as well."

"But you were told not to go inside. And you were new and trained to take orders. This has nothing to do with how many years you had on the job, or if you were married and with children. If your superior tells you not to do something you follow orders, correct?" Julian might be reaching here, but it was all he had to work with, and he thought it made sense.

After a moment's hesitation, Nick gave a begrudging nod.

"Then understand it from that perspective. Concentrate on the good you've been doing; the burn unit and those kids. Maybe you'll want to volunteer at a center to help runaway LGBT kids, like the one Marcus had his fundraiser for."

There was still so much pain in Nick's face, but Julian could see a hopeful glint in his eyes.

"Do you want to know what I've been doing all this time?"

Nick shifted over to sit nearer to him on the sofa. "Trying to get your business back in business?"

"In a way." Julian stood. "Come with me."

He strode to the back of the loft and turned the spotlight on over his worktable. The light hit the various colors in the soft jersey knit, a silk and cotton blend he'd been working on to make sure it would fit with ease and comfort over bandages. It had taken long days and hard lonely nights, and meetings with Jamal to fit the arm and leg sleeves over the bandages.

Julian found he loved working with the young man; Jamal confided to Julian he'd always dreamed of being a model, and had given Julian a wonderful idea to make detachable Velcro cuffs for the bandages, so they would show like a regular shirt cuff. Julian tried to make the fabric light and breathable so it wouldn't add any extra weight, and it had to move easily with the limbs' range of motion.

"What do you think?" Nervous now, showing off his work, Julian stepped back and allowed Nick to stand in front to view the samples.

After several moments with nothing forthcoming, Julian grew nervous. "Um, are they that bad? I mean, they're a first try and can be changed if you think—"

"No." The word came out soft, yet stopped Julian from speaking further. Even more to his surprise, Nick spun around and grabbed him by the shoulders, fingers digging almost painfully into his arms. "I thought you'd forgotten about it, or decided not to do it. I'm speechless at what you've accomplished."

Warmth flooded through Julian. That praise from Nick

meant more than any critic's from one of Julian's shows.

"I worked with Jamal, and with Kayla too. They're inspirational." Almost afraid to move, Julian wanted nothing more than to prolong this closeness between the two of them. It wasn't just because he loved Nick and wanted to keep him close. If Julian wanted to admit it to himself, he'd probably never stopped loving him.

He recalled how Nick had shied away from others invading his personal space when Julian had met him at the club, and how he didn't like to be touched. Now that Nick was the one doing the touching? Yeah, Julian liked that very much, and wanted Nick to keep touching him. Tentatively, holding Nick's grave blue gaze with his own, Julian placed his hands on Nick's shoulders. A slight tremor rippled beneath his fingers, but it was a small victory, as Nick didn't move away from Julian's touch, and to Julian's surprise, spoke.

"I think you've inspired them more than I've been able to. They're thinking beyond the pain of today and looking toward tomorrow and beyond."

"Isn't that what we should all do?" As he spoke Julian slid his hands across Nick's collarbone, keeping his touch deliberately light. "Look ahead?"

Nick's expression darkened, his eyes turning hungry. "I'm thinking about today." He moved even closer, his breath touching Julian's cheek. "And how much I want you. Right now."

Chapter Sixteen

THERE WAS NEVER any choice, Nick thought, as he drew Julian's shirt over his head and dropped it to the floor. He slid his hands up Julian's warm, muscled chest, and knew he could never pretend there was anyone he wanted more than this man. Julian stood still before him, those honest eyes locked with his.

It was Julian who knew him and understood the demons residing within Nick. With his uncanny ability to see through the bullshit and smokescreens Nick threw up around himself, Julian had refused to let Nick be the master of his own demise and instead, forced him to come to terms not only with the trauma from his past, but with his future as well.

All Nick knew right now was, with Julian here in this space, he didn't ever want to leave again. Perhaps sensing Nick's internal struggle, Julian traced Nick's lips with his fingertips.

"We don't have to decide the world tonight. It can just be for us. You and I are all that matters."

He followed Julian to the bed, and they lay together. Nick relished the dips and curves of hard muscles and the roughness of hairy thighs against his own. He loved the sight of Julian's cock, swelling even thicker beneath his sweatpants as Nick watched. Julian rolled on top of him, straddling his hips, brushing his full erection against Nick's own aching cock.

"I'm willing to go as slow as you want to. But I want you. In my bed and in my body."

Those words seared like fire through Nick's veins, and he reached up and dragged Julian close, so close that their breath mingled and their lips brushed together.

"I want you too. Inside me. I want you to fuck me, Julian."

He left no room for questions, no doubts or indecision on his part. This was where he wanted to be and who he wanted to be with. A man yes, but not just any man. Julian. It could only be Julian. Nick took Julian's lips in a hard, punishing kiss, his tongue probing deep inside Julian's mouth, their teeth clashing. After a moment's hesitation, Julian returned his kiss with a wildness that had Nick's cock, trapped between their bodies, thrusting, aching for that much-needed friction.

"Fuck." Wrenching away from Julian, Nick tore at his zipper and took off his jeans faster than he ever remembered doing in his life. He discarded his briefs as well. Why pretend they weren't both going to be naked in a matter of seconds?

He pounced on Julian again and hooked his hands at the elastic of Julian's sweatpants. He yanked them down, his breath growing short in his chest when he saw Julian had on no boxers, no briefs.

"Commando, huh?" Nick growled, and his own cock, the large head already wet, jerked at the sight of Julian completely naked and spread out underneath him. Julian's dark eyes gazed up at him, hungry and feral.

"Yeah. I wasn't expecting company." He licked his lips. "Not that I'm complaining." He reached up to grasp Nick's cock, and with a firm hand, began to stroke him. Nick leaned into that touch, thrusting into Julian's palm.

"I meant what I said before." Nick gritted his teeth as he struggled to keep his voice from wavering. Julian's hands were working him over well. One continued to jack his cock, and the other, wet with Nick's own fluids, slipped down to fondle his aching, tingling balls. "I want you inside me."

For a moment, Julian stilled. "And is that something you normally do?"

"No," he admitted. "But I want it with you."

Julian let go and reared up, grabbed Nick around the neck to tug him close. "It's all I've ever wanted."

"Then do it, Julian. Make me fucking feel again."

Julian kissed him, tantalizingly long, slow, and deep, their tongues tangling. He broke their kiss and scooted over to the night table, retrieving condoms and lube. Nick's heart hammered in his chest, and his face must've shown his fear, as Julian reached up to cup his jaw with a gentle hand.

"We don't have to; *you* don't have to go through with it." He caressed the soft underside of Nick's jaw and goose pimples crept up Nick's arm. "You don't need to prove anything to me."

"I made the biggest mistake of my life because I was too scared all those years ago to be with you. Then I ran from the Towers and didn't save my buddies." The tightness in his throat hurt so fucking much. "I can't do it anymore. I want this—want you." He covered Julian's hand with his own. "I never stopped. I only fooled myself into thinking I could be something I'm not to make other people happy, when all along I've been nothing but miserable."

"Then it's time to make you happy."

The kiss from Julian now wasn't gentle and sweet. It was raw, hard, and searching. Nick fell back on the bed and watched as Julian straddled him, his eyes glowing like emeralds. Julian was naked, but Nick wasn't. Without hesitation now, Nick pulled the sweatshirt he still wore up and over his head.

"You're so beautiful, Nicky."

"You don't have to say it. I know how it looks." He glanced down at his scarred chest; he was like the Scarecrow in the *Wizard of Oz* with all the stitches from his skin grafts sewing him back together. Piece by piece.

"Do you think, even now lying naked with me, that I'm still that shallow man you once thought I was? Seeing you, being with you again . . ." Julian swallowed heavily, struggling to regain his composure, while Nick could only stare at him, hope unfurling the tight bands across his chest. "I see the real you, the man underneath the scars at the surface. Those mean nothing to me. I've looked beyond that. A person's body is merely a place card for their soul, their heart, and their mind. And in that respect?" Julian bent down and kissed him softly. "You're the most perfect man I know."

"Please." Nick whispered against Julian's lips. "Please."

Nothing more needed to be said. Julian held his gaze and kissed a path down Nick's trembling body. With the gentlest of touches he pressed his lips along the ridges of each scar, validating his previous words, showing Nick he didn't care about the maligned flesh. Bit by bit, with each kiss down Nick's body and press of lips upon his skin, Julian took Nick apart until Nick could barely breathe.

Julian reached out to Nick and took his hand, lacing their fingers together, smiling into Nick's eyes. Nick had never known tenderness during sex, and his heart swelled with emotions he couldn't yet put into words.

"How does it feel? Is it okay what I'm doing?" Julian's breath blew damp against the fevered skin of Nick's torso.

"I don't have much feeling there," admitted Nick. "But knowing what you're doing and seeing it fucking slays me. It makes me want you even more."

Julian's lips curved against Nick's stomach in a smile. "I've only just begun to love you." And with that, he engulfed the head of Nick's cock with his mouth and wrapped his hand around its rigid length. He sucked Nick down his throat as far as he could take him, while keeping up the firm pressure of his up and down strokes.

If there could be a more sensual sight than Julian's full lips sliding down his cock, Nick didn't know of one. Then he forgot everything when Julian pushed the tip of his finger, slick and wet, inside Nick's hole. Strange at first as it sank in deeper, it seemed only natural by the time it was buried to the hilt.

"God, Julian." Sensation zipped through Nick and his mind became so jumbled he didn't know what to do with himself. He thrust up into Julian's warm mouth while writhing underneath him, reaching for something he didn't understand. "Please," he begged. "More."

Julian increased his vigorous sucking, swirling his very facile tongue around the sensitive head of Nick's cock, all the while pumping his finger in and out of Nick's passage. A wave grew inside of Nick and for a moment he struggled against it. He never liked being out of control, and he was well on his way to losing his mind completely.

Perhaps sensing this, Julian slid in a second finger and curled them up inside Nick, pressing, seeking—

"Fuck!" Nick cried out, violently heaving his hips off the bed. He felt his cock swell and pulse as he came hard and deep, his warmth sliding down Julian's throat. Julian never faltered and held on, drinking him down until Nick softened in his mouth.

He couldn't catch his breath and tears pricked the edges of his eyes. Watching Julian sit back, a satisfied smile on his face, Nick reached out, and Julian, with that seemingly innate sense he had to know when Nick needed him, took his hand, squeezing it tight. And right then, Nick knew without a doubt, he was out of his mind and completely, hopelessly in love.

"It's going to be fine." Julian smoothed his free hand over Nick's thighs, and even that touch set Nick's pulse racing.

No, it won't, for Nick knew this was the beginning of the end of his orderly life as he knew it. After tonight, he would be irrevocably changed; Nick would never be able to go back to being the man he was before. Before Julian, with his touch and his mouth and those clever, all-knowing eyes, had burst back into his life upending and upsetting the plan Nick had to simply exist.

Nick didn't respond, and watched Julian roll the condom down his erection and slick himself up. He breathed deep, prepared for pain, but Julian bent over and kissed him then, and Nick couldn't help but fall into Julian, ceding the control that had held him within such a rigid grasp for years, to the only man who'd ever made a difference in his life.

"Relax."

Nick couldn't help but smile, even as his body opened up to Julian's probing touch. "Easy for you to say."

"After I'm finished with you, you won't be able to move, and I mean that in a good way." Julian's smug, answering grin was infectious. Nick had never experienced sex where fun and laughter entered into the equation.

"Pretty sure of yourself aren't you." Nick was about to continue when he groaned, the feel of Julian's teeth nipping on the sensitive flesh of his earlobe sending a dark tug of desire through his body.

"Mmm hmm." Julian hummed and pressed his knee inside Nick's thigh, encouraging him to open up. Nick spread himself wide, and Julian's cool fingers touched him. "I can't wait to hear you scream my name."

Nick opened his mouth to respond when Julian entered him, the head of his cock spreading him wide, and instead of a joke, Nick hissed in pain. Though his first instinct was to push Julian off, Nick refrained and forced himself to relax, his passage full and stretched to the extreme as Julian inched himself inside, a little at a time.

"I have to move, Nick." Julian's fierce gaze held his, and he leaned over to take Nick's hands, pinning them to the bed. Sparks shot through Nick's blood.

"Do it." Nick grunted, pushing back against the slight movement.

Julian withdrew halfway only to push back in, finding a rhythm that soon had Nick writhing beneath him. They rocked together and Julian found an unerring angle that hit Nick's sweet spot, and he plunged inside him over and over, their hands clutching each other tight. Julian leaned over and dragged his nose down Nick's cheek, then skimmed his lips across Nick's, before taking Nick's mouth in a hard kiss.

Nick had never known sex could be like this, giving yet so intense he barely remembered his own name. His entire body hummed as if electrified; his balls drew tight and his cock stiffened against Julian's stomach. Julian's tongue plunged into Nick's mouth as his hardness slid in and out of Nick's passage. The bed rocked to the rhythm of their merging bodies, and wave after wave of pleasure rolled over Nick.

"Julian, God," he sobbed, rising up to meet Julian, thrust by thrust, as he took Julian into his body and into his heart. All Nick's fractured pieces settled into place; not perfectly aligned, yet comfortingly right. Julian pumped hard and hot within him, then collapsed with a shudder. He lay on top of Nick, his erratic breathing and pounding heart giving Nick insight that Julian was as affected as he was.

Julian murmured something Nick couldn't make out, then nuzzled into the curve between Nick's neck and shoulder and sighed a happy, contented sound. They lay together for a few more moments before Julian pulled out and stripped off the condom, threw it away, and returned back to the bed to lie next to Nick.

Nick finally found his breath and rolled over on his side to face Julian.

"How do you feel?" Julian traced a lazy circle on Nick's stomach with his finger.

"Is it always like that?" With his body still vibrating, Nick couldn't do more than whisper in the darkened room.

"Like what?" Julian's face was grave but still so beautiful.

"So . . . intense? All encompassing. Like getting knocked off your feet under a tidal wave."

Julian shook his head. "No. Never. This was completely different."

Suddenly unsure whether that was a good thing or bad, Nick had to ask. "Good different? Or different as in 'never again' different?"

Julian cupped his hand around the back of Nick's neck and dragged him up against his chest. "Different because it's never been like this before for me either, different." Cool fingers touched Nick's cheeks, skimmed his jaw and traced his lips. "Amazing and fucking perfect, different."

Julian kissed Nick, his lips lingering close to Nick's mouth. "Different because it's you and me, different." He kissed him again and held him close, chest to chest. "Go to sleep now." He snuggled down on Nick's shoulder and closed his eyes, and for Nick, who'd never slept with another man, holding Julian seemed like the most perfect thing he'd ever done. His eyelids fluttered shut.

Chapter Seventeen

THOUGH THEY'D GONE to bed early, Julian slept the entire night through. He'd have liked to attribute that to late nights working non-stop on the bandage sleeves. But waking up cuddled into Nick's broad chest was the real reason. He buried his nose into the crook of Nick's neck and inhaled, drawing Nick's scent deep into him. It wouldn't have shocked Julian to have woken up to find Nick gone, but to his surprise, Nick had also slept peacefully and looked even better in the morning with his face all stubble-rough and hair sleep-tousled.

And it wasn't a surprise either that Julian had also woken up hungry and demanding for more of Nick's body. So Julian took advantage of having Nick in his bed fast asleep, and took Nick's early morning arousal in his mouth, sucking him down, sliding his fingers over the soft sac to his puckered hole. When he dipped his fingers inside, Nick awoke with a grunt, then arched off the bed with a strangled cry. Julian held him fast with his mouth, moving his tongue up and around the wide head of Nick's cock until the man lay helpless beneath him, writhing and begging, his head tossing back and forth against the pillow.

"Julian, fuck, don't stop, God damn, fuck, there. Yes. God. *Fuck.*" He came with a sharp, piercing cry, pumping hot and thick down Julian's throat.

Julian sat back after he'd finished and gazed down at a sight he never thought he'd see—a blissed-out Nick in his bed, skin glistening with sweat, hair plastered to his head, chest heaving. He looked thoroughly fucked and deliriously happy.

"Damn, you are so fucking gorgeous right now."

Nick opened his eyes, the glow of his smile extending to his eyes. Without saying a word he held his hand out and Julian took it, lacing his fingers together with Nick's, then lying down next to him, cuddling into his chest. For Julian, it was the most profoundly loving, sweetest moment of his life. One he'd cherish forever.

They stayed close together, nesting in each other's arms. Julian hadn't been certain Nick would enjoy the aftermath of lovemaking; it surprised and thrilled him when Nick pulled him close and kissed the top of his head.

"That was amazing; you're amazing."

It had never been Julian's style to be a greedy lover; to him that signified an emotional entanglement he wasn't willing to pursue. But hearing Nick's rapidly beating heart underneath him and feeling the strength in Nick's powerful arms holding him tight, Julian knew he wanted this every morning. Any resistance he had toward Nick was simply futile; only Nick had this power over him. Now he had to make sure Nick wanted it as well.

After another kiss to his temple, Nick groaned. "I have to get up. I have to go home to change, then go back to work." He slid up to a seated position and rubbed his face. "Damn, I wish . . ." With a shake of his head he climbed out of bed and went into the bathroom.

Julian heard the shower turn on and knew morning had officially started. He slipped on his sweatpants and headed to the kitchen to start the coffee. The least he could do was send Nick off thoroughly caffeinated.

Ten minutes later, Nick was out of the bathroom and dressed, and Julian was on his second cup of coffee.

"I won't say thank you because to me that's a sign I won't be seeing you again." Nick drained his cup of coffee and brought it to the sink. He bit his lip. "I liked waking up with you this morning." Julian's best intentions of not loving this strong, walled-up man were obliterated by that simple sentence.

"You've never had a lover then."

"No. I've always been alone."

Without saying anything Julian hugged Nick, burying his

face in his still damp hair.

"Being alone is a choice, being lonely isn't. You can be with someone and still be the loneliest person in the world if they aren't the right person to set you free. I sometimes like being alone, and need to be when I'm designing, but I'm never lonely."

Nick held on to him tight before pulling away, picking up his jacket, and slipping it on. Marcus was right about one thing: a man in uniform, even his tac jacket, was hot as hell.

"I'm alone and I'm lonely so I'm a double dose of pathetic, huh?" Nick shoved his keys into his pocket.

"You're many things, Nick, but pathetic isn't one of them. And I think maybe going forward, we've taken care of the loneliness problem?" Julian leaned against the counter. "I'm not planning on going anywhere. Are you?" The question was pointed and deliberate. Remembering how Nick had pushed him away and ran, Julian needed to know. If it was only a one-time thing, it was fine. Julian could pull back and disengage. But if it was a yes, and Nick was willing to give them a chance . . . Julian's heart hammered as he waited for Nick's reply. And he wondered when the rules of his own heart had changed that he wanted a forever man, a forever life.

Love.

The answer was clear. It was only because it was Nick. And yet Julian still wasn't sure where he stood.

"Yeah. I want this, us. But it'll take some time for me to arrange all the shit in my head and then tell my family. And I want to tell the people at work as well. Are you willing to give that to me? Time? The time I need?"

Relief flooded through Julian and muscles he wasn't even aware were clenched, relaxed. "I've got plenty of time, as long as the end result is you staying and not running away this time."

"I won't fuck up again." Nick kissed him. "Maybe if I'd stayed the first time my life might have turned out different. I'll never know."

"We've been given a second chance. Some people never even get a first. Do you know how lucky we are?" There was the world in Julian's question, and it wasn't until Nick nodded that Julian released his breath.

One last kiss and then Nick left. It was heinously early to be up, but Julian couldn't go back to sleep. The designs he worked on last night still needed some finishing touches. Today he planned on showing them to Helena, and getting her input and some contacts to show people in the industry what he'd created.

Julian hadn't thought about his regular clothing collection in the past week. Melanie knew what he'd been working on and had taken over the designing and styling for Julian Cornell Designs; he was happy to give her a chance to showcase her talents. From what she'd shown him, her work was excellent, and he gave her carte blanche to do what she could with the little resources they had.

He'd gotten a reprieve from total collapse not only from Helena's loan, but also from one of his buyer friends who knew the background story of Devon Chambers and had persuaded her shop to go with Julian's collection. They were a hit and on their second reorder. It made slow inroads on his debt, but he was able to make the minimum payments on all his credit cards and the bank loan.

His phone buzzed as he straightened out his design table.

"Hey, what's up? Isn't it early for you?" He pushed the speaker button so he could continue working and talking.

Marcus's voice blared out into the apartment. "What's up is breakfast. Eleven o'clock at the usual place on Broadway. We missed you last week, so we're doing an unscheduled second breakfast and this time you'll be here, right? We're doing it in the downtown in the city today instead of Brooklyn to make it even easier for you."

The note of anxiety in Marcus's voice touched Julian. "Yeah, sure. I want to tell you guys what I've been up to anyway." He picked up two of the sleeves, the fabric in the colors of both of New York's basketball teams. Maybe he should think about contacting their corporate offices to see if he could get permission to put logos on them. He jotted that down as a note to himself for the future.

"Yeah. Zach and I were saying you've been holed up in that loft, we were wondering if you had some kind of sex slave operation going on." Marcus chuckled. "And I was getting pissed you weren't sharing."

"You don't have enough pretty boys around you, Marcus?" Julian rolled his eyes. The memory of last night was painted all over his skin; Nick's scent still lingered in the apartment. Julian had no desire to play around with the boys at Marcus's club. Not anymore.

"Variety, baby. Got to keep it spicy, you know?"

Julian heard a voice in the background. "Where are you?"

"In my bed." Marcus couldn't keep the grin out of his voice.

"Do you have someone with you, or is that a stupid question for me to ask?"

"I think you already answered that, right? Now I have to tend to a few things before we meet. See ya later." The phone went dead.

Julian could only shake his head and laugh at his friend's antics. There were things that were certain in life: death, taxes, and that Marcus Feldman would never settle down with one man. He went to take a shower.

AT FIVE MINUTES after eleven he pushed open the door to the restaurant on Broadway in SoHo and spotted his friends right away. Zach, as usual, was on his phone, tapping away at God knows what, and Marcus was talking to some random, good-looking man.

"Hey, guys."

Zach looked up and smiled at him. "Hi. I'm glad you could make it. We missed you last week." His eyes danced with humor. "You owe me for leaving me alone with him and his pick-up lines." With a jerk of his chin he indicated Marcus, laughing up into the man's face.

Marcus gave the man a squeeze on his shoulder, then walked

over to stand next to them. "Pick-up lines?" He pretended outrage. "I don't need to pick up men, they gravitate to me. It's like I'm the queen bee."

"Oh God, I'm going to lose my appetite," said Julian groaning. Zach rolled his eyes and shook his head.

"Juli, you look different today." Marcus studied him through narrowed eyes. "You're happy, yet calm." A sly grin teased his lips. "You got laid last night, I bet. Who was it? Are you holding out on us?"

It would be a cold day in hell before Julian spoke to Marcus about his feelings for Nick. He could hear the snide comments and teasing now.

"Don't be an ass. Did you give our name to Steph?" He motioned to the table where the harried hostess stood. Even for breakfast, this place was jammed.

"Yep. We were waiting for you." Marcus waved at the young woman, and she beckoned to them.

"Come with me, gentlemen. I have your table in the back."

They followed her slim figure as she threaded through the maze of tables to the comfortable booth the busboy was setting up.

"Here you go, guys. Enjoy."

"Thank you, Steph." He smiled at the young woman. They came here often and from what Julian could tell, she never let the crowds get to her.

"I saw your show on television. I loved the collection." She smiled up at him through her fringe of bangs before hurrying back to the front.

"Thanks." At least a few more orders had begun to trickle in, so he wasn't homeless. This month.

Julian slid into the booth, thinking about the calls he needed to make later on today to the contacts Helena had given him. He had to raise the money somehow to make this dream happen. He refused to fail those kids.

"What's going on in that head of yours?" Marcus nudged him with his elbow. "I've known you too long not to see the wheels turning."

Julian sipped his water. "I'm changing course for a bit." He proceeded to outline his idea, leaving out, of course, the personal relationship between him and Nick, but showing his friends the pictures he'd taken of both Jamal and Kayla wearing the prototypes of his "designer" compression bandages.

The waiter arrived and took their drink and food orders, and Julian sat back, waiting for his friends' reactions to his new endeavor. When neither of them said anything, he became nervous and somewhat defensive.

"Okay, so you don't like it. I know it's not what I always said I wanted to do, but I met these kids and they're—"

"Stop." Marcus put his hand on Julian's wrist. "Shut up for a second and let me talk now."

The waiter came with their drinks and the bread basket, and Julian, nervous about what Marcus was going to say, took a big gulp of his vodka. It wasn't necessary for his friends to help with what he was doing, but he always appreciated their support.

"This is a total 180 from what you do, what you've said you've wanted to do your entire life. Isn't your line, 'beautiful clothes for beautiful people'?"

Hearing that tag line now, Julian winced at its utter shallowness. To think that Jamal, Kayla, and the others in the burn unit would leaf through magazines and see his name tied with that—what else could they think but that he was only interested in a person's outward appearance? And up until a couple of weeks ago, they would have been correct. Nick may want to thank Julian for bringing him back to life, but correspondingly, Julian owed Nick as much, if not more, for making him see what was real and important.

"Yeah, but maybe I've had a change of heart. People can change, you know."

"Defensive much?" Marcus murmured. "You're misunderstanding me. I'm not saying that to make you think what you're doing isn't good. Exactly the opposite. Personally, I think it's fucking fantastic." He leaned back in the booth. "Where do I sign up?"

Confused, Julian stared at Marcus. "Sign up? These are for burn victims, not the general public."

Marcus arched a black brow. "No shit." He leaned forward to grasp Julian by the hand. "Juli, how damn dense are you? I'm trying to tell you I think what you're doing is amazing. I'm so fucking proud of you."

In his usual quiet, thoughtful tone, Zach interjected. "Maybe if you stopped cursing every other word people might pay more attention to you."

"Well, fuck me. I think I got schooled." Marcus smirked. "But you love me anyway, Zach."

"Yes, but it makes taking you out in public a very trying ordeal."

The three of them shared a laugh, and with a pang Julian knew Nick had never had the love and friendship of men who understood who he was and knew him like they did their own breath.

This was what he wished for Nick: friends who would be there by his side for whatever shit life threw his way. Julian knew he never could have made it if he didn't have these men as his anchor. No one should have to go through life alone, afraid to be the person they were inside. Nick's only crime was fear. Fear over telling his family, thinking they'd reject him. Fear that the people he worked with would believe he was less of a man because he was gay. And maybe, deep down, fear over letting go of a lifetime of denial, and admitting all of this to himself.

"What I meant," Marcus continued, "was that I think your idea is fuc—um, absolutely brilliant. And I want to invest in it."

Julian choked on his drink. "You do?" His eyes hardened. "I don't want you doing this out of pity. I'm serious about this."

"Don't be an ass," snapped Marcus. "I don't mix business with friendship. This isn't me buying your clothes to wear at my club. If you're planning on marketing this, I want in. I know you, and I know when you're passionate about things."

"Marcus is right, I'm in too." Zach took off his glasses and polished them on a napkin. "I've already paid off my mother's house and sold some apps to big software developers that have me sitting well. I pretty much don't need to work again if I don't want to." He blinked. "Ever. So I have the money to invest in what I want."

He spoke with such nonchalance it took a few minutes for it to sink in—Zach, rich?

"I, I didn't plan on asking you guys for money." Julian licked his lips, nervously. "My business problems are my own."

"Remember when I started Sparks?" Marcus stared at the table, spinning the fork around and around. "I had almost nothing; I begged and borrowed from everyone."

"Sure I do," laughed Julian. "I made all the outfits for the bartenders and the wait staff. Three sets if I'm not mistaken."

"Exactly. Did I ask you to do that for me?"

"Well, no, but—"

"No buts, Juli." Marcus expertly cut him off. "That's what friends are supposed to do. Step in when they can help, no questions asked. You did it for me and now I want to give back to you. I'm not giving you the money, and I don't hear Zach saying he is either. But if we want to invest in your company, invest in you, why not?"

Why not indeed. Julian had no answer and in fact couldn't have spoken at that moment. The hot tears burning his eyes and the choking sensation in his throat made that an impossibility.

"Thanks," he whispered. "You don't know how much that means to me."

"The three of us are family. And family helps each other. So now that that's settled," Marcus's eyes gleamed, "tell us about you and Nick."

He hadn't wanted to talk about this yet. It was so tentative and new, and it may end up burning bright and hot, then fizzle out. It had been a long time for them both. But like Marcus said. Family.

"Well . . ."

"Ha! I knew it. I told you, Zach, didn't I?" Marcus turned to

Zach who nodded and knit his brows together.

"Why are you so hesitant to talk about him, Julian? Is everything okay between you two?"

"I can't say yet. You know he's in the closet. He hasn't told anyone he's gay except for his sister, and the environment he works in isn't the most gay-friendly."

"All that means shit to me. How is he with you?" asked Marcus. "The rest of it is stuff that can be dealt with. Does he care about you?"

And that was the crux of it all. Julian never had to think about things like this before, because he never cared enough to have it matter. One man was the same as the next. Deep down it was because he was most likely comparing them all to what he'd felt for Nick. It didn't matter that they were teenagers and had never had sex. It was a connection Julian had never felt with any other person.

"I think he does. But I don't plan on rushing things. Nick has been through a lot, and that's all I'm going to say on the matter." He cut off Marcus who'd opened his mouth. "No, I won't go there. It isn't anything to make light of and say he'll get over it with a wink and a nod. What happened to Nick and how he's dealing with it is his own personal story. One I'm not able or willing to talk about."

"You really care for him?" Zach held his gaze and smiled into Julian's eyes.

"It's that obvious, huh?" Julian tried to cover up his weak laugh by taking a deep swallow of his drink.

"Don't let him have everything, Juli. Hold back a piece of yourself until you see he's for real this time." Marcus was unusually sober.

Too late, Julian wanted to answer. But all he could do was nod and hope that it would all turn out for the best.

Chapter Eighteen

THE RIDE HOME to change was perhaps the longest one in the history of man. Accidents, road construction, and general traffic made Nick want to rip his hair out. It wasn't until he was merging onto the ramp for the Brooklyn Bridge that it hit him like a fist: he'd gone down the elevator in Julian's building without a second thought and by himself.

To some, it was no big deal. To Nick, it was the world. If he could do that, without him needing a nursemaid, a drink, and a recovery period, maybe he *was* recovering. He pressed the button on his hands-free device to call Dr. Landau.

"Doctor's Office. May I help you?"

"Hey, Shena. It's Nick. Does he have a minute?"

"One sec, let me look. Yep. His next appointment is running late. Hold on."

After only a brief hesitation, the smooth voice of Dr. Landau filled Nick's car.

"Hi, Nick. What's up? Everything okay?"

"More than okay." He proceeded to tell Dr. Landau about what he considered his breakthrough. When he'd finished and the doctor didn't speak right away, Nick grew nervous.

"I know it isn't much, but to me, it meant a lot."

"Nick. Don't think like that. I was trying to gather my thoughts to let you know how incredibly proud I am of you."

Landau's warm voice kindled a warmth within Nick. It was good to have someone praise him for once. It was an emotional moment for Nick, realizing he could conquer a fear, small as it might be to some. It proved that he could overcome the blackness and pain he'd submerged himself in since 9/11. Some but not all of the credit was due to the reemergence of Julian in his life and the talks they had about forgiveness and recovery. He knew it wasn't the time to tell his doctor this, not over the phone.

"I'd like to make an appointment to talk to you about some things that have happened to me in the past week or so." His appointments had gone from twice a week in the beginning to once a week after a few years. He'd been going once a month for the past year, but Nick wanted to talk to Dr. Landau separately about Julian. And he was hoping Julian might want to go with him.

"Sure. I have your schedule. I'll have Shena set something up and email you, how's that?"

"Perfect. Thanks."

"Thank you for calling me and telling me the good news. These are the types of calls I like taking."

After sharing a laugh, Nick clicked off. He exited the bridge and joined the line of cars waiting to enter the expressway, where, after about twenty minutes he exited onto the city streets. He drove through the familiar neighborhood where flags were going up in preparation for Veterans Day. This was a pretty conservative, blue collar area of Brooklyn, and Nick's stomach twisted at the thought of the inevitable conversation with his parents.

Not today, however, as he saw their car was absent from the driveway when he pulled in. Even though he'd showered at Julian's he took another one at home to relax himself, then dressed in fresh clothes, listened to the news a bit, and went through his mail. His phone rang with an unfamiliar number.

"Fletcher."

"Mr. Fletcher, this is Ms. Cruz at the Human Resources Office. I'd like to discuss these papers you filled out yesterday."

"Yes. I was planning on contacting you to see the procedure."

"Can you come in today?"

He checked his watch and to his surprise it was only ten o'clock. He'd been up so long he thought half the day had passed. Then he recalled how Julian woke him and heat flooded through him.

"Um, yeah. How's in about an hour?" Nick adjusted himself,

squeezing the hard-on he seemed to get every time Julian was around. Now the mere thought of the man caused his balls to ache with a painful intensity. Shit, he was in deep trouble.

"That's good. Thank you."

Nick hung up and looked down at the bulge in pants. "Down boy. You already got your action today." But he gave himself an extra squeeze and willed away the uncomfortable thought that he missed Julian more than he'd thought possible.

An hour and ten minutes later he was walking into the office of Ms. Ana Cruz, Senior Investigator with the FDNY's EEO office. Ms. Cruz was in her mid-forties, with a tight bun, and an even tighter smile.

"Mr. Fletcher, what I'm seeing here in these papers is a very serious accusation. One that if the department doesn't act upon immediately, could result in a lawsuit not only against the City, but against several high ranking members of the department as well."

Damn. Well he was certainly going from behind the scenes to on stage without any rehearsal. All it took was remembering the hurt in Barton's face as he stared at his locker for Nick to know he was doing the right thing. People like Jensen couldn't be allowed to bully their way through life, and if it meant Nick would be outing himself because of it, then so be it.

"Whatever I have to do, Ms. Cruz. Tell me what I need to do."

After an hour of questions, filling out more forms, and writing up another, more detailed statement, Nick was finished. Ms. Cruz promised to be in touch and told him to keep everything they'd discussed confidential.

He thanked her and left, completely drained. He stood outside, taking in deep breaths of air, thinking how fast his life had moved lately. A sudden urge hit him to talk to Julian, and without thinking, he pulled out his phone and called him.

"Nick? Is everything all right?" There was noise behind Julian's voice.

"Am I interrupting you?" It occurred to Nick he didn't really know much about Julian's life.

"You couldn't. I'm finishing up breakfast and then I'm going to make some phone calls and work on the prototypes. I'm hoping to be at the burn center later." His voice dropped a notch, growing warmer and more intimate. "Will I see you there, or do I have to wait until later tonight?"

There was so much promise in Julian's voice, Nick's breath grew short, the blood beating fast and hot through his veins. Was this because it was so new with Julian, or was he going to want to be naked with the man every time he saw him? "I'll be at the center, though I may be late." He explained to Julian what he'd been doing all morning.

"I'm so proud of you. That takes courage."

Though the praise filled Nick with a sense of accomplishment, he felt he hadn't done anything yet. "I haven't told anyone yet."

"That you're gay, you mean?"

"Yeah." Nick entered his car and blew out a noisy breath. "It wasn't necessary at this point."

"What will you do if something happens again to Barton?"

"I don't know, okay? Why is it so necessary to tell them all I'm gay right away? What purpose does that serve? The main thing is to stop the bullying, I thought."

Julian sighed heavily into the phone. "Of course it is. But if others see what gay people can accomplish, it gives them hope, you know? And you being a firefighter and coming out has more of an impact than me being gay as a fashion designer."

The edge of condemnation in Julian's voice set Nick's back up. "I didn't sign up to be the poster boy for the fire department. This is all happening so fast; I have to think of my family and my job."

"How about us, Nick?" The tired resignation in Julian's voice squeezed Nick's heart. "Have you thought about us or was that all too fast for you as well?"

A voice screamed inside his head: *Tell him he's wrong. Tell him you're going to tell them when you get to the job, and tell your parents when you get home.*

Instead Nick said nothing like that. "It's not that easy."

"I see." Julian's cold, hard voice indicated he thought Nick was full of shit. "Is it all a game to you, then?"

"What are you talking about? You know—"

"I don't know shit." Julian swore viciously. "I know you and I fucked our brains out last night, and I thought it meant something. Instead you go away for two hours and suddenly you're afraid. Are you also regretting us? Do you regret last night?"

Struggling against his own anger, Nick gasped. "No, of course not. It was perfect. It's just that, I . . . you and me . . ." He leaned his head against the steering wheel. "I'm so confused, Julian," he whispered. "I don't even know myself anymore."

The silence lasted so long on the other end of the phone, Nick almost thought Julian had hung up.

"I get it, Nick. I don't want you thinking I'm a complete bastard; I'm not."

"But you're afraid. Of me."

"Not of you, but that you'll draw me into your life again, then disappear."

Considering what had happened before between them, Nick could understand. "I promise I'm not going anywhere. It may take me a while, and it may take me away from everything I know, but in the end, I won't be leaving. I'm coming back to you."

"That's all I needed to hear," said Julian in a soft voice. "I'll see you later then?"

"Yeah."

Nick hung up, drained and exhausted, yet he still had to go to work and run drills today. He drove away toward Randalls Island, thinking about his life—what he wanted, and whom he wanted in it. In every scenario, Julian was standing at his side, proud and unafraid of who he was.

By the time he pulled into his parking space, Nick was running about ten minutes late. He hurried into the locker room, changed into his gear, and found his team practicing unconscious firefighter removal when he joined them on the field. For these drills he'd normally work the sidelines, allowing Jensen and Carlos to take the lead, but in light of his progress today, he wanted to see how far he could take it.

He joined the crew and watched as the two teams entered the building and began searching for and carrying out the life-sized dummies set up in strategically located places. His eyes narrowed watching Jensen whisper and smirk as Barton was the last to enter the building. Deep inside, Nick had a bad feeling, and he stormed over to where the two men stood.

"Time to teach the fairy a little lesson, wouldn't you say?" Jensen gave a signal and one of the other trainers tossed something inside which set off a flash bang along with a choking plume of smoke. Nick watched in shock and horror as the trainer threw the lock on the door, despite the radio call from Barton inside, asking for information as to what was happening.

"You bastards, what the hell are you doing?"

"Oh cool down, Nick. Just teaching the queer a lesson. We'll let him out in a little while."

"Listen to me you asshole and listen good. You either open that door right now so I can get Barton out of there, or I'm going to call the cops and have them haul your ass off to jail. Got that?"

Nose to nose he stood with Jensen; Nick could barely see for the blinding rage that coursed through him.

"What's it gonna be?"

"What's the matter, Nicky? Got a thing for the kid? Don't tell me you like taking it up the ass too?"

Unable and unwilling to control himself any longer, Nick grabbed Jensen's shirt and twisted it in his hands, bringing the man's startled face flush to his.

"And what if I am, you fucker? What're you gonna do about it?"

Chapter Nineteen

IT WAS QUITE possibly the best day of Julian's life. After breakfast with his friends he returned to his loft and finished the prototypes for the sleeves. Then the calls he thought would prove stressful and problematic ended up with pledges of support, money, and resources. Once executives heard it was for victims of fire, these people were hell-bent on opening up their wallets and their hearts with offers of not only money, but also the promise of space when Julian was ready to show the line, a catering company to feed the guests he invited, and an advertising company donating their services.

Before he had a chance to check his watch it was three thirty. Damn. He'd been at it all afternoon, and aside from his omelet that morning, he'd eaten nothing. After making himself a protein shake, Julian checked his emails and turned on his phone. A text marked urgent popped up from Melanie.

> *Devon Chambers is spreading a rumor that you're closing up shop. How do you want to handle it?*

By fucking killing the bastard, was Julian's first thought. He pressed Speed Dial and Melanie's voice filled the loft. Julian had to put her on speakerphone, since he couldn't sit still and needed to pace while he was ranting and raving.

"What did the fucker say, Mel? Tell me everything."

"He's told at least three buyers I know of that you haven't recovered from the show and you're winding down operations." The anger in her voice was uncharacteristic for Melanie, who normally saw the good in everything. "I have to say, Julian, the fact that you haven't been seen or heard in your usual places since the show isn't helping this any."

Julian ran his hands through his hair as he paced the floor. "I've spent the entire afternoon on the phone with investors and people willing to help me with this project. The more I think about getting back into that scene full of sharks and backstabbers, the less I'm inclined to do so."

"So you're giving up?" Mel's voice rose high with incredulity. "You're letting Devon Chambers win. I can't believe it."

Julian slumped onto his sofa. "It's not that at all. I'm so focused on this, Mel. It means something, not only to me but to those people. If I don't have a collection next fall, it wouldn't affect anyone. If I put this project aside however, I fail the kids and men and women I'm trying to help. And I'm not willing to do that; I can't. They feel lost and uncared for as it is."

"What about me, though, Julian? Where do I fit into your plans?" Melanie's soft, sad voice hit Julian like a punch in his stomach. "Are you cutting me loose?"

"Shit, no. Of course not." The last thing he wanted to do was lose Melanie. She was one of his best friends. Maybe he hadn't told her how much he needed her. He hated that she might not know.

"Sweetheart, I could never do without you. I'm sorry I haven't brought you into my life more these past few weeks. I have an idea, though."

"What?"

"Meet me at my loft in an hour. I want to take you somewhere."

"Where?" There was no hesitation, only curiosity. Melanie would never try to dissuade him from his dreams. And if he could succeed with these kids, it might open up a future for all of them that no one had ever anticipated.

"I want you to meet some people." It was imperative for Melanie to understand that even if she wasn't part of the creative development for this project, she was still part of his team. Without her handling Julian Cornell Designs, he couldn't fully focus on this project. He owed her everything.

"Really?"

He heard the excitement bubbling in her voice and regretted not doing this sooner.

"Mel, I'm sorry I haven't included you more. I've been so wrapped up in the project I forget the important stuff. But I don't want you to ever think I don't need you. Eventually, when you leave me, I know I'll never find another person like you."

She sniffled into the phone and Julian smiled. She always was a big softie.

"I'm not leaving you, Julian. No matter what happens, I'll always be with you."

After he hung up with Melanie, Julian wished he could be as sure about Nick and their relationship as he was about his and Melanie's. He shouldn't have more faith in his assistant sticking by him than his lover, Julian mused, as he wrote down all the businesses and people he contacted earlier, and what they'd promised to contribute, donate, or help him with. While he waited for Melanie, he sent emails to everyone, confirming their conversations.

His phone rang and seeing it was Marcus, he picked up.

"What's up?"

"You're not closing down, are you?"

Julian sighed. "Shit, not you too. Of course not. I left you only a couple of hours ago, don't you think I'd have told you?"

"It's in the *Post*. Listen."

Julian heard the paper rustling as Marcus turned the pages. "Here it is: *Did Julian Cornell walk his last runway? Sources close to the trend-setting designer, whose latest show fell flat to everyone's surprise, have told us the designer isn't planning any new shows, and may be closing up shop for good.*"

Furious, Julian wanted to find Devon Chambers and rip his throat out. "It's that fucker, Chambers. He's trying to sabotage my whole company."

"Why does he hate you so much?"

It boggled Julian's mind that even after all these years, Devon kept a grudge. "We were in the same class at FIT. We dated a few times, but nothing serious." Though it had been a few years by that time, Julian was still mourning the loss of Nick, and had vowed to concentrate solely on his studies. "He took it more seriously than I did and was so relentless that when we were assigned a project together, I asked the professor to put me with someone else. Ever since then, he's done nothing but bad-mouth me and put me down."

"What a bastard. He can't get by on his own talent, so he steals yours."

"Eh." Julian transferred the phone from one ear to the other. "That's the strange thing. The guy has talent. He's a miserable person."

"So here's what I'm going to do." Julian could hear the grin in Marcus's voice. He truly loved his friends. "I have some connections at Page Six of the *Post*. When the time is right, you tell me, and I will make sure they run pictures of you and the kids and whatever event you have set up for the big unveiling of your project. Plus, I'm going to do a benefit for it and the burn center at Sparks."

All the breath left Julian's body as he fell back onto his sofa.

"Wha-what are you talking about, Marc? Why are you doing this?"

"Because I'm so fucking proud of what you've done. It's time for you to shine, to have the spotlight on you and what you've accomplished."

"Marcus," sighed Julian. "This isn't about me. It's about the kids."

"That's what I mean, Juli. You got brutalized by the press the last time, and I want to make sure that this project gets all the attention it deserves."

Nothing could have prepared Julian for the effect Marcus's words had on him. It was as if a wall inside him crumbled, releasing all the emotion he'd bottled up inside for years. Words failed Julian and he struggled to keep Marcus blind as to how much his words meant. It wasn't Julian's way to broadcast his feelings.

"I appreciate it and thank you."

"I'm not in it for the thanks. I don't like seeing people who deserve the best get fucked over." The grin in his voice was pure Marcus. "My mission then becomes fucking over the fuckers."

Who could argue with that? "Weren't you supposed to cut down on the cursing?"

"Screw that," said Marcus. "That's only when we're out with Zach. He's the only one I'd ever do that for. Otherwise I refuse to censor myself. Anyone who doesn't like it can fuck off."

Julian promised to let Marcus know when he was ready to move on the publicity. The doorbell rang.

"Gotta go. Talk to you later."

Julian hung up and went to buzz Melanie in.

"OH MAN, THIS is awesome." For the first time since they'd met, a spark lit Jamal's eyes. Julian had shown him the sleeves to slip over his bandages, and, as Julian had guessed, Jamal picked the pinstriped one modeled after the Yankees uniform. He allowed Melanie to fit it on him and then stood, admiring his arms in the mirror. Even to Julian's perfectionist eye, it looked pretty damn good. Maybe he should think about getting the bandages pre-printed with the designs themselves. Something to think about. He pulled out his phone and made a note to himself.

"Oh Julian, what a marvelous idea." Melanie wiped her eyes. "I can't believe what you've accomplished in such a short period of time." She hugged him fiercely. "You should be so proud of yourself."

Truthfully, Julian was thrilled. Not only with the results of all his hard work, but with the way the bandages infused Jamal and Kayla with a sense of excitement. They were talking about showing people their bandages, not hiding away in a dark room. He checked his watch, surprised he hadn't heard from Nick since their last conversation. It wasn't that Julian was worried, but deep inside, he still wondered if each time he said goodbye to Nick, it would be the last time he saw him. Old wounds died hard, and Julian couldn't trust his heart to remain his own. From the pain he felt at this moment, cut off from Nick, not knowing if he was once again running and hiding, Julian knew he was royally fucked.

"I spent the day speaking with investors, setting up appointments to show them the prototypes." The satisfaction and pure joy in Jamal's face as he admired his arm in the mirror forced Julian to return to what was important. Jamal and all the other people he'd hopefully be helping with his designs spurred Julian's excitement. "As a matter of fact, Jamal here is going to come with me when I present to the investors."

The smile on the young man's face froze. "I am?"

"You sure are." Julian's smile broadened at the look of wonder on Jamal's face. "Who else could I get to model but the person who inspired this whole operation?"

If he'd told Jamal he'd won the lottery, the young man couldn't have looked more astonished. "Me? You want me to model?"

At Julian's nod, Jamal's eyes turned dark. "But I ain't no model and I'm full of scars."

There was so much the real world didn't know about the sham world of modeling. How imperfections were hidden with tricks of light and Photoshop. What seemed so effortlessly perfect was most often the result of hours of hard work and the luck of a good camera angle.

"Trust me when I tell you: you're the *only* one I'd consider. If not for you, Jamal, this never would've happened."

A look passed between them and Julian could see the young man's inner struggle as he debated whether to open his heart to trusting Julian. There was wisdom and so much pain in the depths of those hazel eyes. Emotions no seventeen-year-old should have. Though Julian couldn't give Jamal back the life he once had, perhaps this could help him on the road to healing.

"This isn't a whim on my part, Jamal. You have to understand I'm all in."

Jamal took his words to heart. "I always wanted to be a model." The grin he flashed was one of pure delight, as he ran the tip of his finger up his bandaged arm. "Wait till the girls hear about this."

Though thrilled beyond belief at how it all seemed to be working out, a thread of worry wormed its way back into Julian's mind when he checked his phone again and there was still no message from Nick. By now it was late enough that he should've been by; he certainly had finished work. Yet Julian hadn't received a text or a phone call.

Where was Nick?

Chapter Twenty

IT HAD ALL come down to this. Nick stood within inches of the mocking face of a man he'd worked with for years, yet now seemed like a stranger.

"I don't need to tell you shit, except when I open that fucking door, Barton better be okay."

Something dark and feral glinted in Jensen's eyes. "This isn't over yet."

"Time and place." Nick poked Jensen in the chest. "Name it. But first I'm doing what I was trained to do."

Nick left Jensen and sprinted to open the door and enter the smoke-filled building.

"Barton, where are you?" Choking on the fumes, Nick knelt low to the ground. He wouldn't go in further without a mask. With the help of a brisk wind blowing in from the river through the open door, the smoky fog dissipated from the rooms and Nick saw Barton, his protective mask covering his face, advancing toward him.

He stood and grabbed the man's arm. "Let's go."

Barton followed him outside, remaining silent until they were several hundred feet from the building. At that point Barton tore off his mask, revealing his smoke-stained face and red-rimmed eyes. He coughed, and one of the men stepped up with a grim face and offered him a bottle of water. Barton drank half and poured the rest over his head to wash his face and probably clear his eyes.

It was painful to stand there and watch Barton struggle to understand what Nick already knew. That Jensen was willing to potentially cause harm to a fellow firefighter, *a brother,* for the simple reason he was gay. There was no sense Nick could make of it; the utter hatred was inconceivable.

A few minutes passed and Barton faced him, still pale, but with a face that looked older than it had only a few short days ago.

"What the fuck happened?"

It took all of Nick's strength not to steal a glance at Jensen, whom he could hear still joking in the background as if he hadn't a care in the world. Adam Barton, though, was no dummy.

"They tried to fuck me over, didn't they?" Those honest blue eyes were clouded with pain and something new. Angry determination.

"They're not going to get away with it, Barton."

"You're damn right they aren't," Barton shouted. That was directed over Nick's shoulder to Jensen and the other men who stood with him. "I'm not letting them, or you, or anyone else tell me I don't deserve to be here." Twin spots of red stained his freckled cheeks. "I earned my spot here like everyone else, and I'll be damned if some bigoted asshole is going to run me out." He threw down his gear and stormed off toward the main building.

A mocking laugh split the silence. "He won't say nothing if he knows what's good for him."

Nick whipped around at Jensen's remark. The smirk on his face left Nick with little recourse. He could either be a man and stand up for himself and who he was, or choose to hide. Thinking back to the morning and waking up with Julian's cocky mouth around his dick, taking him apart, sending him to oblivion, Nick knew he could never go back to the man he'd pretended to be for all these years. Not if he wanted Julian in his life.

And he knew without any doubt he wanted Julian.

The smile faltered on Jensen's face. With each step Nick took toward him, Jensen took one back, until he was trapped up against the fence. Nick breathed down into Jensen's face.

"You want to know about me? Why? Why do you need to know who's in my bed? Who I'm screwing?"

A crafty look lit Jensen's eyes. "You one too, Nick? That's

why I've never seen you with a girl?"

"Cut it out, Jensen. Nick, c'mon. Let's get out of here, man."

Carlos stood beside him, but Nick ignored his plea.

"I'm telling you for the last time: it's none of your fucking business who I have in my bed. You got bigger problems to worry about than mine or Barton's sex life."

His gaze flicked over Jensen, registering nothing but disgust for the man. He'd be damned if he'd be forced to come out to this piece of shit before he had the chance to talk to his parents. And when that happened? Nick knew he wanted, no, he *needed* Julian by his side. Not because Nick couldn't do it without him, but because Julian deserved to be there with him.

A grin stretched across his lips and he poked Jensen in the chest. "I reported you, Jensen. I reported every filthy thing you've said or done since I began working with you. A word of advice?" Nick straightened up and patted Jensen's cheek. "You might want to think about retirement." Without waiting for a reply, Nick spun on his heel and walked away after Barton.

By the time he found Barton in the locker room, the man had changed into his civilian clothes. Best to proceed with caution, Nick decided, noting Barton's stiffened posture and grim face.

"I meant what I said. I reported him to the EEO office."

A flicker of interest passed over Barton's face, but he said nothing. Only the tenseness in his jaw muscles gave a hint as to his true feelings.

"I thought you'd be interested to know."

Anger radiated from Barton's eyes. "Yeah? Big deal. So you did your duty. Now you can say you helped the queer guy." He hefted his bag up onto his shoulder and brushed past Nick.

"Adam, come on."

At the sound of his name, Barton stopped and whirled. "Come on what, *Nick?*" The mimicking tone in Barton's voice saddened but didn't surprise him. "I heard you. You reported him. Did you do it for me, because if so I have a surprise for you. You think that's going to stop people like him from making fun of me? How do you think it feels knowing people wish I were dead because I'm gay? You have no idea what I go through. So yeah, great news. Now I'll get to go sit in an office and tell some strangers about something they have no need to know. My sexuality and who I like sleeping with." His eyes blazed blue fire. "Imagine if you had to do that, huh?"

With that, Barton hurried out of the locker room. Nick didn't try to follow him—what purpose would that serve?

NICK HAD NO recollection as to how he got home; autopilot kicked in and the next thing he knew he had pulled up into the driveway of his parents' house. He vaguely remembered promising to meet Julian at the burn center, but his mindset tonight made that an unwise move. He slammed the car door so hard he hoped it remained on its hinges. It took several swipes with his key before his trembling fingers could unlock the front door. Without bothering to remove his coat, he kicked the door shut behind him and headed straight to the refrigerator where he snagged the entire six pack of beer. Before he left the kitchen he'd finished half of one and was already eyeing the second.

He stripped down to his undershirt and briefs and lay on the sofa, feet propped up on the backrest, a pile of pillows shoved underneath his head. There was a bowl of chips, and the beer was cold and within reach. The television blared some murder show, and Nick was halfway through his third beer, a nice and pleasant buzz settling in his veins, when he thought he heard a banging on his front door.

He cocked his head and listened to the pounding grow more insistent. The blanket he'd wrapped himself in slipped to the floor when he shuffled off to see who was bothering him. Figuring it might be Katie, he opened the door halfway, shielding his lower body so she wouldn't see him in his underwear. To his surprise, instead of his sister, it was Julian.

"Oh, hi."

This was a totally different Julian, however, than he'd seen before. He brushed by Nick and walked in and Nick caught a whiff of his light cologne. The green of the scarf draped around Julian's neck brightened the color of his eyes to emerald, while his normal sleekly styled hair tumbled over his forehead in messy waves that gave him a sexier and rougher look. When Nick had left that morning, Julian had been lounging in a pair of sweats, but upon removing his black trench coat, he revealed a trim charcoal gray suit that fit his lean, muscular build like it was made for him. It more than likely had been, thought Nick, by Julian himself. Nick liked that look. Very much.

The crisply tailored shirt had alternating stripes of green, blue, and white, and was paired with a bright green tie. He looked rich, and mouthwateringly desirable, like a walking advertisement for sex on long, muscular legs.

Legs, Nick mused, that he wanted wrapped around him sooner rather than later. He took Julian's coat and draped it over the kitchen chair, picking up his own jacket which lay in a crumpled pile on the floor where it had landed after slipping off the table.

"Is that all you have to say to me?" Hurt, anger, and surprise all echoed in Julian's question; furrows etched deep lines in his brow. "Oh, hi? Where were you today and tonight? I must have called your phone at least ten times."

Crap. Nick ran his hands over his face, pressing his fingers into tired, gritty eyes. He was so weary of going over this again. "Some shit happened at work, but I honestly don't want to talk about it." He moved closer and dragged his nose down Julian's smooth cheek, inhaling his scent. The man always smelled wonderful, like sunshine, and Nick's inner turmoil settled. "I don't want to talk at all." Nick wrapped his arms around Julian to hug him close.

The silence stretched out between them, with Julian making no move to touch or kiss Nick. His body remained hard and unyielding beneath Nick's touch. "What's wrong?"

A bewildered-sounding laugh broke from Julian's lips, and he eased away from Nick, walking into the living room. "What's wrong? You think it's okay to disappear on me for the day, then not come to the hospital like you said you would. No phone calls or texts? I'm not asking you to check in with me, but . . ." Julian shrugged and sat on the sofa. "Have a little fucking common courtesy at least."

"Why are you so angry with me?" The pleasant buzz from earlier had crashed, and now Nick was left with an aching head and an empty heart. "We talked in the afternoon and I told you where I stood with us. I'm not going anywhere."

"That's the point. You're not going anywhere. You refuse to admit you're gay, yet you say things to me that make me think . . ." In a swift motion, Julian stood and headed for the kitchen. "I'm not doing this anymore. I'm leaving." He grabbed his coat from the back of the chair.

If he let Julian leave this time Nick knew he'd lose him forever. It would be like breathing his last breath. Nick choked out, "Wait, please."

Keeping his hand on the doorknob, Julian hesitated. "Why, Nick? So you can try and convince me that you want me? I know you want me. I want you too. But wanting and needing are two different things."

This was what he should have had the guts to do all those years ago. "How about loving, Julian? Would it be any different if I said I loved you?"

Chapter Twenty-One

FOR FUTURE REFERENCE, Julian wanted to remember everything about this moment, from the clothes he wore to the exact time it occurred. For so many years he'd locked everyone out of his life because Nick hadn't been able to come to terms with who he was. Hearing him now say "I love you" should have flooded him with a sense of joy. Why then, did he wonder if it was real?

Facing Nick, Julian couldn't help but move closer; like water to the thirsty, Julian needed to touch Nick. He smoothed his hands up Nick's chest, following the touch with his lips, hoping he once again proved to Nick he didn't care about the scars underneath. They'd journeyed too far and fallen too deep to remain stranded at the surface of life.

"Say it again," whispered Julian, his lips pressed against the strong, corded muscles of Nick's neck.

"Pushy, aren't you." But there was joy in Nick's voice, a lightness Julian hadn't ever heard. The smile in Nick's eyes promised a world Julian had yet to experience.

"Tell me," Julian insisted. "Say it again."

Gentle hands framed Julian's face, evoking a tenderness he'd never anticipated from the gruff and serious Nick he knew. Those deep blue eyes gazed at him, while a hesitant smile teased his lips.

"I love you, Julian. When the thought of you leaving made me dread life without you, I knew it had all changed. I'm tired of being alone and lonely. I want to count in your life, for the kids, in my job. I don't want to be a nothing anymore."

In an uncharacteristic display of emotion, Nick hugged him close, and Julian held on to him as if he was drowning. The strength it must have taken Nick to admit his vulnerability nearly shredded Julian's heart.

"You could never be a nothing. For God's sake, don't you know you're everything to me?"

Nick groaned, his breath gusting over Julian's skin. "You look so fucking cool and put together, all dressed up in your suit and tie, but I know the real you underneath all this bullshit." Nick pulled the shirt out from Julian's pants while Julian unbuttoned it with shaking fingers. But when Julian went to unbuckle his pants, Nick slapped his hands away. "I know all the hot and sexy things you like to do. And have done *to* you." Warmth circled his belly as Nick's hands roamed his skin. "You're mine tonight and I'm gonna do it all."

Passion spiked, searing between them, and Julian arched up, pressing himself into Nick's cock. With that one short proprietary phrase, he'd grown achingly hard. What would happen tonight would no doubt seal him and Nick together. The risk was enormous to Julian. Though he'd sworn not to fall for Nick, the battle had been lost before Julian knew the war had begun.

But life was made to be lived with risks. Through lowered lashes, Julian watched Nick step out of his briefs, his thick cock standing proud. Being with Nick was the risk he was willing to take. Nick's fingers brushed against Julian's erection, still trapped within his suit pants.

"I want this in my mouth."

"Then take it already," rasped Julian, so perilously close to coming in his pants, he panted with the exertion of holding still. "Do it now before I ruin my best suit."

"If you're more worried about your clothes than what I'm planning to do to you when you're out of them, I'm not doing something right." A seductive, evil laugh passed through Nick's lips and a coil of excitement tightened in Julian's belly. Without warning, Nick yanked down his pants and briefs, grasping Julian's already wet cock in his large palm.

"I changed my mind. Step out of your pants."

Desire sizzled through Julian's fevered brain. In no shape

to argue, he did as Nick asked, and soon he too was naked in Nick's kitchen save for his unbuttoned shirt.

"Spread your legs."

Holy shit, Nick was going to take him bent over the kitchen table. That was hot as fuck. Julian braced his arms on the smooth wooden surface. He waited, wondering where Nick kept his lube, and if it was too soon for them to go without condoms, when—

"Fuuuck." The wet swipe of Nick's tongue in between his ass cheeks sent off an electric current straight to Julian's dick. His balls drew tight and his spine tingled. "Nick." Julian shouted, and with one hand pressed hard on his surging erection which threatened to explode all over Nick's nice clean table.

"Hold it." Nick's mouth nuzzled, then fucking kissed Julian's ass, nipping the cheeks until Julian writhed under him, hips thrusting his cock through his fist.

"I'm trying," gritted Julian.

"Keep trying." Nick spread the globes of Julian's ass and dipped his tongue straight into Julian's hole, delving deep and hard, ignoring the cries and curses streaming from Julian's lips.

"Fuck. Me. Nick, God. There. Right there." Julian pushed back against that wet and wicked tongue, impaling himself, while managing to hold back his orgasm which teetered on the brink of erupting. Julian knew without a doubt if he lived through the pleasure, it might qualify as a miracle.

White sparks lit the corner of his rapidly wavering vision. He cried out as Nick once again swiped his hole, loving him with everything he had.

"Fuck, Julian, I need to be inside you now, but I don't have any condoms." Nick panted, resting his torso against Julian. "The department tests us monthly—"

"Do it then." His voice cracked with greedy hunger. "I got tested at my last physical three months ago. "Get inside me now."

"Bossy bastard." Nick reached around him and took the oil off the table. "This'll have to do for right now because the sight of you bent over my table is too fucking hot. We'll move to the bedroom later." He poured the oil over his cock and trickled some between Julian's ass cheeks.

"Stop talking and fuck me." Julian ground his teeth together. "I'm ready to explode here."

Nick put the thick head of his cock in line with Julian's hole and pushed inside, resting his chest flush up against Julian's back. One large hand held Julian's shoulder, while the other took control of Julian's cock. The roughness of Nick's hand only added to the contact Julian craved, and he surged against the friction, crying out in reckless abandon with the pleasure pain that swamped him.

It took only two or three thrusts of Nick's cock inside him to tip Julian over the edge. His vision blurred and a kaleidoscope of colors burst behind his eyes. Before he collapsed completely, hot streams pulsed out across his fingers and onto Nick's table, and he shouted so loud his ears rang.

"Oh shit, it's so good. So fucking good." Nick drilled deep inside him and came, emptying hot within Julian. He covered Julian with his heavier body and grasped hold of Julian's chin to plant a wet and messy kiss at the edge of Julian's mouth.

Both of them gasped for breath, their bodies shuddering in the aftermath. Nick pressed his face into the curve of Julian neck, the tears on his eyelashes mixing with Julian's sweat. Profoundly moved, Julian held onto Nick's sticky hand and squeezed his fingers tight.

"When we were sixteen and you left me I thought I was going to die. I picked myself up and continued to live, but it wasn't until right now, with you inside me, your taste on my lips that I knew I'm alive."

A harsh breath escaped Nick's lips. "You always were smarter than me. I don't know how to say pretty words. All I can tell you is when I'm with you, it all makes sense. People used to tell me half a life is better than none, but you've made me see everything I've been missing. Loving you has made me whole again."

Julian's one hope was that Nick had broken through the

wall of shame he thought loving a man imprisoned him behind. The two of them alone worked. How he'd feel about being a gay man, out in the open, might be different. Tonight, with Nick still buried inside him and their sweat-slicked bodies plastered together, it was enough for Julian.

Nick withdrew from Julian then and kissed his shoulder. "I'll be right back." He headed toward the bathroom and Julian cleaned up and began to dress. His pants were on but still unzipped when the front door inched open. Julian froze and watched with growing dread as a man with a gun held straight out entered the apartment.

"Hold it right there."

It was Nick's father. They stared at one another, and Julian could see the man's shock at finding a half-naked man in his son's apartment, the unmistakable smell of sweat and sex hanging in the air.

"Uh, hello, Mr. Fletcher, it's Julian Cornell. Remember me?"

The shock was evident in Brian Fletcher's eyes as he looked around the room: at the floor with the clothes littered about and then back at Julian in his disheveled state.

"What the fuck is going on here?"

Chapter Twenty-Two

HAPPINESS WASN'T AN emotion that had ever come easily to Nick. When you lived a lie most of your life, it was hard to dredge up the energy to enjoy your days. The smile reflecting back at him from the bathroom mirror could only be because of Julian. Nick understood now what it meant to have someone in his life whose well-being meant more than his own. Having had everyone concentrate on him and his needs for so many years, Nick wanted to spend some time doing special things for Julian.

Sated and content, Nick slid into his sweatpants, planning a night of loving Julian until the man was incapable of moving from Nick's bed. Sex over a kitchen table was spontaneous and hot, but hell on his back.

Laughing to himself, Nick strode through the living room. "Hey, don't think we're finished for the night . . ." His voice trailed off at the sight of his father standing in the kitchen, holding his fucking gun at his side.

"Dad. What the hell is going on here?"

To give Julian credit, although his face washed out pale, his voice carried strong, without a hint of fear.

"Um, your father wants to know what's going on." The direct gaze from Julian held a world of meaning. Nick knew what Julian wanted. A declaration and validation from Nick to his father. And more than anything Nick wanted to give it to him. But for Nick, the here and now were important. This wasn't a conversation to be held when he and Julian were at the disadvantage of being half dressed.

"What are you doing here, Dad? What made you think you could barge into my home?" Furious at this invasion of privacy, Nick glared daggers at his father.

Finally, his father turned his back on Julian to address Nick. "Your mother and I came home and heard shouting inside here. She was afraid you were having a reoccurrence of those nightmares you used to get, or that you were being robbed." A sneer curled his lip. "It's a good thing I sent her upstairs, so she wouldn't have to witness this." He gestured behind him to Julian and the floor littered with discarded clothes.

For only a moment, shame touched Nick; not at what he and Julian had been doing, but that his mother had to worry about him.

"We're going to have a conversation, but I prefer to do this when we're both fully dressed. We'll come upstairs in a little while." Nick moved next to Julian, who managed a brief smile that failed to reach his eyes.

"You're planning on discussing this with your mother?" His father's voice rose with incredulity. "I don't want him in the house." With a jerk of his chin, his father indicated Julian.

The gauntlet had been thrown at his feet. If his father thought he'd shy away from this, Nick was about to shake up his father's world.

"*He* has a name—Julian. Use it." To his own surprise, he took Julian's hand in his, and he felt no shame in holding a man's hand in front of his father. "And if Julian's not welcome upstairs than neither am I."

Julian squeezed his hand hard. "Can we talk for a moment?" He pointed to the living room. "In there?"

With a curt nod and still holding Julian's hand, Nick turned his back on his father without further word and left the kitchen. Tears threatened to break through his barely-maintained self-control. The one constant in his life, the strength he'd clung to every day, had always been the love and support from his family. Losing it would be a devastating blow.

Julian faced him, concern and tenderness reflected in his beautiful eyes. "Don't do it."

Confused, Nick stared back at Julian. "Huh? Do what?"

Indicating Nick should follow him, Julian sat on the sofa

and waited until Nick settled in next to him. "Don't make our relationship more important than your parents' love and acceptance." He caressed the inside of Nick's wrist with the pad of his thumb, then kissed it.

Julian's lips rested soft and warm against Nick's wrist. "Our love isn't a choice—us against them. I'm perfectly content to wait downstairs and let you have the conversation about you being who you are, keeping it separate and apart from us and what we mean to each other."

"I don't want you to think I'm going to back out now and make excuses. I want you to hear me tell them that I love you."

That smug grin of Julian's resurfaced. "I didn't say I wanted to be left out of that part. I want to hear you say it many times. Everyday in fact." His green eyes grew serious. "We waited a long time for this; I did, at least. Do it the right way so you wind up with everything; your family and me together, not splintered apart."

"And here I thought you were just another pretty face."

Julian laughed, his eyes bright. "I'm not pretty. I believe I've been called 'devastatingly handsome' by at least one fashion blogger."

"It better have been a woman," growled Nick, surprised at his jealousy. The idea of anyone but him touching Julian, or having the same illicit thoughts he did about that smooth body, and wicked, hot mouth brought out murderous intentions Nick had no idea he possessed. "No one puts their hands on you anymore. Only me."

"Go upstairs and talk to your parents. I'm here when you need me." The tips of Julian's fingers ghosted over Nick's cheeks. "I'll always be here. I never left you."

With a heavy sigh, Nick stood. "Yeah, you're right." His footsteps dragged like those of a tired soldier called back to battle. Before he rejoined his father, Nick snagged a tee shirt hanging from the doorknob and slipped it on over his head. No surprise to see his father remained exactly where he'd left him, arms folded now and his jaw clenched so tightly he could crack walnuts with his teeth.

"Let's go see Mom." Nick continued his march toward the door.

"What about him?"

Nick stopped and glared until his father relented. "What about Julian."

"He's staying here for a while, until I call him." His father opened his mouth, and Nick shut him down once again. "Not up for negotiation."

The walk upstairs had the air of a funeral dirge; Nick dreaded what he knew would be so painful for his parents to understand. When he got to the top of the stairs, his mother sprang up from her seat on the sofa and rushed toward him.

"Are you all right? I was so worried and then your father was gone for a while . . ." Her voice petered out when she gazed over Nick's shoulder. "Brian, what's wrong? Nick's fine."

"Mom, let's sit down."

He hated the instant worry that creased her face. "Everything's all right, isn't it? I spoke to Katie and she's on her way over, even though I told her it wasn't necessary."

Fan-fucking-tastic. Then Julian's words filtered through his mind: *"Do it the right way so you wind up with everything; your family and me together, not splintered apart."*

His father went straight for the liquor cabinet. Nick watched him pour a double shot of scotch, the shaking glass a giveaway to his nervousness. Watching his father's apprehension rise, conversely settled Nick somewhat. Nerves he could deal with; irrational hatred and anger he couldn't. Nick loved his father; the man hadn't left his side when Nick was recovering from his injuries. Would that man truly turn his back on his son?

He refused to believe it.

"Can you pour me one too, Dad?"

His father glanced over his shoulder and flashed him a look from sad blue eyes. Nick wanted to reach out, shake him and yell, *"Look at me. I'm the same person you loved this morning; the same man you hugged last night. Why does it matter who I love?"*

But he remained silent, accepting his drink, sitting down with a thump on the club chair.

"Careful. Those old springs could give way at any minute, and you're no lightweight anymore." His mother gazed at him fondly. "You're back to the same Nicholas you were before."

His father choked on his drink, and Nick set his down, untouched, on the end table. "Mom, I came up here with Dad because I need to talk to you." His heart ricocheted in his chest and his mouth dried. Maybe he did need that drink.

"You're scaring me, Nick. You aren't sick are you?" All color drained from her face and her eyes brimmed with tears. "Please. We've only just gotten you back."

"No, Mom, I'm fine, I promise you." He glanced helpless at his father who flexed his jaw muscle, downed his drink, and came to stand by his wife.

"Marilyn, physically, Nick is fine." He slid his arm around her shoulder and led her to the sofa where he sat with her. Unable to sit still, Nick stood, rocking back on his heels.

Confused, her gaze shifted from Nick to his father. "What do you mean physically? Brian, you're scaring me."

Dumbfounded at his father's words, Nick stared at him. "Is that what you think it is, a mental illness?"

"Will someone please stop talking in riddles and clue me in here?"

Nick knelt at her feet and took her hand, his heart jackhammering in his chest. "The reason I've never gotten married or enjoyed being set up on dates with those women you pushed on me, Mom, is that I'm gay. I've always known, but didn't want to admit it, exactly because of the reaction I'm getting from him." He gestured to his father with a jerk of his chin. "But you know I'm still the same person I've always been, the same son you've always loved. Please don't pull away and stop loving me."

Several moments passed and with each beat of his heart, Nick died a little inside.

"When you were born and they handed you to me, all swaddled up with only your perfect little face showing, all I could think of was 'Thank God he's healthy.' You were so beautiful, Nicholas; a beautiful, happy little boy."

Tears fell unchecked down her cheeks. He loved his mother so much and didn't know what he'd do if she turned away from him.

"It's always been my dream to see you married with a wife and children, and now you tell me that isn't going to happen."

"No, Mom, there'll be no wife."

"But you know what's worse for me than you not having a wife and children?" She swiped at her eyes, but the tears still fell. Nick reached out and brushed at the wetness with his own fingers, keeping his fingertips on her cheek.

"What, Mommy?"

Her smile bloomed bright at the childhood endearment he hadn't used in forever. "Not having you at all. You see, I know what it's like to almost lose you. For four days we sat at your bedside, not knowing if you were going to make it. And when the doctors told us you came out of the coma, it was like I gave birth to you all over again."

"Mom." The pain he'd suffered couldn't be any worse than what he'd put his parents through all those years ago. "I'm sorry. I know I'm a disappointment—"

"Who told you that?" Marilyn Fletcher didn't raise her voice often but when she did, only a fool would dare ignore her. Her rage burned bright and fierce as Joan of Arc's heading off into battle. "You are my son. You could never be a disappointment to me. If you think that then I've been a failure as a mother."

"I love you, Mom, and I know it will take getting used to, but I'm the same person I've always been. I was hoping you would be okay with it, even though Dad doesn't accept it."

The withering look his mother shot at his father boded a great deal of unpleasantness to come. "He doesn't? Tell me, Brian, what don't you accept; your son being happy? Would you rather he be miserable?"

Grooves of sorrow deepened on his father's weathered face; in one night his father had become a stranger to Nick instead of the man he'd worshipped all his life. "Of course not. I'm being practical. The boy's a fireman. Do you think anyone's gonna want to work with him, knowing he likes other men? They won't even want to go to the bathroom with him in there." His father had the grace to look supremely uncomfortable, but Nick wasn't about to let it slide.

"I see. So according to your warped logic, every gay man wants every straight man? By that analogy, you should want every woman you see. Should Mom be worried?"

Embarrassment stained his cheeks red, but his father continued his argument. "Don't be ridiculous, you know better than that. Your mother has no reason to ever think I'd look at another woman. I'm not interested in anyone else."

"Then why would a gay man be interested in every man he sees? If I was married, or in a relationship, why would you assume I'd be any less committed to my partner than you are to Mom?"

This time his father's hand held steady as he drank down his scotch and poured himself another, emptying the bottle into his glass. There was no offer to Nick of a refresher for his glass.

"It's not the same."

There was nothing left of the kind and gentle father Nick had toddled after as a child, begging to ride beside him on the fire truck, or help shoot water through the fire hose. Disapproval radiated off Brian Fletcher in almost visible waves; his sad eyes and intractable, stubborn jaw impossible to equate with the loving memories of childhood.

"Is there someone special in your life, Nick?" Curiosity, not condemnation tinged his mother's voice.

Unable to speak for the tightness in his throat, Nick could only nod and hope he didn't cry. That would give his father even more ammunition to throw back in his face. Real men don't cry, after all.

"When can we meet him? If he's special to you, he'll be special to me too."

Nick knew he had to be one of the lucky ones to have been

blessed with a mother who possessed an open and loving heart. For the rest of his life he vowed to make every day Mother's Day for her.

"Are you sure? He's waiting downstairs for me to bring him up here. I wanted him to come with me from the start, but he insisted we talk first as a family and make sure things were okay between us." He swallowed heavily. "Are they? Okay by us I mean." Instinctively his gaze found his father's anguished eyes on his. "Come on, Dad, don't do this."

"All my life I dreamed of having my son follow in my footsteps." The thick emotion in his father's voice rendered his normal gruff tone almost unrecognizable, a quiet whisper in the stillness of the room. "No one was a prouder father when you graduated from the academy and got assigned to your house." He fumbled with his empty glass, then set it down on the side table and ran his hands through his thick head of hair. The silver streaks had become more prominent as of late, and Nick blamed himself for that as well, knowing it was over the worry about his health.

"Before you were injured I thought you'd maybe even make lieutenant or higher. You were that good a fireman, Nick. You're a born leader."

"I haven't changed, Dad. Maybe I can't be the firefighter you thought I'd be, but that doesn't mean I'm not the same man inside. I tried so hard, but the lies to you and mom, not to mention myself were killing me." If he failed to win his father over, Nick wasn't sure he'd have the strength to make his relationship with Julian last. Neither option was acceptable anymore to him. He needed both in his life, standing by his side.

"You keep talking about me being a fireman like that is all that matters. I love the Department, you know that. But that's my job. Being a fireman doesn't define me and who I am."

His dad huffed out a frustrated breath. "I'm getting this all wrong; you know I'm no good with talking." His well-worn, roughened fingers twisted in his lap. "I learned when you were injured that things don't always go according to life's plans. I never looked beyond you being a fireman; I didn't ever think about what you wanted or even thought to ask; it was just the way it was. You were gonna follow in my footsteps."

Witnessing the battle raging inside his father almost broke Nick. He'd already caused his parents so much pain, and this was what he feared. Losing everything he had in his life. Only months before, that life had stretched out before him full of meaningless encounters and lonely nights; a virtual emotional wasteland. Now, it held so much hope and promise, an element of fear hovered over Nick, whispering like a devil, taunting at his happiness. Only Julian had been able to eradicate the devil and the fear with his in-your-face attitude, clever mouth, and loving acceptance. He couldn't give him up, not even for the heartache it caused his father.

"I still look up to you, Dad. You're still the best man I know."

"No, I'm not."

At his father's simple declaration, Nick's stomach clenched tight. Was this really the end? Would he be able to walk out of this house and not see his father again?

"I wanted you to be me. Without any thought as to what you might ever have wanted. They were my dreams. Never yours. Is that being a good father?" A sigh escaped him, and he shook his head. "I don't think so."

Cautious optimism from those words sent adrenaline pumping through his system, but Nick held his nerves in check, not wanting to believe he could be wrong about the way this conversation might be headed.

"It's all you knew, Dad, and you're wrong—I wanted it too. You never forced me into anything. I always wanted to be a firefighter, to be like you—the best. I forgot to say thank you for never letting me fall, catching me, while you taught me to stand on my own. Thank you for giving up your own life to help me with mine all these years after I got injured."

"Don't ever thank me for loving you. It's the easiest job I've ever had."

From the corner of his eye he watched Katie inch her way

into the room to sit beside their mother. Hand in hand, the two women in his family were his lifeline, but Nick wanted it all. He needed his father.

"If that's the case, then the person I am and always was hasn't changed." Nick took his father's hand in his. "You still love me, even though I'm not following what others consider the norm. But it's my normal that matters; a new and different normal. My normal is accepting and open, one that doesn't discriminate or hate. Haven't we seen enough of that already? Shouldn't the normal be love?"

"You always were too smart for me. I'd tell everyone Nick could talk circles around me until I couldn't remember what the original question was."

There may have been four of them in the room, but even the sound of their collective breathing didn't penetrate through the fog of uncertainty in Nick's mind.

"Are we good, Dad? Or are you going to turn me away and make me meet Mom and Katie for dinners and lunches without you?"

Their gazes clashed and Nick held his breath, honestly unsure of his father's decision.

"I don't understand your choice, I'm being honest. I know that's not the correct way to think, but I'm old-fashioned and slow. I don't like change. But I'm not willing to give you up, because you're my son and I love you. So if you can promise to tolerate me getting things wrong sometimes, and know it's an honest mistake, I promise to stand by you."

Both his mother and Katie hugged him, sniffling through their tears. Though he accepted their embrace, he never shifted his focus from his father's face. And at last, what Nick had waited for broke through. A relaxation of the tense lines creasing his father's face; the subtle movement of his lips so that they tipped up in a smile, instead of downward in a frown.

It would be all right, Nick knew, as he returned his father's hesitant smile. It would take plenty of hard work and time, but all things worth fighting for did; he learned that after waking up in the hospital with half the skin on his chest burned off.

"I'll be right back up. Is that okay with you?" Nick walked to the staircase, pausing on the top step.

"Go on, son." The warmth and affection in those three words wrapped their way around Nick's heart. From that moment on, it could only get easier. Why should he give a damn if the people he worked with cared about his sex life? He didn't care about theirs.

Giving his father a thumbs-up sign, Nick headed down the stairs to his apartment. There was a different feeling upon entering, knowing someone was waiting for him. That he wasn't alone and in the dark. The sight of Julian lying stretched out on the sofa, his eyes closed and a slight smile on his face, spelled comfort, home, and love. Careful not to disturb him, Nick made sure to close the door quietly behind him.

"I'm awake."

At the sound of Julian's quiet voice, a need, hot and desperate, rose within Nick to touch Julian and kiss his lips, as if to convince himself it was all real and within his reach. The warm, light scent of Julian's skin filled Nick's senses while he leisurely explored Julian's mouth with his own, their tongues sliding and twisting, hot and slick.

They stayed that way for several moments, enjoying the taste of each other until, with a groan, Julian pulled away. Eyes glazed and slightly unfocused, he backed away when Nick moved close to kiss him once again.

"Stop. You need to tell me what happened up there." A wary expression clouded his face, all traces of desire washed clean. "How did it go?"

The touch of Julian's palm to his cheek warmed Nick through to his heart. If he could be certain of anything, it would be that he must've done something good to deserve a second chance with Julian.

"I'm sorry, Julian."

"For what, baby?"

"For being such a coward all those years ago by sending you

away. For all the wasted years apart when we could have been loving each other. For almost doing it again until you opened my eyes to see that everything is nothing if you aren't by my side, encouraging me, helping me, and loving me."

He framed Julian's face in the palms of his hands. One thing that had never changed was the absolute honesty always present in Julian's eyes. It was there right now, shining and pure, a direct line to Nick's heart.

"And your parents? Things are going to work out with them?"

"Why don't you come upstairs with me and find out?"

Julian's eyes widened, and Nick answered the question hanging in the air between them with a wide smile and a kiss.

"I'm so happy for you," said Julian, pressing short, nibbling kisses along Nick's jaw.

"For us." With reluctance, Nick stood, pulling Julian up along with him. "It's time for me to come out of my closet, but my life won't be complete unless I have you by my side as my partner and lover." He pulled Julian tight to his chest and kissed him. "Ready?"

At Julian's nod, Nick took Julian by the hand, and they walked upstairs.

Chapter Twenty-Three

WALKING BEHIND NICK on that narrow, dimly lit stairway, Julian's nerves kicked in stronger than they ever had before any show or interview he'd ever done in the past. Staring at the flex and bunch of Nick's muscles under his shirt, Julian recalled their stolen afternoons together in high school, and how their desperate kisses and teasing touches had him believing they were in love.

Perhaps it had been the beginning, the uncurling of a blossoming flower, or a newly unfurled leaf, that would have revealed love had it been nurtured and given a chance to grow. Maybe Julian had pushed too hard and too soon; they were kids after all. Had they let their love burn so hot and bright no doubt it would have fizzled out like a used-up Fourth of July sparkler, to lie in smoking ruin at their feet. What the hell had they known about love?

Time heals all wounds, the old saying goes, and Julian didn't necessarily disagree. He'd never considered love to be a wound; yes, his heart had been shredded, but it had a wonderful capacity to knit itself back together. The feelings he had for Nick went beyond love, beyond the physical electricity that sparked between the two of them whenever they were together.

At the top of the stairs, Nick hesitated and glanced over his shoulder to give Julian a wink and a smile. "It's gonna be fine," he whispered. "I love you."

This was "the real." It's what Julian called it when reality was so much more authentic and perfect than anticipated.

Him, Nick, love—the real.

Pressed up against Nick's firm back, Julian inhaled his spicy deep scent. It gave him courage to face what he knew would be the fight of his life—a fight *for* his life; a life he wanted. With Nick.

Had it only been a week or so ago that he sat here and joked with Nick's mother and sister while Nick's father glowered at him from his chair? Who knew he'd be returning now, waiting to receive judgment from a man who Julian knew not only didn't like him, but didn't approve of him. A man who didn't consider Julian a man at all.

And yet Julian couldn't help but hold out hope to one day be a member of this family, maybe even accepted and loved, so he swallowed down whatever misgivings he had and pasted a smile on his face to greet Nick's parents once again. He was good enough; good enough to be part of Nick's life, good enough to keep his business not only afloat, but thriving.

Nick stepped to the side and Julian came to stand at his shoulder. "Hello again, Mrs. Fletcher, Mr. Fletcher." He tipped his head to Nick's father, keeping a neutral expression on his face. "Hi Katie." By the startled intake of breath from Nick's mother and her widened eyes, it became immediately apparent no one had mentioned to her that he was the man in her son's life.

Katie made room for him to sit on the cozy, flowered sofa; however, Julian chose to remain standing, unsure if Mrs. Fletcher would welcome him sitting next to her.

"Well," she said, her gaze flickering between him and her son. "This is a night of surprises." She gestured to the space Katie vacated next to her on the sofa. "I'm not going to bite, Julian. Come sit, and let's talk."

With a comforting squeeze to his shoulder, Nick pushed him forward. "Go on. It'll be fine." A smile rested on Nick's lips, and the laugh lines Julian realized he didn't see often enough fanned out from the corners of his beautiful blue eyes. How had he managed to block this man for all these years, when his very presence now was like water to his dried-up heart?

From his seat in the corner, Nick's father frowned, tense and grim, not offering up a warm greeting like his wife. Julian surmised he'd put up with Nick's gayness if his boyfriend stayed out of the picture as much as possible. After all, as a fashion designer, Julian might as well have GAY written all over his face. Well, fuck it. He'd been out his whole life and never hidden away or kept his life a secret, nor would he allow himself to be shoved in a closet until Papa Bear could come to terms with it.

Struggling against his nature to lash out with a caustic tongue, Julian restrained himself. Anger and arrogance wouldn't help his cause with Nick, nor would it put him in the best light in front of Nick's family. Because the reality check Julian got to his gut when he walked into this home was that if he wanted to make a life with Nick, the goal wasn't to piss these people off, or prove that he was a prick. Rather he had to show them he cared for and about their son by his maturity.

With strong, sure strides, Julian walked over first to Nick's father and stuck out his hand. "Mr. Fletcher. Maybe we can forget our first interaction tonight and start fresh?"

That same blue gaze he loved so much on Nick stared back at him and Julian held his ground, returning the look with a confidence he didn't feel. Julian could only hope that the innate goodness in Nick's father, the core beliefs and strengths that had raised a man as caring as Nick, would come to the forefront, allowing him to have some type of relationship with Nick's father.

The brittle smile on Brian Fletcher's face transformed into one that if not warm and friendly, certainly could be called accepting. "In light of everything, I think that's the best thing." And with that shocking statement, Brian Fletcher grasped Julian's hand. "My family is the most important thing in my life, young man. Like I told Nick, I may not understand, or say and do the right thing all the time, but I'm going to try. First thing is, call me Brian. Mr. Fletcher makes me sound like an old man."

Dumbfounded, Julian nodded, unable to speak, as everyone else in the room exploded with relieved laughter.

"Dad, you've done the impossible. I've yet to see anyone able to make Julian speechless."

It was almost anticlimactic in a way, that the meeting ended up as easy as it did. He and Nick's father—*Brian*—forged a truce around their mutual love for Nick, and Julian respected the man immensely for the way he handled the situation. Minus the gun of course. As shocked as he was by Brian, Julian hadn't noticed Nick's mother standing next to him until she slipped her arm through his.

"Now come with me to the kitchen. That's where we bring family."

Hot tears rushed to his eyes, and he blinked furiously to keep them at bay. The last thing he wanted was to cry like a baby in front of Nick's parents, especially his father, but the thought behind what Nick's mother said to him brought more comfort to his heart than anything anyone else could have done.

Love and acceptance radiated from her softly lined, beautiful face; no hesitancy or shadows dwelled behind her eyes. With his artistic sense quickening, Julian planned to make her a scarf swirled in blues and violets, colors that would perfectly match her slate blue eyes and fair skin. He'd make a tie for Brian in the same pattern.

"Thank you."

They shared a smile, and walked together to the back of the house. Knowing that this was Nick's childhood home, it gave Julian insight as to his upbringing. Julian had never been invited over, and while he understood and never resented it, a piece of who Nick was had remained a mystery.

Until now. The kitchen, obviously remolded since Nick's childhood, boasted a large stainless steel refrigerator and matching dishwasher. The countertops were tiled in pure white, and a parade of red and yellow roosters adorned the tiled backsplash. Matching rooster dishtowels and potholders hung from wooden hooks. Fluffy white curtains hung over the large picture window that Julian envisioned overlooked the backyard.

When Marilyn went to put the coffee on, Julian whispered to Nick, "I see now where you get your obsession with cocks." Lucky for him, no one was within earshot for Nick's murmured response.

"Only yours. Which I intend to have inside me later tonight after we go home to your apartment."

Julian sat down, as he couldn't afford to shock Marilyn with the sight of how hard he'd gotten from that one simple sentence from Nick. Putting on a smile, Julian accepted his coffee from Marilyn, and reached for a cookie from the plate Brian had set before him.

They'd all settled around the table, and Julian imagined this was how Nick and Katie had grown up; an intact family, surrounded by love, with dinner on the table at six, and bedtime hugs and kisses every night.

"Tell us a little something about yourself, Julian. I don't remember your mother or father from any school events."

Marilyn couldn't know her innocuous question sent all of Julian's old insecurities rushing to the surface. He didn't want to explain he had no father, and how his mother had been forced to work late hours to scrape by. She hadn't had time for after-school play dates and chorus, or to see Julian's art work at a school exhibit. Before he could respond, Nick's hand slid on top of his thigh, resting there as a comforting weight, and a reminder he was loved.

"I never knew my father. My mother worked to support us since he left before I was born. She couldn't get time off to come to school; she was always afraid she'd lose her job. I transferred in junior year of high school, and she died right before my graduation. I went to FIT, took some college courses, then on to Europe to study. Then 9/11 hit."

Nick's hand tensed on Julian's leg, and now he was the one to offer a reassuring touch. Julian placed his hand on top of Nick's, entwining their fingers, both of them needing the connection.

"I wanted to come home. I called you," Julian said to Nick. "I checked on everyone I knew still left here. I tried this number for four days but no one answered, so I figured you had moved."

No one said a word. The muffled sound of a car passing by the house filtered through, then silence dominated once again.

"After Nick was injured we both stayed in the hospital.

Marilyn refused to leave until he woke up, and I wouldn't leave either one of them." Brian's haunted gaze stared unseeing at the wooden table. "It took four days before he came to, and another day until he recognized us." Marilyn took her husband's hand and held it tight. "My family means everything to me. So we wouldn't leave him until we were certain Nick knew who we were, and that we were coming back to him."

The strength of Nick's family astounded Julian, bringing with it more clarity as to what happens when the cameras leave and the news stories fade away. "I can't imagine what you must've gone through."

"I couldn't work in the firehouse anymore; I had nightmares, and the stress was off the charts. I took three years off, but after more therapy than I will ever admit to, I had to go back to work." With each word, Nick's voice grew stronger, the passion for life and his job evident to Julian. "I asked to be put back on active duty, but the department felt I'd best help doing training and tactical."

"But you miss it? The firehouse?"

"Julian—" Marilyn spoke, but surprisingly Nick cut her off.

"No, Mom, you've pussyfooted around this since my accident. Of course I miss it. Every God damn day. I miss my guys and the whole camaraderie of the house in general." Nick's voice caught in his throat, the words lost in a shuddering sob.

Fuck. He hadn't meant to dredge up this shit storm for Nick to deal with. Oblivious to everything except Nick's pain, Julian didn't think twice about putting his arms around the man he loved and holding him. Even if it was in front of Nick's family. "It's all right, baby," he murmured, rubbing Nick's back. "You're strong now. You beat it."

Several minutes passed, and when Julian let go of Nick he froze, the extraordinary realization that he'd hugged Nick in front of his family—his father, no less—sending shooting threads of nerves up his spine. Julian mentally prepared to be if not sneered at, then at least given a lecture on how the family wasn't yet up to dealing with such overt public displays of affection.

There was none of that to his amazement. Instead, Marilyn's face glowed with approval. Katie he had no worries about; she already was like a sister to him. Focusing on Brian—the man cocked his brow and gave him a smile Julian could only think of as quizzical.

"Did you think I was gonna be upset that you touched him in front of me? You look like a guy who stands up for what he believes in, and you say you believe in my son. All the talk in the world is just that, talk. I need to see it for myself before I believe it."

Julian hardly registered Nick's broad shoulder pressing up against him, or that their fingers remained laced together in his lap, so completely was his attention focused on Brian.

"You proved that you didn't give a damn what any of us thought and your only concern is Nick. Just like my only concern is my wife and my kids."

Before Nick had burst back into his life, Julian hadn't ever thought of a family or a forever. But sitting here now in this warm kitchen, surrounded by years of home-cooked memories and so much love and devotion that to anyone else it might seem smothering, Julian found his heart.

"I've loved Nick for as long as I can remember, and no matter how hard I tried to forget him, it didn't work, something pulled me back. Deep down inside, I think I was always coming back for him."

"Oh, Julian," sniffed Marilyn. She got out of her chair and without any reservation, slipped her arms around his neck and kissed his cheek. "I know I can't replace your mother, but if ever you need me, I'm more than happy to be a stand-in."

He will not cry. *No, no, fuck it, not going to happen.*

"Thank you," he whispered, unwilling to trust his voice.

"Tell me, Nick, are you planning on telling them at the department?"

That was a mood-killer. Julian suspected Brian Fletcher wasn't a man who discussed his "feelings," and likely wanted all the practical discussions of his son's new-found sexuality dealt with as quickly and smoothly as possible. Unfortunately for him, Julian knew it wouldn't happen so neat and clean; this was far from a perfect world they lived in, and God knows the men Nick worked with were far from being allies or even receptive to homosexuals.

"I filed a report against Jensen; he could've had Barton seriously hurt with that crap he pulled today. That man is a disgrace to the department."

"Just be careful, son. I've known that man for years; he hasn't been the same since he lost his son in the Towers."

Nick pushed back from his chair to pour himself another cup of coffee, and brought the pot back with him to freshen everyone else's cups. "It doesn't give him the right to bully others. He's gone too far this time, and he has to be stopped."

They finished their coffees in silence and despite the caffeine, Julian yawned. A quick glance at his watch startled him; it was almost midnight. With regret, he stood and brought his coffee cup to the sink.

"I'm sorry, but I have to head back home. I have some meetings scheduled for tomorrow that I haven't had time to prepare for yet."

After he kissed Katie good-night and promised her to let Melanie know she'd text her about dinner, Nick's parents walked him back to the living room. They reached the front door, and after Marilyn kissed him good-night and Brian shook his hand, Julian assumed Nick would remain with his parents, although he wished Nick would come downstairs for a more private goodbye.

"I'll speak to you guys tomorrow."

Staring at Nick in surprise, Julian couldn't hold back an amused smile. "Coming downstairs with me? I can find my way."

"I think we need to talk a little as well."

Chapter Twenty-Four

WITH JULIAN'S HAND firmly in his grasp, Nick walked down the stairs back to his apartment. The evening had been a success; a miracle. His mother's easy acceptance had been somewhat of a surprise, although he never thought she'd turn her back on him.

Seeing his father with Julian, knowing that the two most important men in his life put aside their wariness and differences and forged a tentative connection over their shared love for him nearly broke Nick. In all the scenarios he'd played over in his mind he'd never anticipated this result, and he knew the deep bond his parents had instilled in him and Katie had resulted in their family remaining not only intact, but stronger for having included a man like Julian.

"I hate to leave you, but I have to go home and do some work. I have investor meetings tomorrow and—"

Nick cut Julian off with a kiss that turned passionate so quickly he'd better stop or he'd be on his knees in his parents' stairwell. That thought alone proved to be enough of a lust killer to get his brain back in gear again. "I want to go home with you. I can pack my stuff for tomorrow and leave from your apartment."

Julian's eyes glowed with happiness. "I'd like that," he breathed, sliding his arms around Nick's neck. "I like waking up with you in the morning. And," he said with a wink and a grin, "getting to see you all dressed up in your uniform? Major hotness."

"You're insane." But Nick made certain not to forget any of his training gear as he quickly packed his bag once they reentered his apartment. Within ten minutes they were in his car and on the highway heading back to the city.

Julian relaxed in the seat next to him, staring out of the window into the blackness of the night. "I never expected what happened tonight to go the way it did, you know. I thought your mom would eventually come around, act a little skittish when she saw me, but we'd be cordial and somewhat friendly. But your father?" His fingers drummed on his thighs. "That was crazy."

"Yeah." A smile broke across Nick's face. "I was kinda shocked at how you two got along once it was in his face."

"He's a pretty amazing guy. I see where you get your devotion to family from, and it's inspiring."

Nick took his hand off the wheel to take Julian's. "You want to know what's inspiring?"

"My cock?" Julian spread his thighs, giving Nick a side-eye view of the thick bulge in his pants. Deliberately teasing, Julian cupped his crotch and rubbed. "Cause I have to tell you, I've been hard as a rock for you since we left your apartment, and as soon as you stop driving like a grandmother and get to my place, I'm going to jump your ass."

It might have been a record, but Nick made it from the exit off the bridge to Julian's loft in eight minutes flat. Of course he skirted quite a few yellow and red lights along the way, but Nick didn't plan on wasting valuable time looking for a spot. He pulled into a 24-hour garage, threw them the keys, then he and Julian walked the few short blocks to Julian's apartment in anticipatory silence.

The banging and lurch of the large elevator didn't bother him any longer, and Nick made a mental note to tell Dr. Landau in their therapy session. He wondered if Julian would want to come with him. Julian slid open the door, and they hurried into the apartment. Nick tossed his overnight bag on the sofa and grabbed Julian by the arm, yanking him up against his chest. Funny how having Julian pressed up tight and snug enough to interlock their muscle and bone structures no longer bothered him. Nick needed the feel of this man.

"Come take a shower with me. I never got to take one after

this afternoon, and I want you wet and dripping when I'm sliding inside you." Julian smiled and began stripping off his clothes.

Heart racing with excitement, Nick slipped out of his sweatpants and pulled his sweatshirt over his head. A move that to everyone else was second nature, but to Nick indicated how far he'd come that he didn't think twice now about standing naked before Julian. Instead he reveled in the intensity of Julian's hungry emerald gaze as it raked over his body, its focus resting on his rapidly stiffening cock.

Forcing himself to walk away in a nonchalant manner, Nick headed for the bathroom, a smile residing on his lips. Never in his wildest dreams did he imagine he'd live a life of normalcy; in love, with his secret revealed, and his family rallying behind him and Julian. He chased away the thought of telling the people at work, for the time being, when Julian came right up behind him, already naked and very, very warm to the touch.

"I don't know what I like better, the front of you all hard, or the sight of your sweet round ass walking away."

Nick reached behind him, bringing Julian's hand to his stiff dick. "You can have both if you're good." He shivered, Julian nipping his earlobe while giving the head of his cock a wicked little twist. Nick couldn't hold back the groan of pure desire that burst from his lips. The slow steady ache of arousal pulsed upward from Nick's groin through his chest, while Julian's fingers continued to torment his cock.

"Are you sure you want me good?" Another wicked twist, and Julian nuzzled Nick's neck, the rasp of his stubble abrading the skin along his collarbone. He nipped at Nick's collarbone, then his tongue licked the spot, its wet heat lessening the sting. "I'm better when I'm evil."

Nick knew Julian's teeth would leave a mark on his skin and didn't give a damn. He loved the different sides to Julian; the suavely sleek businessman in his perfectly tailored suits made an appearance in public, only to be replaced by the darkly decadent lover in private, possessing the most wicked mouth Nick had ever been blessed to have tasted.

"Mmm. I don't care, as long as you keep doing what you're doing. Good, evil; I only know if you stop, I may have to kill you."

Julian laughed and backed him into the shower stall. He turned on the jets and warm water spilled over them. The steamy heat only added to the pleasurable haze surrounding them, and Nick found himself sagging into Julian's arms.

"Come sit down."

Nick allowed Julian to lead him over to the catty-cornered built-in bench. Julian had certainly thought of everything, including the most wonderful smelling body wash which he poured over Nick's body, slicking it into a rainbow of soapy bubbles. The misty heat combined with the slippery sounds of the body wash sent Nick into a fever pitch of arousal. His eyes widened when Julian dropped a thick towel on the floor and sank to his knees.

"Spread your legs."

Julian's mouth was still inches from Nick's cock, yet Nick could almost feel the imprint of those lips around the crown. The blood rushed to his groin; in all his life Nick had never been as turned on as at this moment. A dripping wet Julian, full mouth open and green eyes fierce with passion, stirred up a primal need so raw within Nick, he teetered on the brink of orgasm, and had yet to be touched. He opened his legs wide.

"Fuck it, suck me already."

Julian needed no further invitation, and Nick bit back a cry at the first touch of Julian's lips sliding down his cock. Nick knew it wouldn't take long, not with Julian's soapy-slick hands rolling his balls, while his mouth and tongue played havoc with Nick's cock.

He dug his fingers into Julian's wet hair, twisting his fingers around the strands, and thrust his cock into Julian's mouth. He needn't have worried if Julian could take his length; from the encouraging noises he made, Julian was a more than willing participant.

"Fuck, yesss," Nick hissed.

Julian squeezed Nick's balls, at the same time scraping his teeth gently over the ridge running down the length of Nick's cock, and Nick was lost. His hands gripped the edge of the marble bench and his ass clenched tight as he pumped hot and hard into Julian's mouth. Spots danced in front of his eyes and his breath stuttered in his chest as he shattered, completely undone.

"Julian." Nick's voice trembled on a sigh. It took him several moments to regain his wits and open his eyes. Julian sat back on his heels, a self-satisfied smirk on his face. He brushed a hank of wet hair off his face and pushed himself up from his crouched position.

"So was that good, or evil?" Julian's amused voice penetrated the fog still hovering in Nick's head. Julian took Nick's hand and placed it on his own erection, their hands sliding together as they stroked him to a shuddering completion. Like a happy drunk, Julian's head fell forward onto Nick's shoulder, his fingers digging into the meat of Nick's biceps.

"Good." Nick kissed Julian's drenched head. "So very, very good."

MORNING CAME TOO quickly for Nick; his brain registered a large bed and a warm body snuggled up against his; no matter the time, he couldn't bring himself to move and start the day. Had it been up to him, he'd have stayed where he was, face-planted in Julian's down pillows, under luxurious, thousand-count sheets. They'd only fallen asleep when their bodies became so sated and limp from their love-making, it was impossible to move.

"Nick."

Julian's lips moved against his back and Nick shivered.

"Nick, are you awake?"

"Mmph." Nick really didn't want to get up, but given the heavy thickness prodding him in his back, there might be a future benefit to his waking.

"I have meetings later today, but I have to meet the guys for breakfast. They're going to invest in the business, and I told them I'd give them an update before I meet some of the other investors that my friend Helena put me in touch with." Julian kissed his shoulder, tracing his spine with flicks of his tongue.

His own cock full and aching, Nick rolled over to face Julian, and captured his face in the palms of his hands. With his tousled hair and heavy-lidded, sleepy eyes, Julian was a gorgeous sight to wake up to, and Nick was in no mood to have a conversation. He could think of a much better use for Julian's talented tongue.

"You can be late." He crushed his mouth over Julian's, sliding his tongue inside to tangle with Julian's. They rocked their pelvises together, their hard shafts sliding against each other. The friction created a pleasurable drag, heightened even more when Nick reached between them to collect some of the fluids leaking from their tips to spread around his palm, before grasping both their cocks in his hand. With Julian gasping hotly in his ear, Nick stroked them both to a mind-numbing release.

They lay cocooned together under the comforter, Nick stretching, relishing the sight of Julian lying next to him, as blissed out as he felt.

"What I was saying before you so rudely interrupted to use me for your sexual pleasure," Julian said, his eyes remaining closed but with a smile on his lips, "was that I have to meet the guys, but I want you to come with me." He opened his eyes then, and turned his head on the pillow to catch Nick's gaze. "They need to meet the man in my life, and I want you to get to know them as well."

It would be the first time out as a couple for them and immediately Nick tensed, hating that he did, but knowing it would take more than the support of his family for him to be at ease in public with his new status. Perhaps sensing his hesitation, Julian sighed and got out of bed.

"It's all right. It was only an idea." He headed toward the bathroom, and Nick remained in bed, ashamed by his cowardice, and wondered what he was really afraid of.

By the time Julian returned, fresh from the shower and dressed in a suit, Nick had made up his mind.

"I'm going with you. I have a simulated burn today in Brooklyn, but not until the afternoon, so I don't need to prep before 11:00." He cupped the back of Julian's neck and drew him close to kiss him, but Julian pulled back and met his gaze with an unusually sober regard.

"I'm not trying to force you. If you aren't ready, tell me. I have no desire to bully you into doing things you aren't comfortable with."

"It's not that." Nick dropped his hand and raked it through his hair. "I'm not ashamed of us and being with you. I love you. It's taken me half my life to get to this point."

"Then what?" Julian's brow furrowed in confusion, but his eyes never left Nick's face. "I must be missing something."

"It's me; I've spent my whole life in the closet. Give me a little time to work my head around all of this. But none of it means I don't want to be with you, or that I'm ashamed of you, all right?"

But even though Julian agreed, Nick could see the shadow of doubt in his eyes.

Chapter Twenty-Five

HE HADN'T BOTHERED to tell the guys ahead of time he was bringing Nick. Julian figured it would give less chance for Marcus to think about some shenanigans to play on him and Nick, however good-natured it might be. What he didn't expect was Marcus's sullen attitude, but Julian chose to ignore him rather than engage. Marcus never had a problem revealing his feelings, so Julian was certain he'd get an earful of whatever was bothering his friend when Marcus was ready.

"Zach, do you remember Nick?" With a lift in his heart, Julian watched as his lover and one of his best friends shook hands, before they took their seats at the usual corner booth. Within moments the waiter appeared, and he and Nick ordered their coffees and accepted the menus.

"Sure. We met briefly at Sparks the night of your show." Zach's sweet smile lightened his normally quiet expression. "I don't know if you remember me though."

That was Zach, always self-deprecating. Before Nick had a chance to respond, Marcus cut in.

"Why would he? He ran like a bat out of hell at the end of the night if I recall."

Zach flushed and sat back in his chair, retreating as usual, rather than answering Marcus. Julian had no problem butting heads with Marcus and his anger rose over Marcus's brush-off.

"Something crawl up your ass and die?" The waiter approached and he ordered his eggs and waited for Nick to finish ordering before directing his attention back to Marcus. "What's gotten into you?"

"What, or should I say who's gotten into *you*?" Marcus countered. "Or do we even need to guess, Juli?"

Nick flushed, but Julian had no intention of holding back their relationship from his friends. If he and Nick were to be together, Nick would have to get used to his friends, like Julian had to put up with Nick's parents. These men were Julian's family.

"Nick and I are together. We've worked through some unresolved issues from our past, but we're in a good place now."

"That's wonderful. I'm happy for you two. I know you both have a history together. There's nothing like giving love a chance all over again." Zach's genuine delight kindled a warm glow of happiness in Julian that unfortunately, Marcus's cold eyes put a chilling effect on.

"So are you playing at being gay, or did you finally open your closet door?" The sneer in Marcus's voice rankled Julian. What the hell was going on? Marcus didn't have to love, like, or even approve of Nick, but what he did have to be was respectful.

"Marc, what's wrong with you? Nick's been through enough. He doesn't need your bullshit."

"I can handle myself." Nick braced his elbows on the table, lacing his fingers under his chin. "You think I'm gonna hurt him, right? That I'm gonna run if it gets too tough."

"Yeah, I do." Marcus ignored everyone, concentrating only on Nick. "I've known guys like you before. Too many."

"Well, I'll tell you. I've spent my whole damn life running. At the end I've gotten nowhere—I'm in the same place, and I'm still alone. I've finally stopped long enough to figure out what and who I want." He picked up Julian's hand and squeezed it hard. "This man. I disappointed him and hurt him, so yeah, you have a right to be leery of me. But I promise you that I'm going to make it up to him and love him. He fucking owns me."

Surprise flickered over Marcus's face, along with another emotion that if Julian didn't know his best friend so well, he'd swear might be envy. Julian dismissed that thought as foolish, since Marcus Feldman was the last person to think about being in a monogamous relationship. For God's sake, the man bought into a condom company because he wanted to make sure he always had a fresh supply.

Was that a symbol of a man who wanted a relationship?

Unable to talk and unsure how Nick would take receiving a kiss from him in public, Julian placed a discreet hand under the table and squeezed his lover's powerful thigh. No one had ever said how much they loved him and in such a forceful manner. Desire shot through Julian, knowing Nick wanted him so much.

He cleared his throat before speaking. "None of us ever lets everything out. We always keep a piece inside that's just for us. Nick was that piece of me I held the closest. Maybe that's why it was impossible for me to let him go."

"Jesus, the level of sweet is enough to give a man diabetes."

The laughter in Marcus's eyes signaled to Julian that things would be okay between them.

"Oh, fuck off. I'm trying to be deep and bare my soul to you, and this is what I get?" Julian tossed a sugar packet at Marcus who flicked it at Zach.

"Hey." Zach blew his straw wrapper back at Marcus, and they all began laughing, Nick included. When they reverted to acting like teenagers was when Julian knew everything would be right in his world.

Julian caught Nick's bemused glance at their antics and shrugged. "Since I got back from Europe, we make sure to meet for breakfast once a week either in the city or in Brooklyn. The three of us never let work interfere with our friendship, so get used to it, since you'll be coming with me when you can."

"It worked out well for me today, since my training is across the street in the park." Nick lounged back in his seat, his arm draped across the back of the booth behind Julian.

"Oh, does that mean hot firemen available for the looking?" Marcus sipped his coffee and finished off the last of his omelet. "Maybe I'll become short of breath, and they'll need to give me mouth to mouth."

Nick's eyes danced with evil glee. "I'll make sure to send Big Frank to help you then."

"Big Frank?" Marcus's eyes lit up. "Ahh, sounds like my kind of guy. Details, man. What are we talking about here?"

"Oh, he's around fifty-five, about 5'8" and 350 pounds. A real sweetheart of a guy. You'll love him."

Coffee sputtered out of Marcus's mouth, while Zach howled with laughter.

Julian listened to the back and forth, good-natured teasing between the two men, and nudged Nick's foot with his own. At Nick's raised brow, Julian winked and squeezed his thigh again.

"Thank you," he whispered so only Nick could hear. "This means more to me than anything."

"I know." Nick pressed his thigh hard against Julian's. "That's why it means so much to me too."

They finished off their food in relative silence, and Julian let his eggs get cold answering texts from several sponsors who, to his growing excitement, not only agreed to allow him to use the team logos, but wanted to know how they could help with either tickets for events to the families, or sponsoring other fundraisers. Unable to keep the news to himself, he shared it with the guys and as usual, Marcus the businessman took the idea and ran with it.

"Let's do a massive holiday fundraiser at Sparks; a Winter Wonderland theme. All the NY sports teams can join in, and I'll get my liquor distributors to contribute as well." He tapped his chin, and Julian as always marveled at his friend's business acumen. Who knew beneath that heart-stopping smile that got almost any man in his bed, there was a brain that rivaled any Wall Street mogul?

"Plus, you can get the kids from the center to model the prototypes—you should have quite a few by that point, and we'll invite not only industry people from the medical field, but those fuckers who pretended to be your friends while circling you like the vultures they are, ready to pick the bones of your company."

"Marcus, you are absolutely amazing." The respect he had for his friend grew exponentially with each idea he tossed out. "I love each and every idea, and I know the kids are excited about modeling." Julian turned to address Nick. "Yesterday I told Jamal I wanted him to model, and I thought he'd jump out of the bed he got so excited."

"Sometimes out of the worst experiences, people find the best in themselves." Nick pulled him close and hugged him, unashamed to show his affection in this public place.

"Oh for Christ's sake. Is this what I have to look forward to from now on?" Marcus rolled his eyes and nudged Zach. "Warn me if they're going to start kissing and say 'I love you.' I may become violently ill."

Zach shrugged. "I think it's wonderful that Julian and Nick have come together after all these years. It's like a movie."

"That's 'cause you watch too much of that crap on Lifetime with your mother. You need to watch some good old-fashioned raunchy porn with me."

Zach turned beet red and mumbled something into his coffee cup that sounded like "I do all right." He kept his gaze trained on his plate and ate the rest of his meal methodically, in quick, precise bites. Julian watched him thoughtfully, and not for the first time wondered what his friend did after leaving their weekly breakfasts. Zach was so super secretive about his life and even his job.

Nick whispered in his ear, "I gotta go to work, babe."

Nick slid out of the booth and said goodbye to everyone, promising Marcus and Zach to bring them FNDY shirts and caps the next time he saw them. Julian walked him outside.

"So what's the plan? Are you going to speak to that guy Jensen and tell him to shove it up his ass?" Personally, if it were up to him, Julian would walk up to the man and call him out in front of the whole group. Nick, however, wasn't as comfortable in his skin to be so forthright.

Nick shifted on his feet. "I'd rather play it by ear, see how it goes today."

Perhaps Julian's eyes reflected the skepticism he held back, for Nick found the need to defend himself. "I need to talk to Adam Barton first." He blew out a breath. "I feel like I owe the man an explanation, separate from me confronting Jensen."

That made sense. Julian's hope was that Nick wouldn't

chicken out when confronted with Jensen's ugly mouth and prejudices. "I'm not going to pressure you to do anything you feel uncomfortable with. All you need to know is that I'm behind you, one hundred percent, all the way."

Watching Nick walk away to the park across the street, Julian wasn't sure what Nick would do. What Julian did know was he wouldn't let Nick go again without a fight.

Chapter Twenty-Six

WALKING UP TO the park, Nick ran through different conversations in his mind as to how he planned to approach Adam Barton. Nick fully anticipated the man to view him with some hostility, yet he held out hope that Barton would at least listen to him and his explanation.

He'd deliberately arrived early for his shift; Nick had hoped to find him in the locker room, but there was no sign of him, nor did he find him in the lounge. He did find Jensen and several of his lackeys, hanging around, drinking coffee, and watching the television mounted up on the wall.

"Feeling better today, Nicky?" The smirk curling Jensen's lips belied any real concern he might have had for Nick's actual welfare.

"I wasn't the one with the problem. Back off from me, Jensen. I'm not in the mood." Cold air blew in from the opened front door, and Nick scanned the group of people who'd walked in. Spotting Barton with his friend Gentry, who Nick remembered from the incident in the locker room, he hurried away from Jensen and his group without bothering to say anything further.

Once he'd reached Barton, Nick faltered a bit, unsure how to start this conversation. Barton, however, solved that problem easily enough.

"Excuse me, Fletcher, I have to get changed." Without a backward look, he walked away from Nick and headed to the locker room. Nick started after him, only stopping when he felt a restraining hand on his arm. Gentry stood scowling by his side.

"Leave him alone. He's had enough to deal with in his life, and your interference isn't helping any."

"I'm only—"

"Yeah, yeah," said Gentry, folding his arms and glaring at Nick. Gentry's firehouse was out in Queens, and Nick hadn't had much interaction with him this training schedule. They were around the same age, although Gentry looked younger. He hadn't been with the department as long as Nick, coming on about five years earlier. With his sandy-blond hair, freckled face, and wide blue eyes, he looked better suited to working in a cornfield than on an engine, but from what he'd heard, the man had a good work ethic and was calm and steady in the field.

"I know what you're gonna say. You're only trying to help him. Everything's gonna be fine." A bitter laugh escaped him. "Blah fucking blah. Cut the bullshit, please."

"It isn't bullshit, and you have no idea what I'm going to say to him, so I'll thank you to keep out of my business." Nick pushed past Gentry and headed toward the locker room. Barton had already changed into his training uniform and was arranging his bag when he looked up and met Nick's eyes. It hurt Nick to see a wall of anger and hurt shutter down over the man's face, knowing it was caused by Nick's own cowardice.

Not anymore. Bring it on.

Funny how after a lifetime of hiding, it could suddenly be so very freeing to let go and tell the truth.

"Can we talk, please? Or," he said hastily, watching Barton's mouth tighten to a thin white line, "if you're not interested in talking, will you at least listen to me?"

Barton's gaze clashed with his, and Nick breathed a sigh of relief at the quick nod of acquiescence from the younger man. Nick sat at the end of the bench and gathered his thoughts, piecing together how he wanted the conversation to go. Barton raised a brow.

"Second thoughts?"

"Look," Nick began, rubbing the top of his head with his hand in a nervous gesture. "I'm not good at this stuff."

"Stuff?"

"Talking about personal things. I've had enough therapy in my life and spent enough time having my head shrunk that you would think it would be easy by now, but it isn't." He took a deep breath and stared Barton straight in his eyes. "Especially when it comes to who I am, and how I've been hiding things, from myself even, for almost my whole life."

Barton, however, wasn't going to make it easy on Nick. From the flare of interest in his eyes, it seemed Barton knew what Nick was saying without Nick having to come out, so to speak, and say it in exact words.

That was a coward's way to handle it, and he was no fucking coward. Accepting his right to have survived and be alive had taken Nick years of therapy to figure out in his head. God only knew he was still a work in progress. But loving Julian and receiving his love back in return had filled in all the remaining pieces of Nick's fractured life.

"What are you trying to tell me?" Barton stood and zipped up his bag. "I don't have all morning, and I don't want to be late for training and get called out for that."

"Barton—Adam. I'm not going to let anyone bully you anymore. Being gay doesn't give anyone the right to harass or intimidate us. Right?"

Barton's eyes widened at Nick's choice of words. "So you're finally willing to admit it out loud?"

Nick rubbed his chin and slanted Barton a rueful glance. "I have to hand it to you, you won't back off until I come right out and say it. Yeah, I'm gay. I've spent my whole life hiding it from my friends, family, and myself even."

"You must've been very lonely." Adam sat back down on the bench and put his training bag on the floor. "I came out in high school, but my parents were cool about it."

"I hurt someone very special to me in high school because I was too afraid to admit who I was." Nick stood and jammed his hands into his pockets. After all these years, his stomach still turned at the disbelief on Julian's face from the betrayal. "After he left, nothing mattered to me anymore. I thought I could fake it with a woman and eventually get married, but after 9/11, everything got so fucked up." He shrugged, not willing to let those memories suck him under anymore. He had Julian now, and his family was intact. As far as Nick was concerned, he'd conquered the world.

"It's not that easy, is it? For a while things were okay here, but now with Jensen, he's making it impossible."

Damned if he'd let that bastard run people out of the department. Nick didn't care what his father said; losing someone didn't give Jensen the right to make other people miserable, or put their lives at risk. The man needed serious help, but right now, Nick needed him off his and Adam Barton's back.

"Don't you worry about him," assured Nick. "I'll take care of Jensen."

"You will, huh?" Jensen stepped inside the locker room, his ever-present entourage behind him.

"I'm sorry for your loss, Jensen, but it doesn't give you the right to bully Barton. Or myself." Nick planted himself in front of Jensen and looked him straight in the eye without flinching.

That foxy gleam entered Jensen's eyes. "So I was right."

Nick shrugged. "About what, that I'm gay? Yeah, so what? You're straight. Doesn't matter to me who you sleep with as long as you do your job."

Barton and now Gentry stood beside him. Nick searched the crowd and saw Carlos watching him through narrowed eyes, and his heart sank. For some reason he'd thought Carlos would have his back.

"It matters to me. I don't want to work with someone who wants to suck my dick."

Despite the gravity of the situation, Nick burst out laughing. "Are you fucking crazy? You think all gay men want you? You're not my type." Still laughing, Nick turned around to head to his locker, when Jensen grabbed his shoulder.

"Don't walk away from me; I'm not finished with you yet. Maybe you took a knock in the head all those years ago and it made you think something stupid. Whatever it is, I ain't working with a faggot."

"Jensen, man, that's cold. Leave Nick alone; no one has a

problem with him."

Finally. Carlos met his eyes and nodded.

Disbelief tinged Jensen's words. "No one has a problem? I have a fucking problem."

"Screw you then. That's your issue." Nick fiddled with his locker and opened the door. Without warning a shout rang out; he glanced back to see what the commotion was, and his head snapped back, hitting the locker. Pain radiated up his jaw as he slumped to the ground.

"Fuck." Blinking hard, he shook his head in an attempt to clear the ringing in his ears and his vision. When he opened his eyes, Jensen stood over him, hands on his hips and a sneer on his lips.

"Get up, pussy."

Carlos stepped in between them, even as Nick struggled to stand with the help of Gentry and Barton.

"Don't do it man. Don't throw away your whole career over bullshit. Leave Nick alone."

"It isn't right. It shoulda been him, not my Tommy." Jensen cried out, his fists clenched. "My son lies dead and they're—he's . . . Tommy didn't deserve to die. He was gonna get married. Now I've got nothing."

Nick stared at Jensen in horror as the man pounded on the lockers, then collapsed on the wooden bench. Where only seconds before Jensen had seemed in complete control, Nick knew from experience the man was a hair's breadth away from a total breakdown.

"Get the lieutenant," he whispered to Barton who seemed dumbfounded by the events. "And tell him to have a doctor available."

That woke Barton up from his trance. "What? Why?" He glanced over his shoulder at the broken man slumped on the bench. "Fuck him. You heard what he said? That he wished it was you and not his son? How can you even think of helping him?"

"How can I not?" An ineffable wave of sadness swept

through Nick. How much pain had Jensen kept inside since Tommy's death? He knew Tommy Jensen well; they'd come up through the academy together. He knew the man was supposed to get married; his girlfriend had only found out she was pregnant right before he was killed. The news of Tommy's death had been too much for her to bear, and she'd miscarried not long after.

Jensen lost not only his only son, but his only chance at a grandchild as well, since Tommy had no siblings. He couldn't imagine heartache like that. Nick knew about pain; the bone deep, soaked to the skin, and beyond everything imaginable pain that eviscerates you from even the tiniest of movements until even breathing hurts so badly you think about holding your breath for forever. Anything to stop the pain.

"I knew his son, but I didn't know Jensen still had trouble dealing with his loss." Knowing the man, he was probably too proud to go for counseling through the department. "Had I known, I might've handled all of this differently."

"Okay." Barton glanced over at Jensen. "I'll go get the lieutenant."

Nick didn't even realize he was bleeding until Gentry came over to him with a wet washcloth. "For your face," Gentry indicated and held it out.

He took it and after he touched it to his swollen lips, looked and saw the blood. With the pads of his fingertips he gingerly touched the side of his jaw and his mouth, the puffiness evidence of where Jensen's fist had landed. Lucky for him, no teeth had been knocked loose, but Nick knew he'd have a hell of a black and blue mark by tonight.

It only took a few minutes before Barton returned with Lieutenant Delany, and Nick didn't relish the thought of explaining the fight and what led up to it.

"Fletcher."

"Yes, sir." Nick set the washcloth down and approached his lieutenant, coming to stand before him. In his early sixties, Delany boasted a head full of black hair and sharp blue eyes, and Nick knew him to be straight-forward and to the point.

"Explain what the hell is going on here."

"Jensen and I had a disagreement." He bent closer to Delany. "I think he needs counseling, sir. He's pretty close to losing it."

Delany turned his attention to the bench where Jensen sat, and Nick watched Jensen pull himself together under his lieutenant's probing gaze. To his shock, the man stood and walked over to them.

"I apologize for hitting you, Fletcher." No other apology seemed forthcoming, and in spite of his earlier words Nick grew angry. No one had the right, no matter what happened in their lives, to call him names and hit him.

"Is that all? You try to break my jaw, call me a faggot, and think it's going to get swept under the rug?"

Delany threw him an unreadable look, then returned his focus to Jensen. "Is what Nick said correct?"

Jensen hesitated, and Delany took the opportunity to interject.

"There's a room full of witnesses. Don't lie, or it will go even worse for you."

"I had my reasons, Lieutenant. I can't work with him. Come on, Eddie." He gave Delany a grin, like they were two buddies sharing a beer. "We go way back. You wouldn't want to work with no faggot neither."

Delany grinned back at Jensen, and Nick's heart fell.

"You're right, Stan. We do go back a long way. But that's where it ends. Want to know why?" The grin faded from Delany's lips, and they tightened to a thin, hard slash in his face. "Because my brother is gay; he was afraid his whole God damn life to tell anyone, and waited until he was fifty-one years old to say it to his family. Now he finally got married last year. And I couldn't be any more fucking happy for him and my new brother-in-law."

Jensen blanched. "Eddie . . ."

"So this is how it's going to go." Delany continued as if Jensen hadn't spoken at all. "Effective immediately you'll be on administrative leave, during which you're going to get psychological counseling and anger management training, for which you'll be required to show proof of attendance. After thirty days we'll see if you're ready to return."

"But . . ." Jensen looked to Delany who glared back at him with hard, unforgiving eyes. Nick gained a whole new measure of respect for his lieutenant. The man didn't raise his voice. He didn't need to. Delany continued to speak in his well-modulated, almost reasonable tone. As if they were discussing where to have breakfast, or if they should see the Yankees on opening day.

"If you fail to do so, we will bring you up on departmental charges and fire you, and it will be a stain on your personnel file." It was at that point that his tone softened. "Is that really how you want to end your career with the department after over thirty years?"

It was like watching a balloon deflate. Without saying a word, Jensen shrank within himself, requiring the help of another firefighter to leave the room. Delany remained silent until the door closed behind them with a decisive thump, then faced Nick with a stern look on his rugged features.

Delany hadn't made it as high as he did in the department without mastering the art of the quelling look. "Care to explain?"

Perhaps recognizing Nick didn't need to have this discussion in the public locker room, Delany glanced at his watch. "My office in ten minutes. Hernandez?"

"Yes, sir," answered Carlos.

"Take over the training today."

"Yes, sir."

He turned on his heel and left Nick in the room with everyone else. All those eyes staring at him, judging him, assessing him. Nick had had it.

"Yeah. I'm gay. No, I'm not interested in you. Any of you. I'm not looking at you in the shower, and I don't dream about your asses. For the record, I have a partner, and it's serious. If I want you to meet him, you will." Ignoring his sweaty palms and rapidly beating heart, he stared each man down. "Any further questions? No? Good."

He stalked out, heading to the lieutenant's office with a smile curving his lips. He couldn't wait to talk to Julian and tell him what happened. Freedom had never tasted so sweet.

Chapter Twenty-Seven

THANK YOU, LADIES, gentlemen. We'll be in touch." Julian came around the boardroom table to shake hands with the men and women he'd spent the better part of the afternoon with. It had all been worth it when he signed the paperwork for the licensing deal that would allow him to use league-approved logos from all of the New York area sports teams—baseball, football, basketball, and hockey.

The amount of corporate sponsorship they were offering was astronomical—it seemed everyone wanted to help these very special victims. They'd brought in their team physicians for consultations, and all were very excited to jump on board and help in any way possible. Julian had done deals with all the major department store chains, yet it was this deal that gave him chills down his spine.

He left the offices in midtown, and though the cold snapped at his cheeks as it whistled around the corners and down the blocks, Julian walked with no particular direction in mind. Excitement pushed him downtown, his mind replaying the events of the day. Everything good began with Nick; waking up with him, making love in the early morning, and sharing his friends; all had led him to the remarkable dealings with the business moguls.

Finding Nick had found Julian his purpose.

Over the course of the past week he'd met with his lawyer and arranged to hand over the designs of Julian Cornell to Melanie; she'd been flabbergasted and refused at first, insisting she was happy to help him in any way possible.

"Mel. I've barely thought about the clothes since I started working with the kids. They've taken a hold of me, and I can't imagine going

back to that den of vipers in the industry."

She laughed, her eyes bright with joy. "I haven't seen you this excited about anything in years. I'm happy to hold down the fort for you, because I don't think you're done with designing collections no matter what you say."

"I'm not giving up, but I want you to be fairly compensated. In the next few weeks we're going to meet with my lawyers to discuss restructuring the company."

He'd brushed aside her protestations.

There was no concern on his part. He had every confidence in the world in Melanie, and with her in control of the company, and Julian doing the work of his heart, all his troubles, beginning with that night of his show, evaporated, leaving behind a life Julian hadn't imagined possible.

"Julian Cornell, finally out of hiding."

Jerked out of thought, Julian warily took in the sight of Devon Chambers, who'd planted himself in front of Julian, barring his path. When Julian gave him no more than a thin, wintry smile and tried to step around him, Devon moved with him to continue to block his progress.

"Come on, Julian. Don't be like that. I haven't seen you since the night of my show." He flashed a grin. "I mean our shows. I keep forgetting; it's been such a whirlwind since then. I've done *Esquire Magazine*, *WWD*, even *Men's Health*." He smirked. "They want to know my secrets for staying so ripped."

"Fascinating," said Julian, hoping his bored tone indicated how much he truly gave not one shit about this conversation.

"I could hardly tell them it was having a parade of models in my bed that keeps my ass so nice and tight." Devon laughed at his own joke, his white teeth flashing in his tanned face. Julian figured Devon must've been spending time in the Caribbean this time of year, shooting new ads for the summer magazine issues.

He didn't miss it at all, especially after last night and this morning with Nick. Hopefully all went well at work today, and the two of them could enjoy a quiet dinner at his apartment. It amazed him, when he'd once been one of the city's biggest partiers, how much he now looked forward to staying in for the night.

"Good for you, Devon. Sorry to be short, but I'm late." Not really, but he had no desire to stand on a windswept corner when he had places to go. Like the hospital to give them the good news about the endorsement deals. He smiled at the excitement he knew that would bring to everyone, especially Jamal. And wait until the boy found out he'd be meeting several of his sports heroes.

"I hear you're working on something brand new, Julian."

Julian slowed his steps, but didn't stop. His heartbeat faltered for a moment. "Not really. I'm reassessing things, that's all."

"Hmm. You're so secretive; don't you trust me?"

Like I'd trust a thief to hold my wallet.

"It's nothing like that. I have someplace to go, and I can't be late." Spotting a cab up the avenue with its light on, Julian stuck out his hand to hail it. It whizzed over and pulled up at the curb.

With a huge fake smile, Julian opened the door and hopped inside, slamming the door behind him to prevent Devon from following him into the vehicle.

"So long, Devon." He leaned forward to give the cabbie instructions to take him to the hospital, then settled back to check his phone. At the message from Nick, Julian couldn't help but smile.

Believe it or not, it all worked out. Tell you tonight at dinner. Your place?

Julian tapped out a response.

Great. Yeah, my place. And don't plan on going home so bring reinforcements.

If Julian had his way, Nick would be staying for a very long time.

"ARE YOU SHITTING, sorry, I mean kidding me?"

As Julian had predicted, Jamal was over the moon and half-way to the Milky Way at the thought of meeting his favorite sports legends. He cautioned the young man.

"Remember though, you are there representing the product and representing yourself. So leading up to the show we expect you to keep up with your school work and your exercises." He raked a critical eye over Jamal. "How is physical therapy coming along?"

With a nod to his mother, Jamal stood up and took several steps, and even though he winced when he bent his damaged knee, Julian could tell how far he'd progressed from the defeated young man he'd been when they'd first met.

"Jamal, that's amazing. By the time you're ready to walk the runway, you'll own it."

Jamal's mother, Sonia bit her lip. "I'm not sure about all this."

"Ma," groaned Jamal in an exasperated voice.

"Let her speak. She's your mother and she's looking out for your welfare." Julian patted Jamal's shoulder as he passed by on his way to sit next to Sonia. "Tell me your concerns."

Her dark eyes held his, and there were new lines of strain across her smooth brow. "He's just a boy, for all he pretends to be so grown-up. I don't want him involved in all the things I've heard about with that industry."

"Like what?"

"Drugs," she stated bluntly. "I've read enough about that lifestyle to know about the partying and the drinking. I can't have him involved in all that. Yet I can't hold him back from an opportunity like this."

He took her hand. "I promise I'll take care of him. I wouldn't allow him to do this for me if I thought it would expose him to any danger."

Her tentative smile didn't dispel the dubious glint in her eyes. "How can you guarantee he'll be safe? You can't be with him all the time."

"But I can and will be."

Nick?

At the sight of his lover, Julian broke out in a huge smile that faded almost immediately at the sight of the bruising along his jawline and the cut at the side of his mouth that had him running to Nick's side.

"What happened to you?"

With gentle fingers he touched Nick's jaw; if they weren't in public he'd kiss the cut on his lip. As it was, he cupped Nick's jaw on the pretense of examining his face, but needing to touch him.

"It was nothing, really." Nick smiled briefly into Julian's eyes, then went to greet Jamal and his mother.

That didn't fool Julian, but he knew it was neither the time nor place for them to talk about what happened.

"I explained to Jamal's mother how I was going to keep him safe from the decadent lifestyle of the fashion industry."

"Trust me, Sonia." Nick dropped into the chair next to her. During Jamal's convalescence, Nick had spent so much time with him, Sonia had come to rely on Nick for advice and guidance in raising a teenaged boy. Pride rose within Julian, knowing his lover, and now he, would be making a real difference in someone's life.

"I'll make sure to be there every step of the way with him. Don't worry." He squeezed her hand, and the look of trust that passed between them almost broke Julian's heart. "I won't let you down."

"Please, Ma?" Jamal pled from his chair. "I promise to double up on my exercises so I'll be perfect for the show."

"Hey, Jamal," said Julian, "I don't need perfection. Be yourself and you'll be perfect, okay?"

Jamal's eyes remained fixed on his mother. "Ma?"

With one last look at Nick who gave her a reassuring smile, Sonia nodded. "Good luck to you, Julian. I hope you know what you're getting yourself into with these kids."

The mood in the room lightened dramatically; Jamal prattled on to his mother about who he would meet, and how all the kids at school would be so jealous of him, and Julian took that opportunity to pull Nick aside.

"Care to tell me about your new facial decoration?" He touched the cut on Nick's lip. "Can I hazard a guess someone didn't take your coming out too well?"

Nick leaned into Julian's touch, and Julian couldn't resist placing a quick kiss to the black and blue mark on Nick's jaw.

"It looks worse than it is. Jensen and I had a difference of opinion when I told him. But in the end, I felt sorry for him."

"You did?"

Nick shot a quick glance to Jamal and his mother. "Maybe we can discuss this later, like over dinner." His blue eyes darkened. "At your place? We can rent a movie, or something."

Still upset at Nick's injury, Julian was no fool. Nick in his apartment, hopefully for another entire night? There was no way in hell he'd turn down an invitation like that.

"I'm all about the 'or something.'" He kissed Nick on the uninjured side of his mouth. "Let's go."

Chapter Twenty-Eight

THEY'D PUT SOME movie on television, and after settling onto the sofa with their Pad Thai and beers, Julian challenged him with a stare.

"Tell me what happened. Obviously that fucker hit you."

The problem was Nick didn't want to go over it again. He wanted to eat his Pad Thai, get a little buzzed, and have mind-blowing sex.

"I'm fine, honestly. We argued, he hit me, but in the end I kind of felt sorry for him."

Almost choking on his beer, Julian sputtered. "Sorry for that bastard? He's a homophobic asshole who hit you. I hope he loses his job."

"I don't." Nick gazed at his beer bottle without seeing it. "You don't understand."

"Enlighten me then, because want to know how I see it?" Julian tucked his feet under Nick's ass.

"Not likely you'd keep your opinion to yourself."

Julian arched a well-defined brow, and Nick wondered if he waxed his eyebrows. He wouldn't be surprised, considering the fashion industry's obsession with appearances. Then he recalled the smoothness of Julian's chest beneath his hands, and couldn't care less if Julian waxed his balls.

Julian wiggled his feet under Nick's ass and Nick growled, "If you want me to listen, cut that out."

"You'd been afraid all along to tell those men you're gay. The next thing I know, you show up with your face bashed in, and yet you feel bad for the man who hit you?"

Nick knew it would be hard for Julian to understand. He set his bottle on the coffee table. "I told Barton, and Jensen overheard us. The man went off on me, and when I turned my back he punched me."

"This forgiveness you think I should have toward Jensen?" Julian shook his head. "Not feeling it."

Nick leaned his head back to stare up at the ceiling. "He broke apart; lost it completely. See, Jensen lost his son, Tommy, in 9/11. Tommy Jensen and I came up through the academy together. He was a good guy, a really good guy, Julian." He punched the pillow at his side. "I fucking hate what this did to people."

"Shh." Julian slid next to Nick and took him in his arms. "I know, I know." Nick held on, wishing Julian did know.

It was hard for people who hadn't lived through it to understand the depths of the despair. Because he functioned day to day, didn't mean he wasn't hurting. Loving Julian had given him back his life to the extent he could love again and think about a future instead of sifting through the ashes of the past, but nothing could ever bring back the innocence lost, the pureness of heart, and the beauty of that endlessly blue sunny sky.

"You don't need to talk about it if it upsets you still."

"It's never not going to upset me, Julian. That's something you need to understand. I may function normally, but it's always going to be there with me, like a living, breathing thing."

Instead of a quick response, Julian blew out a measured breath. "Am I not enough for you?"

Angry with himself for allowing Julian to have doubts, Nick grabbed Julian's shoulders and pulled him close. "Don't ever think that. I've only begun to climb my way out of hell. You're more than enough. You've made me look forward to waking up in the morning, and evenings like this, with just the two of us." He kissed Julian then, rough and deep until they both were left gasping. "Fuck it, Julian—not enough? You're God damn everything."

"Then tell me," begged Julian. "Make me understand."

"My father knew Jensen and said he was never like this before, before Tommy died. And then I found out Tommy's girlfriend was pregnant and lost the baby." Nick stood and paced the loft, ending up at the windows overlooking the street. "I can't imagine losing your only son, then your grandchild, the last link to your only child. I'm not a cruel person. The man needs help."

Julian's harsh breathing resonated through the loft. "Life is fucking unfair, isn't it? I lost my mother, but I don't think I ever really had her, since she worked so hard to pay the bills, I barely saw her."

"So then maybe you can understand about forgiveness. I don't need to hurt the man any more than he's already hurting. Maybe this will get him the help he needs to come to terms with what's happened; I'm not looking to get him fired. Help and education can go a long way."

Julian's warm body pressed up against Nick's back as he wrapped his arms around him. "And here I thought you were simply another pretty face. Who knew you were so sympathetic and caring?" Julian kissed his ear. "I understand what you're saying and you're right. I don't believe in handling intolerance with more intolerance, so if you think this man can get help, then I'm all for it. Now I can tell you my news."

They returned to the sofa, and Nick picked up his bowl of Pad Thai, digging into the spicy noodles. "Tell me." He chewed and swallowed, then washed it down with a gulp of beer.

After Julian conveyed the results of his meetings and showed Nick the signed paperwork, they celebrated with Nick giving Julian a blowjob on the sofa. They lay together, relaxed and sated, with Julian unusually quiet.

"What's the matter?" Nick nudged him with his foot.

"Hmm? Oh, I was thinking about all the changes in your life. I don't want you to think I've forced you into anything. Did I make you do anything you didn't want to?"

Instead of answering him, Nick said, "You know what I'd like?"

"What, babe?"

"I have my therapy session with my doctor tomorrow." It would be the first time anyone had ever come with him, if Julian agreed to go. "Would you, if you're not busy of course, would you come with me?"

A beautiful smile broke over Julian's face. "I'd love to. Thank you for including me in the important parts of your life."

He kissed the damp whorls of hair at Julian's temple, losing himself in the intoxicating scent of this man. "You are the most important part of my life."

INEXPLICABLY NERVOUS, NICK fiddled with the zipper on his jacket.

"Stop it already, you're going to break it, and I'm not giving you one of mine; I like you in your official jacket." Julian's green eyes glowed with humor. "It's every man's dream to have a hunky fireman as his boyfriend."

"Sometimes I think you wouldn't be half as anxious to jump my bones if I wasn't a fireman."

Julian's lips curved in a smile. "You're lucky I like you out of your uniform as much as I do in it."

"Nick?" Shena called out from the receptionist's desk. "Dr. Landau is ready for you."

"Thanks." He headed to the office, Julian at his side. "Shena, this is Julian Cornell. My partner."

It was amusing to watch her reaction; her mouth formed an *O* when she understood the connotation of the word "partner," and her eyes widened with recognition at Julian's name.

"Julian Cornell, the designer?"

Turning on his ever-present charm, Julian leaned over the desk and chatted up Shena for a few minutes before trailing after Nick. "She loves me," he said with a smug grin.

"Somebody has to." Nick grinned at Julian's outraged huff and kissed his cheek. "Make sure you don't become too loveable to anyone but me."

They were both smiling when they entered Dr. Landau's office. Nick shook his hand and introduced Julian.

"Julian Cornell? I think I'm wearing one of your suits if I'm not mistaken."

Did everyone in New York City know his boyfriend? For the first time, Nick wasn't so sure he liked this public side of Julian.

Dr. Landau waited until they were both seated, then faced Nick with a quizzical smile.

"Something you'd like to tell me, Nick?"

Funny how only last month he'd have been too ashamed and afraid to sit and discuss his sexuality. Now Nick was proud to sit beside Julian and claim him as his own.

"Part of the reason I think my recovery has been hampered even after all these years was my inability to admit, even to myself who I was." Gazing into the kind eyes of Saul Landau, Nick knew there'd be no judgment, only acceptance. "When we were sixteen I turned Julian away, knowing how much he loved me, knowing I loved him, but being too ashamed and scared to stand up for myself and choose my own path; I chose to hide and fake my life rather than come to terms with who I was."

"That's a hard choice to make at sixteen. Most people don't know what they want at that age, or who they are."

True. For most people. "But I did. I knew who I was and who I wanted." Without looking, he reached out his hand for Julian. The difference in Nick's life now was that he didn't have to see, because he knew Julian would always be there by his side to grab hold of him. "I threw it away, threw Julian away. I treated him like trash instead of the gift he was."

"Yet here you both are after all these years. Together."

"Life is funny isn't it?" Julian spoke for the first time. "Over the years I imagined Nick married with children; living the life he said he wanted. When we met again, and he behaved like an arrogant ass, assuming things about me, judging me by how I looked, I figured he'd buried himself deep and would never admit to being gay."

"You make me sound so shallow," said Nick, but Julian spoke the truth. "In many ways I judged people by how they looked, but in the opposite way from your world. I figured anyone who cares so much about their clothes was shallow, conceited, and didn't have the character of a person I'd want to know, or have as a friend."

"I was that person for many years. I'd thrown myself into a world where no one looks beyond the surface. They live mediocre lives, content to judge people by the visual, rather than forging friendships based on true character. Reuniting with Nick changed my life. He's taught me so much about the strength of human nature and the will to persevere; I don't have the words."

Warmth flooded through Nick, and he squeezed Julian's hand. No one had ever made him feel as important as Julian had in this moment. "Because of my relationship with Julian, I've found my courage. I've come out to my family, and the people at my job. I've even progressed to the point where getting into elevators isn't a thing of dread."

"You've always had the courage, Nick. It didn't simply pop up one day because you fell in love. You learned to recognize it again within yourself and accept it." Dr. Landau gazed at him with almost fatherly affection. "For years I watched you beat yourself up and smother any sign of life inside yourself. Seeing you today full of acceptance in who you are gives me great happiness."

"As you can see by my face however, there's still a long way to go in terms of others accepting who Julian and I are."

"Will that deter you?" Landau's sharp gaze challenged him.

"Not anymore. I'm done with pretending. It hasn't brought me happiness in life so far; why should I sacrifice the rest by continuing to live a lie?"

"I always wonder," said Julian in an uncharacteristically somber tone, "what life would be like if we didn't take that chosen road. What might have happened if my show had done well instead of being a disaster; would my path have ever crossed with Nick's? After almost every situation where I've been knocked down lower than I ever thought possible, I've discovered even greater success in the end."

Their session over, Dr. Landau rose to shake their hands. "What might have been, what could have been, you can spend your entire life thinking and living in the past. Embrace the joy you're given. You never know how long you have it for. It's a gift not everyone is lucky to find."

Nick contemplated this all the way back to Julian's loft. When they reached the apartment, Nick barely waited until Julian closed the door. He slammed Julian up against the wall and took his mouth in a heated kiss.

Julian responded in kind, thrusting his tongue into Nick's mouth while he took off his coat and suit jacket.

"Hurry," he urged.

Nick didn't need any further words. Without breaking eye contact, he undid the buttons of Julian's pants and shoved them down to his knees, then sank down in front of Julian and took his engorged cock deep into his throat. There was no time for technique. Nick wanted him raw and hard.

"God, yes," Julian moaned, thrusting faster into Nick's mouth. Nick held onto the base of Julian's cock and noisily sucked, swirling around the thick head, loving the hot musky smell of Julian, and he couldn't stop flicking his tongue against that sensitive spot on the underside of Julian's cock. Hearing Julian moan his pleasure only heightened his own; Nick's dick ached, and he knew he wasn't far from blowing apart.

Nick could feel the trembling begin deep inside Julian; he was so intimately attuned to his body. Julian's cock swelled and the first burst of precome landed on Nick's tongue.

"Come on, give it up to me," he muttered. He stroked the hard length. "Fuck me, I can take it."

Julian gazed down at him, eyes wild with desire. "Fuck, Nick." He dug his fingers into Nick's hair and, holding back nothing, shoved himself deep into Nick's throat. Nick took it, loving the hot slide of Julian's length in his mouth, the pleasure swamping through him until Julian cried out and came, arching his back, shooting down his throat. After Julian's hips ceased pumping and he softened and slid out of Nick's mouth, Nick took care of his own aching cock, ripping open his zipper to free himself.

He locked gazes with a panting Julian, his own hand stroking his dick until with a harsh sigh he came, pulsing hot and sticky in his hand. Julian knelt beside him and kissed his fingers, licking at them, then kissing him.

"If I had to do it all over again, I would, if it would bring me right back here with you and this moment."

There was nothing Nick could add to that except one thing. "I love you too."

Chapter Twenty-Nine

FOUR MONTHS LATER

HIS HEART BEATING madly, Julian whipped past the hair stylists curling the last of the models' hair, and the make-up artists putting the finishing touches on their faces, to peer between the curtains at the crowd. What a difference it made from the glittering array of celebrities and scions of the fashion industry who normally filled the seats.

Today there were representatives from pharmaceutical companies and healthcare corporations, doctors and nurses, sitting side by side with select fashion bloggers whom Julian had forged relationships with. All of them expressed excitement over his ideas; the healthcare industry professionals promised increased assistance for the burn victims, while the bloggers agreed to feature stories about the patients in the burn unit and their lives. He had shown them that beauty is more than skin deep, that they needed to look past the scars of a body hard lived.

Various sports figures showed up with their friends, and he was touched that many of the men and women had brought their wives, husbands, and children along. Marcus, as usual, had done an amazing job of transforming the club into a fashion runway. The music was pumping, and the corporate sponsors had done a fabulous job of setting up a non-alcoholic bar, as well as putting together the swag bags and the decorations. Zach sat behind the scenes, working the computers and sound and the different color lights. He'd promised Julian this time to come out and enjoy the party for a while. The place was jammed, but to Julian's shock he'd managed to pick out Devon Chambers sitting in the second row.

"What's that fucker doing here?"

Melanie stood behind him and massaged his shoulders. "One of the bloggers brought him. Don't worry; I've been watching him all night. I won't let him cause any problems."

He turned and kissed her cheek. "Have I told you lately I adore you? How lucky I am to have you in my life?"

Her lower lip wobbled, and she blinked furiously. "Don't make me cry, you'll ruin my makeup." But she kissed him back and hugged him hard.

They'd come a long way since he hired her from the group of student interns he'd been sent from FIT. Over her protests he'd given her forty percent ownership of Julian Cornell, and she'd outdone herself with the designs for the collection she showed him. They planned a showing in Paris for the summer, and he was sending her on her own for the first time to handle it all.

"Hey, what's going on here?" Nick sidled up behind Melanie, Katie at his side. "Are you putting moves on my guy?" He winked and wrapped Melanie in a hug, before moving to stand next to Julian. "You look gorgeous."

Julian kissed him, inhaling his spicy scent. "Mmm, you're pretty hot yourself." He ran a critical eye over Nick's suit and tie. "Why are you wearing that?" Julian grinned at Melanie and Katie. "I wanted him to show up in his uniform. So hot."

Nick rolled his eyes. "You're insane."

Katie nudged him. "You know everyone has a thing for a man in uniform, Nicky. You can't help it if your boyfriend thinks you're a hottie."

Ignoring her, Nick peeked through the curtain. "Are Mom and Dad here?"

Julian pointed them out to Nick. "I have them sitting in the first row in the VIP section. Your mom is next to Helena." Julian had known that would be the perfect place for Marilyn, and he was right. The two women were happily chatting away, while Nick's father, looking a bit out of place, stared in awe at the latest pitching sensation of the NY Mets, who was there with several of his teammates.

"I hope your father won't mind that I got him signed balls and bats from the members of all the NY teams." Julian smirked at Nick who stared at him goggle-eyed.

"Are you shitting me? You'd better have gotten me that too." Nick pouted, and Julian thought he'd never looked more adorable.

"How about dinner with all of them tonight, is that good enough?" He loved teasing Nick, and the sight of the man, excited as a child over dinner with his sports idols made him happier than he thought possible.

"Are you serious? YES!" He fist-pumped and pulled out his phone. "I'm going to go plug this in to make sure I have enough battery. Wait until the guys find out."

"Why don't you go tell them? They all just walked in." Julian pointed them out, and with a hurried kiss, Nick threaded his way through the crowd to reach his friends.

A warm feeling stole through Julian watching Nick interact with the guys from the fire department. Almost everyone on his team had come; Jensen excluded. Over the past few months, Nick had introduced him to the guys he worked with, and though there were a few awkward moments, for the most part Julian felt he'd been accepted. Especially when the men came to him for fashion advice, or what to get their wives, girlfriends, or mothers for Valentine's Day and birthdays. He supposed it was a learning process.

"He's almost back to the old Nick, you know. All because of you."

Katie stood at his shoulder, and they watched Nick laugh and joke with his FDNY buddies as they headed toward the bar.

"Not me. He did it all himself. I was lucky to have found him at the time when he needed to make that change."

Katie smiled at him, her eyes so like Nick's but without that tinge of sadness Nick still carried with him. "Why are the nicest guys either married or gay? I should be as lucky as my brother to find a guy like you."

"Whoever gets you will be the lucky one. You and Melanie.

Now go sit. The show's about to start." He gave her a final hug and kiss, then went backstage again to find Jamal.

The nervous young man sat in a chair; a hairstylist worked on him to make sure his sideburns were even, while the makeup artist added pencil to his brows and powered his face to keep down the sheen of sweat from the bright lights.

"How's it going, kiddo?" Julian gave Jamal's mother and sister a kiss hello. His little sister looked adorable, and had charmed the hairstylist into putting multi-colored bows in her braided hair.

"Are you sure I can do this? There's a lotta people out there. What if they laugh at me 'cause I can't walk right?"

Julian dismissed the stylists and sat down next to Jamal. "Who decides what walking right is? This is more than a fashion show. It's a show about taking back your life, about coming back after adversity. You're a winner, Jamal. You and all the others who are doing this. I created these designs so that you wouldn't feel as self-conscious in public and could be a little more fashion forward. But you are the only one who gets to decide what to do with your body."

"I get it. Yeah." The light of understanding flared bright in Jamal's eyes. All the therapy and exercises helped but only to a point. The measure of a person was how they handled their roadblocks in life. They could lie down and let the world happen all around them and do nothing, or they could learn, adapt, and seek to make a difference in the world. "I wanna do this for you and me, but also to show the kids who couldn't make it today that they got something to look forward to."

Julian met Jamal's eyes in the mirror. "Remember what we said about looking forward?"

At Jamal's nod he continued. "Four months ago, would you have ever thought you'd be a model, walking a runway in one of the trendiest clubs in New York City, and meeting all these ball players?"

"No way, man. I still don't believe it."

"Well believe it, buddy-boy." Marcus stood at the doorway,

dressed in a shirt decorated with every New York sports team, and his usual skinny black jeans. "And from the crowd gathering out there, it's more than you thought it would be as well, Juli."

"What are you talking about?"

The smile grew on Marcus's face until his eyes gleamed. "They're all here. The magazines, the newspapers, all the ones who wrote about your demise after they wrote off your last collection, the bastards are out there."

"Waiting for me to fall on my face, I bet," said Julian grimly.

"Then go prove them wrong. What you've done here is amazing, Juli. I'm in awe of your ideas and creations. Of you. I knew you could do it."

Tears rushed to Julian's eyes at Marcus's praise; his friend wasn't one to give compliments lightly. He had no idea how he would've made it through without his friends.

"Yeah, Julian. When you told me what you wanted to do, I thought you were another rich guy making promises." Jamal touched the new compression bandage on his arm the doctor had put on that morning. He'd picked out a black background with multi-colored stripes up the arm, and for his leg he'd chosen an iridescent blue, like ocean waves. "These are so awesome. I thought it would be slipovers; I didn't realize it would be the actual bandages themselves."

Neither had Julian. But when he'd met with the healthcare industry people, they'd worked with his ideas to tweak it so it could work best for the patients. He still planned on slipovers for the bulkier compression bandages some patients might need, but he loved being able to imprint right onto the bandage material itself.

"It's more than I ever dreamed when I first thought about it." There was a lump in his throat when he thought how close he'd come to missing out on all of this; helping these people, finding love, finding himself. Julian had always laughed at the talk of fate before, but damn if he didn't count himself as a believer now.

"Juli, it's time." Marcus hugged him tight and gave him a kiss on the cheek. "Knock 'em dead, break a leg, or whatever the fuck you creative types say. I'm going out front to keep an eye on things and watch the show."

And probably ogle some of the new models, knowing his friend. Julian laughed to himself. Marcus couldn't help it; the man was a walking hard-on, content with his life as a man-whore.

"Hi."

Nick stood at the entrance to the styling area and a rush of longing swept over Julian; he wanted to hold Nick and bring back the laughter to his eyes and heart. When Julian met Nick's blue-eyed gaze, he understood what it meant to have found a home. Whatever Nick might need from him, Julian would give; Nick had already given him so much. Family, trust, and a way back to a life of meaning and purpose. But most of all Nick gave Julian his heart, and let Julian see him, all of him.

And Julian loved him more, if that were even possible.

"Hey, babe. The show is about to start. I have a seat for you next to Katie and your mom." He cupped the back of Nick's neck, fingers twining in the curling tendrils at the nape. Julian loved the freedom they had now that Nick had come out to touch each other in public.

As if to prove his point, the music switched over to a livelier beat and the lights dimmed over the audience, spotlighting the runway Marcus had set up. Nick, however, held on to Julian, slipping his arm into the crook of Julian's elbow.

"I want to see it all unfold with you. I'm so amazed and proud of you and what you've accomplished here." Nick took Julian's face in between his hands. "I love you, and when you walk that runway at the end of the show, I want everyone in New York City to know who you belong to."

A thrill shot up Julian's spine at Nick's possessive words. "I'd like that more than anything. Let's go watch them."

He took Nick by the hand and moved closer to the back of the stage where the models walked from. He'd managed to snag several top models, both male and female, despite it not being a fashion show per se. Once the word on the street got out that this was helping burn victims, they were eager to help.

But in his eyes the real stars of the show would be Jamal and Kayla, who, to Julian's delight had insisted on a hot pink color for the bandage across her chest. She'd pinned flowers along the neckline, and Julian spied her innate talent and had plans for her when she graduated high school and college.

The models took their turns and walked, highlighting the bandages and demonstrating their flexibility and the range of motion it afforded their arms and legs. Some of the models wore the removable sleeves, and showed the audience that removing them required a simple pull of a Velcro tab. Everything easy and stylish for the person wearing it.

With each model, the response from the crowd was instantaneous, the applause ringing in Julian's ears. He could see the approval in the faces of the healthcare executives, and the fashion bloggers were furiously taking notes.

"All for you." Nick wrapped his arms around Julian from behind, engulfing him with his warm body. "Without your ideas, none of this would have happened. I'm so proud of you."

But Julian couldn't speak, so mesmerized by the crowd's acknowledgment, and the models who believed so much in what they were doing, they stopped on the runway to applaud Kayla and Jamal who walked out, hand in hand, to a standing ovation from the crowd.

Beautiful Kayla, with her cornflower blue eyes and heavy red-gold hair; she floated down the runway, her gauzy dress sailing behind her, looking like the angel she was. She no longer hid her scars from the fire, but wore them as a symbol of her courage.

And Jamal, who inspired it all, his hazel eyes wide as a deer's but with the beginnings of a self-assured smile lighting up his face, showing off his arm with its racing stripes, and posing to display his bandaged leg. He wore shorts so that people could have the full effect. Julian loved that Jamal had paired the blue bandage with a pair of neon green and blue sneakers.

To the crowd it looked like Jamal wore a leotard or a wet suit, but Julian, Nick, and those who knew Jamal, Kayla, and all the other burn victims knew what they'd endured to get to this moment.

And suddenly all the models, plus Kayla and Jamal, began clapping and calling out his name to come on the stage. Nick took his hand and together they walked out on the runway, stopping halfway to greet people, then proceeding near to the edge to wave at the crowd. The lights hit them full on, yet Julian had no problem spotting Nick's parents in the audience, both with smiles on their faces. Next to them Katie and Melanie stood crying and clapping. Marcus of course was at the bar surrounded by good-looking men, but his face was wreathed in smiles and he clapped along with the crowd.

Even shy Zach, as promised, had come out from the sound area to stand with his mother, who wore the scarf Julian had made for her, and waved madly at Julian. Julian blew her a kiss and waved at Zach who had been grabbed by Marcus to stand with him in the crowd of men.

And as if the night itself was not enough of a success, Julian's eyes widened at the sight of the mayor of the city with his security detail standing with the Fire Department commissioner and other high-ranking members of the fire department.

"Whoa, babe. You hit the big time. Those are the big guns at the department." Nick leaned over to whisper in Julian's ear, but Julian hardly heard over the pounding of his heart and the music.

It wasn't him. He was the catalyst, but Jamal, Kayla, and the others were the real winners tonight. It was because of them and their courage that he found his inspiration. Life can be cruel and harsh, but even out of tragedy and loss, sometimes good can often be scratched out of the muck and dirtiness. A wave of protectiveness surged over Julian and he vowed that when the bright lights shut off and the music slowed down, when the cameras disappeared and the accolades quieted, he'd still be there with these people.

Him and Nick, together.

The applause died down and someone, he had no idea who, thrust a microphone into his hand. To his surprise, he didn't know what to say; overcome with emotion for the first time in his life, he turned to Nick with a plea for help in his eyes. Seeing his obvious distress, Nick put his arm around Julian's shoulders.

"Say what's in your heart."

His heart was full to nearly bursting; how to explain that? But one look at Jamal and Kayla and the courage they'd showed tonight, and Julian knew he wasn't the focus—it was these people and their stories.

"Thank you all for coming and making this night a spectacular success. When I first met Jamal here he thought I was another rich snob, who would be a drive-by type of personality; pass by once or twice, make him promises, then disappear, never to be seen again." He glanced at Jamal with affection. "But now that you've met him and Kayla, you can see how that would be an impossibility. Once you meet these guys, they burrow under your skin and latch onto your heart. And then there was Nick."

He hadn't discussed talking about Nick ahead of time and he froze for a moment, wondering if he'd made a mistake, until Nick took the mic and the crowd grew quiet.

"Thank you everyone. Let me introduce myself. I'm Nick Fletcher. I'm a proud member of the FDNY, and I am Julian Cornell's boyfriend. On 9/11 I lost most of the guys in my firehouse and I myself was injured very badly. I spent months in the hospital and weeks in the burn unit, so I'm very familiar with what these people have to endure."

Julian's throat closed up. No matter how often he heard Nick's story, knowing how close he'd come to losing this man never failed to make him emotional.

Nick continued, unfazed by all the attention focused on him. Julian noticed Dr. Landau sitting at the bar, a smile of obvious pleasure on his face.

"I couldn't have made it through without the help of my family; my parents, Brian and Marilyn Fletcher, my sister Katie, the guys I worked with at the FDNY, and Dr. Saul Landau, my therapist. But something was missing. I'd thought once I started volunteering at the burn center I'd find whatever I'd need. But I was wrong."

He picked up Julian's hand and laced their fingers together.

"Years ago I lost my courage to say what was in my heart because who I loved wasn't acceptable. I let the best thing in my life disappear, and I was miserable, knowing I'd lost a shot at my happiness."

Julian couldn't believe Nick stood in front of his family, his bosses, the press, and spoke so open and from his heart. Courage, indeed.

"When Julian reappeared, it forced me to reevaluate my life. And I knew if I let him go again because of my fear, I'd never have that chance again."

There were over two hundred people inside the club, yet there was no sound, only the frantic beating of Julian's heart and the grasp of Nick's hand to ground him to reality.

"He'd moved on to this world of beauty and fashion where appearances mean everything, and I almost let fear sink its teeth into me again. Because you see," Nick dropped his hand, gave him the microphone and unbuttoned his shirt, baring his chest and his scars for the audience to see, "I know personally what these people have gone through. My fear of rejection for my outward appearance almost ruined my second chance with Julian—why would a man who made his living surrounded by perfection and beauty be interested in someone like me?"

Without thinking, Julian spoke directly to him as if no one else were in the room. "Because you are beautiful. Your body tells a story of a life worth living. And you've taught me more about beauty in these past few months than all my years in fashion ever could. That true beauty isn't seen; it's something intrinsic, bone deep and worth delving deep beneath the surface for. To me, you are beautiful, more perfect than when we were young."

He put his arm around Nick's waist and hugged him close.

"I love you."

"I love you too." Nick buttoned his shirt up and together they walked off the stage to join the throngs waiting to speak to them.

Immediately Julian was grabbed for interviews by television news crews and bloggers. Then he had to pose for pictures with the mayor and fire commissioner, and take other publicity shots. It seemed like where he once was a pariah, overnight he'd become the darling of the media. Fickle bastards; he'd forgotten how much he hated sucking up to the press.

Through it all, he kept his eye out for Nick, who'd been swallowed up by the crowd, catching glimpses of him with his fire department crew, and sometimes with Zach, Marcus, and his own family.

He spotted Jamal with his mother, sister, and Kayla talking to some of the baseball and football players. Even at this distance Julian could see how starstruck Jamal was, and wondered how he would react when all the players showed up tomorrow at the hospital's burn unit for a meet and greet with the staff and patients. At a tap on his shoulder he spun around, expecting it to be Nick, but instead he came face to face with Devon Chambers.

Instinctively his guard came up and he girded himself for a fight.

"What is it, Devon? I'm busy here." Julian's attempt to brush past the man was met with Devon laying a restraining hand on his arm.

"What you've done here is amazing. I know it will help so many people feel better about themselves."

Shocked at the seemingly serious tone of Devon's voice Julian nevertheless managed a brief smile. "Thanks." Devon tightened the grip on his arm.

"My sister . . ." Devon drew in a deep breath and squeezed his eyes shut for a moment. "My sister died in a fire at college. Even though it was over fifteen years ago, my parents never got over it, and it changed me. Made me hateful and angry at the world." He brushed his hand over his eyes. "I'm sorry I fucked you over."

"So you admit it." Julian could hardly comprehend he was having this conversation. "I want to hear you say it."

"I took your concepts and added a few changes so the similarities wouldn't be so blatant, but the ideas were yours. And I thought it would make me the happiest man to be on top of the heap, but you know how the business is; you're only as good as your last collection."

"No ideas, huh?" Julian couldn't help the dart of satisfaction that pricked his insides. It may not be nice, but in truth he had little sympathy for Devon Chambers, the designer. But, Julian could feel the man's pain as a human being and sympathize with him.

Devon shook his head. "It's like all my mojo deserted me. I heard Melanie is taking your collection to Paris."

"Do you really think I'm going to talk to you about my collection after everything you did? I'm sorry to hear about your sister, but I have no desire to talk or be your friend. We weren't close before you ripped me off, and we have nothing in common now." Spotting Nick, Julian shook off Devon's arm. "Bye."

He hurried over and joined Nick who was with his training group. Julian greeted them, and they made small talk as the crowd began to thin out. They were joined by Nick's parents, and Julian listened with half an ear as Nick's father talked fire department gossip. Nick slipped his arm around Julian and whispered in his ear.

"Can we leave soon?"

"Nick."

Both he and Nick turned to face an unsmiling gray-haired man. Nick's entire demeanor changed from relaxed to tense. His shoulders drew up, and the smile on his face faded.

"Jensen, what are you doing here?"

Shit. So this was the guy who gave Nick such a hard time. Defiantly, Julian stared him in the face, pleased at the man's discomfort.

"Can we talk in private?"

"No." Nick hugged Julian closer. "This is my partner, Julian Cornell. It's his night, and I won't have you ruin it with your hostility, ignorance, and blatant disregard for our human rights. If you came here for a fight, leave."

"I came here to apologize."

Julian thought he might be in an alternative universe. First Devon Chambers, and now Nick's enemy. Jensen had returned after a two-month leave, and Nick had told Julian he'd given a wide berth to both him and Barton. Deciding to believe the best in people and not the worst, like he normally did, Julian remained silent.

"Go on, we're listening."

For a moment Jensen fidgeted, unsure what to do with his hands. Finally he laced them together behind his back. "I was wrong to hit you and to say what I did. I'm not gonna make excuses for myself because of Tommy, because I still don't get it . . . this gay stuff."

Julian bristled, but Nick held him back. "You don't have to 'get it.' What you do have to do is treat me with the same respect you give everyone else. Get that?"

Jensen glanced briefly at Julian who glared right back at him.

"Yeah, all right. I don't think they're gonna assign me to work with you anytime soon anyway."

Nick shrugged, then took Julian's hand. "We have to go." Without a backward look, Nick almost dragged Julian back behind the stage.

"What's going on? What's the—"

Nick's mouth covered his in a hard hungry kiss that nearly brought Julian to his knees. As it was, he barely had time to grab hold of Nick's shoulders and dig his fingers in, holding on for purchase. Nick's lips moved across Julian's, his tongue sweeping inside Julian's mouth, stealing his breath, while his hands drifted downward to cup Julian's ass in his large hands.

"Nick, what's going on?" Julian could barely breathe, the need for Nick so heavy in his blood and brain it was as if he'd been injected with a drug.

"I saw you tonight, and knowing you're mine after all the years we were apart, knowing we were free to stand like everyone else and not be judged, I needed a few minutes alone with you, to prove that it's real and not something I'm dreaming about."

Julian gazed up at Nick's face, those beautiful blue eyes finally clear and hopeful, instead of helpless and lost, and once again, Julian wondered about the world and the mysteries of life and fate.

"I love you. I've loved you since those long-ago days on that scratchy old sofa in my basement, through all the men who came and went through my bed without me ever giving a thought to their name. I've spent over half my life in love with you, and that's never going to change. I've changed in the process and so did you, but it all worked out for everyone in the end."

"Yeah," Nick smiled, tracing his knuckles down Julian's jaw. "You, me—together. Forever."

"Come live with me, Nick. Move into the loft so we can start our life together."

He held his breath, wondering if Nick was ready. The smile he loved, the one that lit Nick up from within, burst over Nick's face.

"I'd love to, but are you sure?"

Julian kissed him. "Letting you walk away from me was the hardest thing I've ever done in my life. Now when one of us leaves, we'll always know we're coming back home to each other."

Nick brushed his lips to Julian's, then held him tight, their bodies fitting together as perfectly now as they did all those years ago.

"I love you, Julian. No matter where I am, I'll always be coming home to you."

Together, they walked back inside the club, hand in hand.

The End

About the Author

FELICE STEVENS HAS always been a romantic at heart. She believes that while life is tough, there is always a happy ending just around the corner. She started reading traditional historical romances when she was a teenager, then life and law school got in the way. It wasn't until she picked up a copy of Bertrice Small and became swept away to Queen Elizabeth's court that her interest in romance novels became renewed.

But somewhere along the way, her tastes shifted. While she still enjoys a juicy Historical romance, she began experimenting with newer, more cutting edge genres and discovered the world of Male/Male romance. And once she picked up her first, she became so enamored of the authors, the character-driven stories and the overwhelming emotion of the books, she knew she wanted to write her own.

Felice lives in New York City with her husband and two children and hopefully soon a cat of her own. Her day begins with a lot of caffeine and ends with a glass or two of red wine. She practices law but daydreams of a time when she can sit by a beach somewhere and write beautiful stories of men falling in love. Although there is bound to be angst along the way, a Happily Ever After is always guaranteed.

www.felicestevens.com
Facebook
Twitter
Goodreads

Other Titles by Felice Stevens

THROUGH HELL AND BACK SERIES

A Walk Through Fire

After the Fire

Embrace the Fire

OTHER

Rescued

Memories of the Heart

One Step Further

Made in the USA
San Bernardino, CA
24 February 2016